Dangerous TEMPTATIONS

Annie Jocoby

VINCI
BOOKS

By Annie Jocoby

Temptations

Dangerous Temptations
Twisted Temptations
Dark Temptations
Wicked Temptations

Vinci Books

vinci-books.com

Published by Vinci Books Ltd in 2026

1

The publisher and the author have made every effort to obtain permissions for any third party material used in this book and to comply with copyright law. Any queries in this respect should be brought to the attention of the publisher and any omissions will be corrected in future editions.

A CIP catalogue record for this book is available from the British Library.

Paperback ISBN: 9781036703110

The EU GPSR authorised representative is Logos Europe, 9 rue Nicolas Poussion, 17000 La Rochelle, France contact@logoseurope.eu

Chapter One

Run Serena run. That refrain was going through my brain like a mantra as my tired, blistered feet pounded the pavement outside my beach house where I was staying, temporarily, with some surfer friends who I met through Craig's List. I tried to run at least 5 miles a day. It kept me in shape, to be sure, but I craved the physical pain that accompanied it, just because it helped me forget the psychic pain for just a moment. I could concentrate on how my lungs were burning, how my muscles were screaming in protest, how the blisters on my feet were joining in the pain chorus. So, I ran every single morning before work, rain or shine. I would get up at 5 in the morning to run, then hurry home, into the tiny shower in the two bedroom bungalow that I called home, then throw on some clothes and head to work.

It was during these times – when I was running or working – that I was able to come to terms with all that had happened to me in my life. All that I had lost. I never thought that I could fill that space, and, indeed, I didn't even try. I had to continue on with my life, of course, because the alternative was something that I couldn't bear.

I ran my five miles, and then came in the door, where I was greeted by Donny. I was surprised that he was awake that early, because he and Michael usually didn't get started surfing at least until 9.

"Hey girl," he said to me over his bowl of Cheerios. "S'up."

"I'm surprised to see you awake this early. Weren't you and Michael up late last night?"

He nodded his head. "Yeah, but, for some odd reason, I couldn't sleep, so I decided just to stay awake. I know that I'm going to pay for that tonight when I go into work though."

I knew the feeling. Ever since I'd been going through hypnosis and counseling, I found myself waking up really early, having had a vivid nightmare. The nightmares weren't exactly about the incident or what had happened to me as a baby, but, rather, were more coded. I would dream that I was going into an exam, even though I hadn't been to class all semester. Or I would dream that I forgot to put on any clothes at all, and I was standing in the middle of a busy street, buck naked. I would try to hide in a storm drain or wherever I could but, of course, there was never any hiding. Sometimes I would dream that a giant spider was on my pillow, or that there was bleach in my mouth and I knew not to swallow. Then I did swallow, and I would wake up with a start.

I was surprised that my dreams weren't more detailed. As an empath since birth, I was constantly in touch with the pain of others. I never wanted to be, and I couldn't understand why I was. What I always knew was that I was affected more than most when people around me were suffering, and it was always something that I had tried to block out. My hypnotherapist was helping me to understand this ability and how it had always affected my life, and why I, ironically enough, acted in ways that showed the world that I just didn't care.

My life would have been more balanced, for sure, if I didn't also have the ability to tap into the spiritual world. That was something that really drove me crazy all my life, and it wasn't until recently that I was able to accept this aspect about my psyche.

I stared at Donny, and sensed that nothing was really wrong with him. He just probably ate something he shouldn't have, and it made him insomniac for the night. "You probably need to lay off the sugar late at night," I told him. "I have to always remember the Jordane thing."

Donny smiled. "Yeah, guilty as charged. Some idiot coworker brought in these rad cupcakes from Babycakes. Like I can resist something like that. But you're right, I shouldn't overindulge in such things right before I go to bed."

Donny did tend to overindulge in cupcakes and other such delights, whether it was late at night or during the day, but you would never know it by looking at him. He was amazingly lean, as a surfer must be.

He put his hand in his long blonde hair, and pulled it on top of his head in a makeshift pony tail. "What about you, Miss Serena? How come I never see you eat cupcakes?"

I shrugged. "I do. I just have to make sure that there are no animal products involved, that's all. Most of those things are made with butter, you know."

He nodded his head, a lazy grin displayed on his handsome face. "Oh, right, right. I guess you have to make yours with oil or trans fat. I keep forgetting that all animal products are off-limits to you."

I rapidly showered and changed into my suit, and came out to grab my keys, which were on the table. "I'm going to be late coming home tonight," I told him. "I need to see another house." I was looking for a new home in the Solana Beach area. I craved living near the water, which was why I had moved to San Diego in the first place from New York. I missed my family, of course, who were scattered among the East Coast cities of Boston, New York and Portland, Maine. I especially missed Luke and Dalilah, two people who I had grown extremely close to in the past few months, but it couldn't be helped. My therapist told me that I needed to live by water because it was so calming for me, and, I had to admit that he was right about that.

"We're going to miss you when you go," Donny said. "I don't know anybody who can cook a better vegan meal than you."

I smiled. "It's California, trust me, there are lots of people who can cook a better vegan meal than me."

He shrugged. "Can you make sure that your replacement is one of those people?" he asked.

I gave him a look, but knew that he wasn't serious. "Yeah, Donny, I'll get right on that." Then I picked up my keys and got into my new BMW SUV and drove off to my law firm.

I took a deep breath as I walked into the gleaming high rise where my new law firm was located. I was only a junior associate at the firm, of course, and even that was pending my passing the California bar exam that June. I knew that I would pass, of course, but, at the moment, I wasn't able to appear in court.

"Hi Serena," Anna called to me. She was my paralegal, and was an extremely efficient one at that. "There's been an emergency meeting with the partners. They asked that you be there," she said as she took my briefcase and purse from me. "I'll put these in your office. They're waiting on you."

I nodded my head. *Great, just great. Couldn't anybody have called me about this?*

I went into the conference room, where the 20 senior partners were sitting around a table. I didn't really belong there, as I was only a junior associate, and not even really that until I passed the bar, so I was more than surprised that I was to be included in this meeting. Not just included, but apparently I was important to the meeting, as they were waiting for me to show up.

"I'm so sorry," I said. "I didn't know that there was a meeting, otherwise I would have tried harder to be on time." I felt annoyed again that nobody had told me about the meeting. Ordinarily, my being a bit late wouldn't have been a big deal. Today, however, it clearly was a big deal, judging by the temperature in the room.

I tried to shake off the tension I was feeling from the men and the three women who were staring at me, but it was difficult. I, once again, cursed my "gift." Stress hormones flooded through my body, and I took an enormous breath.

"Have a seat," Malcolm, the managing partner, said to me, pulling out my chair. "Now that you're here, we can call our meeting to order."

"Thanks," I said, and then closed my eyes. I tried to block out the voice that was coming from one of the women. I couldn't read thoughts all the time, but I definitely could read feelings, and these feelings were often presented to me in words. *Stupid woman,* she was thinking. *I have no idea who died to make you so important to this firm.*

I glared at her, and she gave me an innocent look like she had no idea why I would be giving her the stink-eye. I bit my lower lip and shook my head, and was glad that she didn't have the Jordane ability to read *my* feelings about *her.*

"Serena," Malcolm said to me politely. I got a read on him and he wasn't covering up annoyance, so I was happy about that. "This firm has just been retained on the Slade Bridgewell case. That is the reason for this meeting."

I nodded my head and thought about what a coup that was. Slade Bridgewell was a billionaire who had been accused of offing his business partner. The media was obsessing over the case and had been for days, ever since his business partner was found bludgeoned to death at the corporate headquarters of Bridgewell Industries, which was an international pharmaceutical company that had just been taken public with an IPO of over $10 billion.

I was ashamed to admit that I hadn't been following the case all that closely, unlike the rest of the free world. The details of the case had been breathlessly reported on every major news station pretty much 24/7 since the incident had occurred. Every time I turned on the television, they were talking about the handsome mogul, but I usually just changed the channel.

He looked guilty as sin in my estimation, simply because he had that look. The look that exuded arrogance and privilege. For one thing, he was extremely handsome and charismatic, more handsome and charismatic than anybody had a right to be. With his dark wavy hair and piercing green eyes, he looked like an unusually good-looking male model. For another, he seemed entirely too laid-back, considering what the was charged with. I hated the way he was always smiling, even after the arrest, with his gleaming, perfect teeth and full lips. Hippy surfers like Donny and Michael had a right to smile like that, not wealthy men who were possibly facing the death penalty.

Of course, I hadn't actually been around the guy, so I wasn't actually able to pick up on his vibrations. Therefore, I didn't necessarily know that he was guilty as hell. I just had the feeling from looking at his visage on television. His looks certainly didn't help his cause, either, as that was part of the reason for the obsessive media coverage of his case. A guy who looked like that and was as self-made wealthy as he was at the age of 28 was a target for media attention anyhow. God knew that most billionaires didn't look like this guy, so he, and his playboy lifestyle, were fodder for the tabloids since day one. It seemed like every actress and supermodel in town had been on his arm at least once. From that, I surmised that he was probably gay and utilized a multitude of beautiful beards.

"That's a coup," I finally said to Malcolm, who appeared to be waiting on my response. I still had zero idea why I was brought in on this case, so I hoped that it would all be explained to me in short order.

"Yes," he said, and then looked around the room. "So this meeting is the initial strategy session for his case. He has a PR firm on top of his image issues, of course, but, nonetheless, we need to be a front line on that as well. We need to prepare a statement for the media, which is camped out in front of the courthouse even as we speak. Mr. Bridgewell is going to be arraigned this morning, and Jonathan is attending that hearing."

Jonathan nodded his head, and everyone got to work preparing what was going to be said to the media. It was the typical statement that every lawyer ever said to a shitload of cameras who were thrust into their face since time began. *My client is innocent until proven guilty, and we ask that his privacy be respected during this difficult time.* There really couldn't be much more said in this statement, because to tell the media what the evidence was going to show would be tipping the hand to the prosecution on what the defense was going to be. That, of course, was verboten.

Cindy, the girl whose thoughts I had read earlier, raised her hand. "I think that it's time that we go over his preliminary defense," she said.

"We need to get his whole story," Malcolm said. "Which is where Serena comes in."

Cindy gave me the stink-eye to end all stink-eyes. "Serena?" she protested. "I was hoping that I could do the initial interview with the client."

I tried to shake off the dark vibrations that she was shooting into me, but it was very difficult. This bitch was throwing me signals, right and left, and I took a deep breath and tried to clear out her negative energy. I was getting better at doing that than I was before, which was why I was, generally, in a calmer head space than when I was growing up and was tormented by the dark energy of others, not to mention the energy, both light and dark, of spirits who were constantly trying to use me as a medium against my will.

Malcolm raised his eyebrows. "Serena will conduct the interview," he said. "And Serena, I know that this is going to be an odd request, but please go into that interview blind. I don't want you to know too much about this guy before you talk to him, so do not do any independent research on him. I need your intuition for this, only your intuition, and if you go into the interview with any preconceived notions, it might interfere."

I nodded my head. It had all become clear. Malcolm was one of the few people in the firm who believed in my gifts. He evidently thought that I'd be able to get at the truth of this matter, which was going to be crucial. This Slade looked like he would be a glib liar, because he just had that type of demeanor and charm. It was naturally important to know the truth. I could read Malcolm's energy, which told me that he thought that I would be able to get at this important truth.

I took a deep breath, hoping against hope that Slade was able to be read. I sometimes had problems with people who were blocked off from their own feelings, as I had been for so many years. If this Slade had any kind of a defense mechanism surrounding his aura, I didn't think that I would be able to achieve what Malcolm was obviously wanting me to.

Of course, if he were a sociopath, I also wouldn't be able to get a read on the guy. A sociopath, a true sociopath, would be one who was not at all in touch with his or her feelings, namely because they didn't have true ones. No feelings, no emotions…just void. I had met more than one person like that in my life, and they creeped me out way more than the ones who were exuding negativity. At least with the really negative people I knew where I stood, and I had learned to deflect their energy. With a sociopath….I shivered just thinking about it.

I stood up, prepared to protest my selection in this matter. "Malcolm, I thank you highly for your vote of confidence. I really do. But I'm the most junior member of this firm. I think that there are much more qualified people than me to handle a case of this magnitude. But I'm very, uh, flattered that you would think of me first."

Truth be told, I didn't want to be the one who would

interview this guy, because I didn't want to be the one who would find that he was guilty. I knew that my law firm needed to know that, because it would direct how the defense would proceed. But I wanted to be far, far away from this case. If I went to meet with this guy, and every hair on my body would tell me that he was guilty, then how could I possibly feel safe? I knew that I was going to have to meet with him alone, too, because if there was anybody else in the room, I might not be able to get a good read on him. I got a good read on Cindy with others in the room, but that was only because she was terrible at covering up her feelings. I had the insight that Slade would not be the Jordane, so I was going to have to really concentrate.

Cindy smiled. "Okay, Serena has declined. I'd like to be the one who will conduct the interview."

I shook my head. I knew why Cindy was so chomping at the bit – she was anxious to meet with a man as handsome as Slade. I knew that she was shallow, but I had no idea....But I could see it in her eyes. She looked like she wanted to bed our client right there in the conference room, and she probably would if she got the chance.

"Serena will conduct the interview," Malcolm said, obviously not brooking dissent. "And then, once she gathers the information, we'll begin preparing our defense in this case." At that, he signaled that the discussion of Slade Bridgewell's defense had come to an end. "Until Serena has conducted the interview, it is pointless to belabor this case," he said. "So, I'd like to discuss other matters on our agenda." Then he looked at me. "Serena, you may wait for me in your office. We'll go over the specifics of where you are going to meet with Mr. Bridgewell and when."

I nodded my head and headed to my office and sat down behind my desk. I had piles and piles of research projects as well as files for other clients who was going to have to interview, none of which were nearly as important as Slade's case. Our firm did a mix of white collar and lower-level crime, as well as quite a few mob cases. I didn't relish meeting with the mob clients, but, at the Jordane time, I usually got along with the wise guys, so it wasn't such a bad thing. We also took on quite a few high profile cases, sometimes *pro bono* if the defendant was particularly notorious and broke. Malcolm was nothing if not an opportunist, so, any time he could get his firm into the news, he took it, even if the case brought in no money at all. He figured that such cases pay off in spades in terms of the firm visibility, and he was right, of course. His machinations had put his firm on the map.

I could just imagine how giddy Malcolm was when Slade decided to retain our firm. That was the get to end all gets. This case was shaping up to be one of the biggest murder cases since Casey Anthony, as far as media attention was going. There was even talk that it might blow up into OJ levels, although that speculation was far-fetched. The media circus over OJ was something that couldn't be duplicated, but this case might give it a run for its money.

After about an hour of looking over files, trying to prioritize them, and doing online research on case law regarding various legal points, Malcolm peeked his head in my office. "Do you have a minute? I need to talk to you about the Slade Bridgewell case."

I nodded my head and gestured to my chair, and Malcolm sat down. "I'm not going to beat around the bush," he said to me. "I'm sure that you figured out why I've chosen you to do the initial interview with Mr. Bridgewell."

"Of course," I said. "You need my particular area of expertise."

"Yes," he said, and I suddenly got the feeling that there was something more to the story. I couldn't quite pinpoint it, though. There was something that felt just a tiny bit off about Malcolm as he sat across from me.

But, whatever it was, he wasn't going to divulge it just yet. "I believe in your intuition, of course, and I always have. I think that you're uniquely qualified to find out exactly what we're dealing with regarding Mr. Bridgewell, and then, after you deliver your report, we'll know how we're going to proceed."

"That's what I thought," I said. "Listen, Malcolm, I hope that you know that my intuition isn't perfect by any means. True, I do have insight that others don't, but there are plenty of people who slip in under my radar. I just want to manage your expectations on how much good I'm going to be able to do."

"Nevertheless, I expect a full report on Monday morning. You have a week, Serena, to get to know this guy. Find out everything that you can. What makes him tick. How he thinks. How much negative vibes you get off of him, and why. I know that you can do this, better than anybody else in this firm."

"Okay," I said, shrugging my shoulders. "When is he coming to meet with us?"

"You're going to him," he said. "I need for you to meet him at his home in LA, and I need for you to stay there for a week."

Chapter Two

I groaned inwardly. "A week. You want me to stay for a week with a man I don't know? I have a life, you know. I'm trying to find a permanent place to live, so I need to close on a house soon." I looked over my real estate listings, houses that I was going to visit that week, and felt enraged. "You can't just upend me like this."

Malcolm shook his head. "You don't have any children," he said. "I don't see what the problem is."

"I was also looking to get a dog," I said, which was true. As soon as I closed on a house, I desperately wanted a French bulldog to keep me company. Actually, I wanted two French bulldogs, litter mates, because I firmly believed that dogs were only happy if they had company during the day.

"Do you currently have a dog?" Malcolm asked me pointedly.

"No," I said. "But I have my eye on some dogs that I found out about through a rescue agency, just as I have my eye on a house in Solana Beach that probably won't be on the market in a week. The owner is motivated to unload it for a song, and it is a once-in-a-lifetime opportunity."

The house that I was looking at was a fixer-upper, as much of a fixer-upper a home in Solana Beach could be, which was why it was so undervalued. I had some experience with fixing up older homes, and I had hoped to take on this home as a project. I always had to have a project to keep my mind off of the obsessive thoughts about my past and about the incident I was trying desperately to forget, the incident that happened right before my mother's murder.

I tamped down the rising panic that was forming in my throat. I could see on Malcolm's face that he wasn't going to let me out of this, but I had to try.

"Listen, Malcolm, I really just can't leave town on a dime." I didn't want to tell him why – that I was terrified that, if I got out of my perfectly designed routine, I would backslide into the way that I was. And going to stay at the Los Angeles house of a billionaire who was accused of murder would certainly qualify as my breaking my routine.

"I don't understand, Serena," he said. "Please help me to understand why you can't do this."

I looked down at my wrists, where the scars had finally faded. The scars on my arms weren't quite as old as the ones on my wrists, nor were the scars on my legs. Fortunately, my pant suit effectively covered all that up. I shivered as I remembered how I got these marks on me. I hadn't been brave enough to do all of that to myself, so I frequented an underground club in New York City, where the people, men and women, were more than happy to do these things to me.

I had left all that behind when I came out west to San Diego. That's why my life was so structured - running at 5

AM, get to work by 8, home by 6. Hang out with either Michael or Donny - it depended on who was home in the evening - watch some television, go to bed. My life in New York City wasn't like that – it was crazy and chaotic, and the craziness and the chaos led to my never being able to fully heal myself.

I was finally finding my center, and now Malcolm was asking me to uproot this.

I took a deep breath, and found that there was no way that I could tell him the truth. He would freak out completely. He probably would never trust me with a major case, that was for sure. "I just think that you need to send a seasoned investigator to talk to Mr. Bridgewell," I finally said. "And, besides, I need to study for the bar exam. It's coming up in another month."

He shook his head. "You got this. You passed New York, which is just as hard as the one here. And you did quite well on it, too."

"Even so, I don't feel confident," I said, which was a lie. I felt more than confident that I could ace the exam. Malcolm was correct – I passed the New York bar with flying colors, and I barely had to study to accomplish this feat. I had no doubt that I would do the Jordane with the California bar. But I didn't want Malcolm to know this. I needed him to believe that I had to stay around to study, not go gallivanting up to Los Angeles to stay with this Slade Bridgewell.

"I've heard nothing from you yet that will change my mind," he said. "You're going to Los Angeles, you're going to interview Mr. Bridgewell, and that's that." Then his face softened. "I understand your reluctance. I really do. But, Serena, you have a gift. You might or might not be able to get a good read on this guy. If you don't, you don't. But I need your insight. The last thing that I want is to defend this bastard, only to find out that he's guilty as hell."

I cocked my head. "What does that matter? We defend guilty as hell people all the time. That's what we do."

"Even so," he said, "I need to know. I usually don't, but, in this case, I do. I don't want to be a laughing stock like OJ's Dream Team was after they got him acquitted."

"They weren't laughing stocks," I said. "They were admired and revered. They did the impossible, getting off a guy who was guilty as the day is long."

Malcolm stared out the window. "It just wouldn't be good for the firm's reputation. Ordinarily, you're right. I couldn't care shit less if the client was guilty or innocent. But this case is too big, Serena. If we get him acquitted and then he goes and does it again..." He shook his head. "There would be hell to pay."

I suddenly understood. "Your fancy friends might not invite you to so many parties if that happened, would they?" I shook my head. I had no idea that Malcolm was so concerned about his image and his social standing, but he apparently was.

He looked embarrassed. "I don't care about all that, but my wife does. She's trying to be a doyenne."

I nodded my head. "Good reason," I said sarcastically. I was going to fall on my sword so that his wife could save face at the Country Club. I shook my head.

It looked like I was going to be going to Los Angeles to meet with this asshat Slade, no matter how much I protested. I could always quit, but this was a very prestigious firm and they handled a multitude of complex and interesting cases. The cases were interesting enough that I might, just might, be able to continue to try to forget about my inner wounds by concentrating on them. Besides, I had to admit that I was intrigued by this Slade case, and I really did want to be a part of it.

I wanted to be a part of it, not be in the middle of it.

But it was beginning to look as if in the middle of the Slade case was where I was destined to be.

I hadn't met the guy, but I already despised him.

Chapter Three

I packed up the Beemer and prepared to meet with Mr. Bridgewell, but I first had to do something for me. In a small act of rebellion, I called the French Bulldog rescue and arranged to meet the two Frenchie sisters who were rescued from a delapidated home that was serving as a puppy mill. As I was telling Malcolm, I had my eye on these dogs, and I felt like I couldn't wait to get them.

I ran it by Donnie and Michael, and they were thrilled to be getting new puppies in the house. "Just make sure you clean up after them," Donnie had admonished, and I promised him that I would.

I had to admit that there was a large part of me that wanted to piss Mr. Bridgewell off. He was just sooooo special that he couldn't be bothered to come to the law firm like a normal person. No, I had to kiss the ring, and I resented it thoroughly. If he had been a normal guy, my life wouldn't have been uprooted. I'd be talking to him at the firm, perhaps over dinner, and my comfortable, safe existence could continue on. But no…he was an entitled jackass, and I had to go to him.

If I had to go to him, then I was going to put him out just a little by springing these two doggies on him. So, I went to the house of the lady who was fostering the two little dogs, Sadie and Gigi. She lived in an elaborate beach house in La Jolla, which was an upscale beach community. I often went to the La Jolla Cove to watch the sea lions, who fascinated me to no end. The animals were not afraid of humans in the least, and they would sun on the rocks and let people take their picture all day long. I often got close to the sea lions, but, one time, one of the sea lions literally barked a warning at me, and I backed off.

If I would have thought that I was bothering the animals, of course, I would never get close to them. I always felt animal suffering in my bones, even more than the suffering of humans, so I never would distress an animal in any way. But these guys more than held their own against the onslaught of fascinated people, and they genuinely didn't seem to mind the attention. So I often found myself going to see them and hang out with them. That's when I knew how desperate I was for a pet of my own, which led me to the Frenchie rescue and Sadie and Gigi.

My plan was to get the two dogs, head down to the shores to see my sea lion buddies, and then head up the five highway towards LA. I would get to this Slade jackass' house around 10 PM that night, and I hoped that I'd be inconveniencing him in some way. I'd be mightily disappointed if I showed up there and he was just waiting for me. I wanted to catch him in some compromising position or with a guest or, better yet, trying to sleep. Then I would ring the doorbell and piss him off, which would delight me to no end.

Yeah, it was immature of me to think that way, but, dammit, if I was going to be put out, so should he.

I arrived at the house, which was a modern glass and stone home that was built like a series of cubes. The woman, Evina, answered the door, the two little dogs in her arms. "You must be Serena," she said. "Come in, come in." She stepped aside, and I entered the foyer of the house. She handed me the two dogs, who were puppies, to my surprise. I thought that they were fully grown, but they clearly were less than two months old.

I stood there with the two dogs in my arms, reveling in their puppy smell and puppy breath. Nothing smelled better to me than those two scents, and these two little girls emitted these smells in spades. I put my fingers in Gigi's mouth, and her tiny body wriggled with delight while her sharp puppy teeth found my fingers and chomped down excitedly. While Gigi delightedly made mincemeat out of my fingers, Sadie excitedly licked my face. No doubt about it, these two little baby girls were pure love and joy.

"Here," Evina said, giving me a box filled to the brim with toys and blankets. "These are their things. Feel free to change their names if you wish. They're only around 7 weeks old, so they don't really know their names yet."

I nodded my head. "You have their shot records, right?"

"Yes."

"Awesome," I said, giving her the $500 rehoming fee that she had asked for. These animals were a steal for that money, plus I got the satisfaction of saving them. Not that I really was saving them, of course, because if I didn't come along, somebody would have snatched them up quickly. Frenchies ordinarily cost around $2,000 apiece. But perhaps they would've been separated if somebody else had adopted them, so there was that. I was keeping them together, and that meant a lot to me, and probably to them.

Evina handed me a folder that had all their shot records, and showed that they were also de-wormed. She had tears in her eyes as she petted the two dogs, putting her face close to their beautiful scrunched up snouts.

"Now you be good with your new momma," she said, as the two dogs licked her face and tried to bite her hands. They wriggled so much that I had a hard time trying to control them, but I managed to keep ahold of them anyhow. "I'm going to miss you two so much, but I know that you're going to be in great hands." She looked at me. "I go through this with every adoption, but it's a necessary thing. As much as I always end up wanting to keep my little babies, I know that I have to give them up so that I can foster others. There are so many who need it."

I smiled and thought that I would love to do what Evina was doing. Fostering animals. Giving them a temporary home away from a shelter while a forever home was being located. If I didn't have a such a demanding job, I probably would do just that when I finally got my new home.

"Thanks," I said, and Evina took the box of toys and goodies out to my car. I had picked up a large carrier to put them in for the trip up the coast. I put Gigi into the carrier, and as I prepared to put Sadie in there, she peed on me. Evina looked at me with horror on her face, but I just laughed. "Guess she's excited. And that's my fault. I really need to let these two little girls go to the bathroom before putting them in there. I can't believe I didn't think about that." At that, I brought Gigi back out, and put a harness on her and Sadie. The dogs sniffed around the front yard and finally they both did their business. I brought out a poop bag and picked up the mess, and Evina helpfully took the two bags and offered to dispose of them.

"Do you need a change of clothes?" she asked me with a worried look on her face. "We look about the Jordane size."

I shook my head. "Actually, I have an overnight bag in the car filled with clothes, but I'm fine."

"Well, then, you need to come into the house and change," she said.

I raised my eyebrows as an idea formed in my head. I could just leave the peed-on clothes on, which would gross out Mr. Bridgewell, which would be one more way that I could get my revenge on him for putting me out this way.

Then I thought better of it. Really, the only person who would truly be hurt in that scenario would be me, because I would be the one in pee clothes for the two hour drive to Mr. Bridgewell's home. "Thanks," I said, "I'd like to change in your bathroom if you don't mind."

"Of course not," she said. "Here, let me help you put the two girls into the carrier, and then you can change and be on your merry way."

I went and changed into some new clothes, putting the old ones into a laundry bag that I had packed in my overnight bag. Then I emerged with fresh clothes and gave Evina a quick hug. "Thanks so much," I said. "You can rest assured that these two little girls will have a wonderful home."

"I know," she said with a sigh. "But I'm going to miss them so much all the Jordane. I really need to get a puppy of my own, but my hands are so full with my foster babies, I just don't know what to do."

I smiled and gave her another hug. "You take care of you," I said. "You're a saint."

Then I got in my Beemer and left, thinking that people like her in the world gave me a little bit of hope for humanity. However slight of a glimmer that was.

I arrived at the home of Mr. Bridgewell after midnight, even later than I had anticipated. I'd found myself delaying getting to his home. I stopped several times to let the dogs out, and then I stopped for dinner at a Temecula restaurant, lingering over dessert and a few glasses of wine. Ordinarily I didn't drink at all when I was driving, but I found myself curiously nervous. Then I felt slightly buzzed, so decided to wait a few hours until my mind was totally clear. In the meantime, I got Gigi and Sadie out of the car and brought them onto the patio of the restaurant, after having asked the waitress if this would be okay.

"That would be fine," she said. "We welcome dogs here on the patio."

So, I brought them out with their harnesses on, and, for the next few hours, I drank water while one person after another came up to them and cooed, oohed and ahhhhd over them. Everyone commented on how adorable they were, and, for their parts, their little bodies wriggled every time somebody came up to talk to them, and they excitedly licked many faces and nibbled on many arms and hands during the course of those few hours.

Finally, around 11, I left the Temecula restaurant and headed to the address in Los Angeles. It actually wasn't Los Angeles so much as it was Malibu, for this privileged sono-fabitch lived in one of those gleaming houses made of windows that were situated high on a cliff. I had to follow a winding path to get to his house, and then, when I finally got to where he lived, I had to follow yet another winding path to his home. His house apparently sat on several acres of prime real estate, and, I had to admit, he did have an impressive view. Before I actually rang the doorbell of the enormous three story home, I took the girls to the edge of the cliff and looked down. Far below, the ocean was crashing against the rocks, and the sound of it made me feel absolutely, positively calm.

I went up to the door and rang the bell. The chime sounded sonorously throughout the home, and I waited there impatiently for him to answer. Or someone to answer. He probably would get a maid out of bed to answer while he slept, I thought. That would be just my luck. Mr. Fancy-pants probably couldn't be bothered to answer the door.

To my surprise, he did answer the door. In a towel. He opened the door, looking sexier than anybody had a right to be, his dark hair wet and dripping in his face. To my dismay, his features were even sexier in person than they were on the television. His eyes were a piercing green, his lips were puffier than any runway male model. His body was tight and sinewy, like he worked out every day of his life, yet he wasn't overly muscular. He was just extremely lean and taut. My eyes inadvertently went to the small patch of hair that was just above his towel, and I immediately felt embarrassed, so I forced myself to look him right in the eye.

That was a mistake. I felt myself melting right there on the porch when I looked him in those piercing green eyes. He cleared his hair off his face with one perfect hand, and still stared at me.

I opened my mouth, but nothing came out. I'd totally forgotten how annoyed I was to be coming up to his house, and then felt immediately annoyed that I'd forgotten that I was supposed to be annoyed. Who was this jackass, looking like he stepped off the cover of a men's magazine, or out of Calvin Klein ad? Did he think that just because he had more money than God and had the looks that Greek deity would envy that I was just supposed to melt in a puddle at his feet?

And, just like that, I was angry again.

Then he opened his mouth, and I was lost again. "You must be Serena. Well, don't just stand there," he said in a gorgeous, sonorous voice. His words were smooth, like melted chocolate. "Come on in. Make yourself at home. What's mine is yours."

Holy fuck. He looked like the personification of sin, and he had the voice to match.

What was I getting myself into?

I tentatively stepped through the door, with Gigi and Sadie trailing behind, wearing their harnesses and leashes. Mr. Sex-on-a-stick took one look at the two little dogs and his face broke into a huge grin.

"Oh, Frenchies, my absolute favorite," he said. And then he knelt down and put his face right up to Sadie's snout. She licked him furiously, and he laughed and, to my surprise, laid down on the floor. The two dogs attacked him gleefully, their little bodies wiggling madly with joy. Sadie barked, the first time I heard her do that, and she commenced attacking his face, biting and licking madly. Gigi did the Jordane, and tried to push Sadie out of the way. She apparently was jealous that Sadie was getting all the attention, and Sadie, for her part, obliged Gigi, who did the Jordane as Sadie – nipping, licking and generally attacking Slade's gorgeous face.

So much for my plan on annoying the fuck out of Slade. That little plan certainly did backfire, as it seemed that my having these two dogs delighted Slade to no end.

Finally, he got up off the floor. "Oh, I can't tell you how happy these two little dogs have made me. I just lost my Great Dane, Sophie. I was going to get a new dog right away, but these two little girls will do for now." He picked them up, and they commenced to licking his face again. And Sadie, of course, right on cue, peed all over him. She seemed to have a habit of that when she got excited, and I covered my mouth so that Slade wouldn't see that I was trying very hard to stifle my laughter.

Of course, Slade didn't mind. In fact, he laughed, too. "Looks like someone is excited," he said. Then he took the leashes out of my hand and put them on the two dogs. "I'll walk them."

"No," I said. "I'll walk them. They're my responsibility."

He grinned. "It's not a problem," he said. And then he let the towel drop. I caught my breath and looked away modestly, but he didn't seem to even notice that he was buck naked in front of a perfect stranger.

He shrugged. "I'd bother to put my clothes on, but why? It's not like there's anybody around to see me walk these dogs naked, and, besides, they really need to go out, judging from the amount of pee Sadie just poured on me."

"I know, which is why I'd like to walk them," I said. "You need to get some clothes on."

He just grinned and found a pair of shoes. "I'll be right back," he said, the two dog leashes in his hands. "Or you can come with."

I took a deep breath, feeling that I had no choice. I couldn't just pawn my responsibilities onto him. That wouldn't be right. So I followed him out the door and took Gigi while Slade took Sadie.

I tried not to look at his nakedness, but it was very, very

difficult. He was sheer perfection, from head to toe. I caught a fleeting glance at his cock, which was dangling in the wind, and I was more than impressed. It was thick and hung down about eight inches. I immediately felt embarrassed and averted my eyes.

He caught me looking, of course, and he grinned boyishly, but he didn't address my peeking openly. "So, what inspired you to bring these two beautiful girls here?" he asked me as Sadie sniffed around some bushes and palm trees before finally squatting. Gigi was sniffing around flowers and shrubs and then she, too, squatted.

"I had my eye on these two before I came here, and I wanted to make sure I snagged them before anyone else had a chance to," I said. "I'm sorry that nobody warned you about them."

"By nobody, you mean you, right?" he said with a smile.

"Yes, I mean me, Mr. Bridgewell. Malcolm had no clue that I was going to bring them up here, of course."

"Well, I'm glad that you did. You do know that they've done studies that show that dogs tend to lower stress levels of the people around them, right? That's why they take dogs to nursing homes, to cheer everyone up and bring their stress levels down. And God knows I need some stress relief after the week I've had."

I cocked my head at him. "I notice the absence of news people. I'm surprised. I thought I'd have to get through a phalanx of photographers and reporters sticking microphones in my face."

"Oh, you'll see them tomorrow, believe me. I call the police on them all the time, because they can't come on my property, so they hang out on the street outside the gate. They wait to ambush me, and I always say 'no comment,' of course. But I'm always catching them in the bushes and hiding behind trees, so the cops have to come out and chase them away."

I looked around, thinking that there was probably a photographer around. If that was the case, it certainly wouldn't be so great for Slade, being buck naked and all. That's the kind of picture that would go viral for sure.

He seemed to read my mind. "There's nobody around," he said. "Not on my property, anyhow."

"How do you know?" I asked him. "After all, if they're able to sneak onto the property during the day, they certainly can at night."

He shrugged. "Eh, you're right, I guess. If they get a shot of me naked, then they get a shot of me naked. That's the least of my problems."

I nodded my head and said nothing. That was certainly an understatement, that him being naked on the Internet would be the least of his problems.

Then he smiled. "Maybe it would even help my case. You guys can argue that I can't possibly get a fair trial if the jury would be busy imagining me naked. Or maybe the prosecutor could argue that."

"I don't think that it works that way," I said. "But nice try."

"How does it work, then?" he said. "I mean, let's face it. The chances of my getting a fair trial with this kind of obsessive coverage is slim and none. At this point, they could hold the trial in Anchorage, Alaska, and the jury pool would still be completely tainted."

I nodded my head and tried to focus on him. I didn't come up here to drool over his body, no matter how gorgeous it was. I was sent up here for a very specific venture, and I felt completely unprofessional for forgetting about it.

Slade had a way of making me forget about why I was there, that was for sure. He had a way of making me forget my own name.

Concentrate Serena, concentrate. I felt distracted walking next to him, to say the very least. My heart was pounding out of my chest and was almost audible in my ears. My hands were shaking as they held tightly onto Gigi's leash.

Slade paused and let Sadie go number two.

"I'm so sorry," I said, "I'll get the poop bag out."

He shrugged his shoulders. "I'll get Henry to get that tomorrow," he said. Then he glanced at Gigi, who followed suit. "And that, too."

"Henry," I said. "Who is that?"

"My groundskeeper," he said. "Do you think that I can get this topiary done on my own?"

I couldn't see very well, but I focused on the bushes and saw they were, indeed, done in topiary fashion. They were very carefully trimmed to resemble geometric shapes, circles and there were a few that were trimmed to resemble animals. One of the bushes was in the shape of the California bear on the California state flag. Two others appeared to be shaped like two elephants walking on the African Savannah. "Henry is very talented," I said. "I'm surprised that he doesn't mind picking up dog poop, in addition to sculpting these amazing animals out of the bushes."

"You'd be surprised at what people are willing to do when you pay them enough."

"Actually, very little surprises me anymore," I said, and I meant that. There was one thing that I had learned in my life, and that was that people, in general, will shock the hell out you if you let them. So I tried not to let them. I had to remind myself of this, however, as I stood next to the naked Slade.

The dogs, having done their business, went inside with us. I brought in their carrier, put a soft blanket in it, and put them inside. "Night night little ones," I said, peeking at them. Within a few minutes, I could hear both of them snoring. It was an adorable sound.

"Okay," he said. "Let me show you to your bedroom, and, tomorrow, we'll get started on the interview."

"Thanks," I said tentatively. He picked up my bags and led me through the house – past an enormous living area with 30' ceilings and a wall of windows with a fireplace in the middle and a skylight on top. The fireplace was surrounded by a rock wall and the floors were cherry wood. It looked like an interior decorator had designed this room. We also walked past an enclosed pool area that had an Olympic-sized pool, complete with lanes and a diving board. There was also, apparently, a bowling alley, movie theater and game room with arcade games and a billiard table.

I had been in plenty of homes in my life, but nothing quite like this one.

Finally, he showed me to my room. Like every other room in this house, the room had 30' ceilings and a fire-place and was enormous. The bathroom had a 10-person jacuzzi tub that was sunken, and a shower that was large enough to fit a group of people. I put my bags down on the floor and sat on the bed. "Thanks," I said to him. I felt embarrassed about thinking such evil thoughts about him earlier.

"Night," he said, and then simply left.

I sighed and undressed and got into bed. On my computer was a list of questions that I was supposed to ask him, but I always preferred to wing it. Ask questions according to my intuition, let it guide me to where I wanted to go. That always served me well when I had trials in the past, and I thought that it would serve me well here.

And I was going to have to keep it together with this guy. I couldn't let him intimidate me with his looks or his obvious charm. I was never one to let things like that block me, and, usually, things like that didn't block me.

There was one thing that really bothered me about this guy, too. It was the fact that he was so unruffled, so charming. His sense of humor obviously was intact, and, indeed, his demeanor with me told me that he didn't seem bothered by any of this. Not by the media attention, not by the fact that he was facing the possible death penalty. None of it seemed to faze him. Unless he was covering up extremely well, it seemed as if he was just living his life and not caring a damn about what he was up against.

Could he be a sociopath? The classic sociopath was somebody just like this Slade character. Charming and glib, with the ability to lie about anything and everything. All sociopaths weren't violent, although some were – the ones who combined other kinds of mental illnesses with anti-social personality disorder. Really, the person who should be here with this guy should be a shrink, not me. Because one thing was for sure – if he was a sociopath, I was going to be taken in by him. As an empath, I had to be working with somebody who had actual feelings. If he was feeling guilt and remorse over the killing of his partner, if, indeed, he killed the guy, I should be able to pick up on that and follow that feeling where it goes. But if he killed the guy and felt nothing? Then I, too, would feel nothing.

I closed my eyes and tried to summon the spirit of the dead guy, Jordan Harris. I had long since blocked out the voices in my head that came from restive spirits. I had to, for my sanity. I had to learn how to make them leave me alone. Now, I was actually trying to communicate with Jordan, which was dangerous, really, because if I let him in, the floodgates could very well open, and I would be the way that I was before I learned to block out all the noise – going literally crazy, unable to function except if I drank to excess. Then my drinking would get me into all sorts of other problems. I couldn't afford to go there.

After a few minutes, I realized that I would hear nothing from the dead business partner. It was just as well, really, because I didn't necessarily want to risk going back to the way that I was.

Chapter Four

I slept in the next day. I couldn't help it – I was greatly fatigued from the stress of having the responsibility of finding out the guilt or innocence of this guy. It was a lot of pressure, and if I was wrong, it could have disastrous consequences. Not only that, but his bed was so damned comfortable. It was a hand-crafted mattress made in Sweden, as Slade had explained, and the brand was Vividus. He didn't say as much, but I knew that such a mattress tended to retail at around $70,000. After sleeping on it for the night, I would have had to say that the mattress was worth every single penny.

I tentatively went down the stairs and stopped when I heard the sounds of a piano playing. It was probably a recording, but it did sound live. I would imagine that this guy had the kind of sound system wired that would make anything sound live.

As I approached one of the dens, however, I saw Slade behind a grand piano. He was playing a complex classical piece that I recognized as being one of Gustav Mahler's early concertos. He didn't notice me until he was completely finished with the piece. Then he saw me and broke out into a huge smile. "Hey," he said. "Did you sleep well?"

"I did." That was an understatement. That bed was so damned comfortable, I was surprised that I didn't just want to stay there the entire week.

"Where would you like to do this?" he asked me. And then he called on the intercom. "Marina, could you please bring breakfast out to the terrace?"

He then turned to me. "I'm sorry, you probably think that I'm completely ADHD. I can assure you that I'm not. It's just that it occurred to me that both of us need some breakfast before tackling what we need to tackle. I'm sure that you agree."

I was hungry, famished actually, so I simply said "sure." I then went over to the carrier to let out the dogs, but they weren't in there.

Slade came up behind me. "I put them out. Don't worry, I do have a large fenced-in area on my land. I've always had dogs myself, so it's been a necessity to have it. I can either get Sven, my personal assistant, go and get the dogs or…"

"I'll get them." I was feeling a major annoyance already with how he apparently couldn't do anything for himself. Then I reminded myself that getting the dogs out of the fenced-in yard wasn't his responsibility anyhow. It was mine.

He pointed to the area where the fenced-in yard was, and I went over to it. My two beautiful girls came up and eagerly greeted me. I had their leashes and harnesses in my hands, and I put them on them and walked them into the house. They went into the house and immediately started sniffing around and exploring. "I hate to ask you this, but is there an area where we could confine these two?"

He shrugged. "Dogs will be dogs, you know? They'll settle down after they've explored the house, and if they have an accident, I'll..."

"I'll pick it up," I finished for him. I wasn't going to let Henry or Sven or Marina or any of his other peons pick up after my dogs.

"Suit yourself. At any rate, let's go out to the terrace. Marina will meet us out there with breakfast. I hope you like croissants, eggs and strawberries. I forgot to ask you what you like."

I took a deep breath. Croissants were made with butter, and I couldn't eat eggs, either. "My fault. I'm a vegan. I should have warned you about that."

He simply called Marina on the intercom after I said this. "Marina, could you please include regular whole grain toast and veggie sausage links in the breakfast too?" Then he turned to me. "I actually have a wide variety of things in this house that are vegan friendly, and Marina has been trained to cook anything at all. So, it's not a problem that you're vegan." He studied me. "What brings you to veganism?"

"Well...." I thought that I would get the whole reason why I was there out of the way. "I'm an empath. I can pick up strong vibrations that are translated into feelings for me. These feelings are often put into words in my head. It's almost like mind-reading, except it's not. For instance, if you're feeling guilt or remorse, I should be able to pick up on that, and that feeling would be translated into you saying, in my head, that you killed your business partner. That's why I'm here, as opposed to somebody on your team who's a bit more experienced than me."

"I see. And you won't eat animals because you have an unusual bond with them because of your empathic abilities." He said that as a statement, and I was impressed that he picked up on that so quickly and easily. "That makes an awful lot of sense. I admire your convictions, really."

"Thank you."

At that, he got out of his chair. "Follow me out to the terrace," and I obeyed. We got to a table that was small and had a marble top and four chairs around it. Down below was a patio that had a large table with 10 chairs around it, another swimming pool and another sunken jacuzzi that appeared to seat 20 or more. The area was surrounded by palm trees and bougainvilleas, a flower that is native to South America that was ubiquitous in California. They were beautiful flowers that grew into enormous bushes and came in various colors, including red, purple, white, yellow and pink. The bougainvilleas that surrounded the pool area were in every color and extremely mature, so that they really provided a natural privacy fence for that area.

A slight woman with blond hair soon appeared with a tray. Slade took baskets off the tray that were filled with strawberries, muffins, scones, and warm bread. Also on the tray was a plateful of eggs for him and veggie sausages for me, plus a pitcher of orange juice. "Thanks Marina," he said, taking everything off the tray.

"So, Serena," Slade began, "let's chat over breakfast. We can get these preliminaries out of the way, and then I have to get some work done while the workers set up for a party tonight."

I took a deep breath. "You were just arraigned for murder yesterday, and this evening you're having a party? Are you quite sure that's such a good idea?"

"No, I'm not quite sure that's a good idea, but who cares? Life has to go on even if you are suspected of murder. The grand jury hasn't returned an indictment, so, as of now, I haven't been formally charged with anything."

"Nonetheless, do you want the media to get ahold of this? They're going to crucify you."

"Like they already haven't. Listen, I know that you're thinking that I don't give a crap about the fact that I have a murder charge hanging over my head, but you're dead wrong about that. This party was scheduled a month ago, and I couldn't just cancel it. I'm very aware that the people in this country and the media believe that I should be withering away alone behind closed doors, secluding myself and clutching pearls because of what I allegedly did. And my answer to all those people is that they can all go to hell."

I had to admit he had a twisted sort of logic. I dug into my veggie sausages and strawberries. "Are those muffins made with butter or oil?" I asked him. I had to admit that the blueberry ones looked scrumptious – they were enormous, with whole blueberries and a crumble topping. I knew that crumble toppings were usually made with butter and so were muffins, so I was hoping that somehow, someway, they were vegan.

He was studying me carefully, his green eyes penetrating the armor that I'd so carefully built around myself. I suddenly felt vulnerable, like he could see inside of me. Maybe he was the empath, not me, because, thus far, I hadn't had any negative intuition at all about him. "They're made with butter, of course. If you would've sent word about your dietary restrictions, I would have accommodated you better."

"Of course, that was my mistake."

He merely grunted at that, and then summoned Marina to come to the table. She was there in a flash, and, before I had the chance to protest, he was asking her to make special muffins for me. "Marina, could you please whip up a batch of blueberry muffins for Serena? She doesn't consume animal products, so everything must be made with oil, even the topping."

"I'll do that," she said, and she disappeared.

"You didn't have to do that," I said.

"It's not a problem. I pay Marina good money to do things like make special muffins."

I turned my attention to my orange juice and took a sip. I glanced at the grove of orange trees that lay just beyond the pool area and surmised that the juice as freshly squeezed blood orange. "Very good juice," I said.

"I picked the oranges for this juice myself. I didn't squeeze them though."

"It's very tasty."

"Of course it is. My horticulturist is one of the best in the world, so the fruits that grow on the trees around here are truly premium."

I bristled at that, and wondered what was wrong with me. I had to admit that the trappings of wealth was something that didn't come naturally to me. My family was solidly working class, and, even though I made good money as a law partner, my earnings never came close to this guy's. So, everything about his lifestyle felt just a little bit wrong to me.

Marina soon appeared with the special muffins, and I eagerly dug into one. It was delicious, moist and fruity. "Where do you get these blueberries?" I asked him.

"They grow wild on my property. Not this property, but a property that I own in Oregon where it's a bit cooler. I have farmers up there harvesting the blueberries all summer long. There's other kinds of fruits up there as well, as well as hazelnuts and marijuana." Then he smiled.

"When pot was legalized in Oregon, I made a killing, I'll tell you that."

"I'll bet you did," I said. "A lot of people are getting rich off the green."

He shrugged. "It's a nice little side income. The farm is projected to bring in about $10 million this year, and it should be growing every year thereafter."

$10 million was a *side income.* Must be nice.

I ate the blueberry muffin and then helped myself to another. "Marina is an amazing baker," I said.

"Yes, she is. She's an amazing cook anyhow." He studied me. "So, Serena, I know that you didn't come up here to hear me rhapsodizing about blood oranges and pot, so why don't we get down to business?"

I nodded my head. "Yes. I need to know your story about what happened. And please don't lie to me. I'll be able to tell." That said, I was hesitant that I would be able to tell if he were lying. Ever since I met him, it was the weirdest thing. I wasn't getting anything negative from him at all. I couldn't feel even a hint of guilt, remorse or shame from him. No sadness, either, really, and this is what worried me. I hoped against hope that he wasn't a sociopath, because then my own life would be in danger.

The dogs came up to us, having thoroughly explored the house. Slade then summoned yet another person, whose name was Magdalena. She appeared, a beautiful 20ish Mexican woman. "Magdalena, could you please go through the house and make sure that these two dogs didn't create an accident? They probably did, so if you would be so kind as to clean up whatever is there, I would be much obliged." And then he said something in fluent Spanish, and she nodded her head and left.

"I should probably put them in their kennels while we

do this, since I can't watch them," I said, picking them both up in my arms. I walked through the house and put them in their kennels. "You go night night," I said to them. "I'll be right back." I never felt foolish for talking to dogs like some people did.

I went back out on the terrace, where Slade waited for me, sipping his orange juice. He poured me another glass when I sat down.

"Okay," I said. "Let's hear what happened the night Jordan Harris was murdered."

Chapter Five

"Where do I begin," he said. "I'll just start by telling you about the relationship I had with Jordan. He and I go way back to college. He was right there when I decided to start up my firm after got my PhD from Stanford. I was 23, and had big dreams. He had the connections that I needed to get venture capital for the firm, so he was very valuable. I managed to get Ambrose to the market in record time, and we were on our way."

Ambrose was a drug that was taking the country by storm. It was apparently the first anti-depressant that worked for many people who were previously drug-resistant, and it did it with a minimum of side-effects. Once it hit the market, and people were finding relief from depression who were never helped previously, it became an enormous hit.

His eyes were downcast, and I felt sadness emanating from him. I almost gave out a sigh of sheer relief when I felt this vibration, because it showed that he was capable of human emotions. *He's not a sociopath after all.*

Slade continued. "I loved him like a brother," he said. "I

couldn't have done any of it without him. But he suffered, always. He was like so many others who are highly intelligent – he was pretty socially awkward and I suspected that he was bipolar. It was undiagnosed, but the signs were there. He could literally work seven days straight without a break. Seven days without a wink of sleep. He'd call me from the lab at all hours of the morning, excited about some breakthrough. I finally had to turn off my phone while I slept, because he would be calling me at 2 AM, 3 AM, 4 AM. You get the point."

I nodded my head. "I've known people like that myself, so I'm right there with you." I thought of my brother Christopher, who was suffering from a mood disorder and had been ever since he witnessed the murder of our mother. I never knew if he had a chemical imbalance or he was just devastated, but he could be a brilliant song-writer when he wanted to, but that burst of creativity always alternated with crippling depression. He could probably be helped by Ambrose, I thought wryly.

"After the success of Ambrose, we were able to get a team of researchers and developers to patent more and more drugs. Everyone wanted to be a part of our up and coming firm, but Jordan couldn't care less most days. He would definitely come off his high-highs and sink down into the abyss. Our firm was working on drugs that would help cure him of his bipolar, including Chares, which was going to be our newest drug. Now, I don't know if it will make it to the market."

I closed my eyes, trying to feel if there was any deception coming off of him. So far, though, I felt that he was telling the truth. Of course, the most pertinent part of the story hadn't yet come out, so that was probably why he showed no hint of lying or guilt.

"On the night when I found him, he was coming off a 5 day binge where he did nothing but work, literally around the clock. And I do mean literally. Medical interns who work 100 hours a week had nothing on him during this period. I always was concerned about him, though, because I didn't know how he could continue to invent safe drugs while he was in that state. He would start to hallucinate, I guess. Then again, maybe he wasn't hallucinating at all."

"What do you mean?"

He sighed. "It's difficult to say. He became very paranoid, but, you know what they say about paranoid people – just because you're paranoid doesn't mean that somebody isn't actually out to get you." He smiled. "But he was paranoid about corporate espionage. He was also terrified that there was shadowy governmental agencies who were trying to shut us down. I do admit that corporate espionage is something that always concerned me as well. There's always somebody who is looking to rip off a drug that you're inventing and try to get their ripoff to market and to patent it before you get a chance to."

I listened carefully and took notes. The vibrations that were coming off of this guy were slight, nothing that would point to deception for me. "Go on," I said to him.

"Well, Jordan was developing a drug that he was really excited about, but he wouldn't tell me what it was. He said that it was going to revolutionize the industry, though, and it was something that was unlike anything anybody had ever seen before. He was very secretive about this particular drug, however, and I have no idea why he was. I personally was wondering if that drug that he was developing was all in his feverish and paranoid head."

I hung back and just let him talk. This was more important than me interjecting or asking questions.

"Yeah, so he was very paranoid, but brilliant." And then he started to look sad again.

It was then that I felt it. The despair that was roiling beneath his sunny exterior. It pierced my heart to feel that from him. It flooded me all at once, and I felt tears streaming down my cheeks. It was a powerful sensation, one that almost shook me to my core. I put one hand on one of his own, and the feelings became all the more potent.

"Uh," he said, and then shook his head. *I can't unsee what I saw.* I heard those words from him as plain as day. *You don't know how it affects you to see somebody that you care about bloody and broken on the floor.*

He put his thumb and forefinger on his face and pinched the top of his nose, as if he was trying to hold back tears. "I'm so sorry," he said, and I felt his grief. It was just as if I was the one who was grieving.

Then, just like that, I didn't feel anything anymore. It was if he had flipped a switch and his wall was back up again. He leaned back in his chair and finished what he was trying to say.

"Anyhow, I found him the night that I was arrested. His skull was crushed on one side, and he had been beaten up pretty badly. He was in the lab, which had been ransacked. I immediately called the police, and I was brought in for questioning that night. I called my lawyer who was there with me, of course. I thought everything was fine during the interrogation, and then they announced that they had probable cause to arrest me."

I had looked over the file, of course, before I came up to see him. I personally thought that the probable cause was flimsy at best. Apparently, he had motive to murder his business partner on the theory that Slade wanted total control of the company. There was evidence that was presented that Slade was working behind the scenes to oust Jordan from the firm, and that was enough for the police to arrest him.

I took a deep breath. "You were trying to get Jordan out of the company. Tell me about that."

His green eyes looked pained. "Serena, I just told you that Jordan was having some kind of a psychotic breakdown. I just told you that I was worried that he was going to be a danger to the company because he might have been in the lab inventing something that wouldn't have been safe. And a man in that state is a loose cannon, anyhow. I never knew what he would be doing next."

I closed my eyes and tried to feel what he was feeling when he said those words to me, but I couldn't. It was a blank space. I had no idea why, except that he had his defenses up. Why did he have his defenses up? That concerned me, to say the very least.

Slade continued his story. "So, I found him in that state, and I was arrested for his murder. I loved him like a brother, Serena. I wouldn't have done something like this to him."

Once again, I felt grief pouring out of him. But that didn't convince me that he didn't do it. After all, you can grieve for somebody that you killed. I wasn't naïve enough to think that wasn't possible. And the way that poor Jordan was killed was such that it was a crime of passion, in that the person who did that probably didn't go into that lab intending to kill the poor guy. Maybe it was all self-defense – Jordan was in a psychotic state, and Slade went in there, armed with a baseball bat in case Jordan tried to attack him. Then Jordan did attack him, and he had to fight back? That would mean that Slade would be grieving for his friend, because Slade would've felt that he had no choice to do what he did.

Maybe. But Slade wasn't singing that tune. He wasn't saying that it was self-defense, which would have been somewhat of a justification. Maybe not entirely a justification, simply because you cannot use more force than what is necessary to protect yourself, and Jordan was badly beat up. One whack of the baseball bat to send him into the hospital would be all that it would take.

Then I ruminated on Slade's words. That Jordan was a danger and that he might've been developing a drug that would be hazardous. Maybe Jordan was developing some kind of drug that would've given him superhuman strength? And perhaps he had taken that drug at the time when Slade went to confront him? In that case, it would've been difficult to fight him off, and maybe Slade was justified in beating him as badly as he did?

I decided to try to go into that line of questioning. "Okay, Slade, so you found him in that state. Do you happen to know anything about some of the drugs he was developing? Was there perhaps a drug that would increase testosterone to the point where, perhaps, Jordan had increased strength?"

He shook his head. "No. I mean, I don't know. He was developing a drug that he was excited about, but I don't think that this drug has anything to do with increasing testosterone." Then he thought more about what he was saying. "Why do you ask that question? You think that I did this in self-defense? That maybe I went in there, and Jordan was as strong as a bear, and I had to beat him like that?"

I had to hand it to him, he was lightning-quick. "I'm just trying to cover all the angles."

Slade shook his head, and his hand was shaking as he put his glass of orange juice to his lips. "I told you that I had nothing to do with it, and that's that." Then he shook his head. "You're my lawyer. There's nobody else here at the moment. Therefore, anything I tell you will be in confidence. If I did it, even in self-defense, I would tell you. I know how the game works. If a client lies, that client doesn't get a good defense."

"You also know that if I know for sure that you're guilty, because you told me so, I couldn't put you on the stand. If I did, I would be suborning perjury."

"I know that." He narrowed his beautiful green eyes. "Why are you here? You obviously don't want to know the truth if you're telling me that if I did it, I should lie to you. I'm not lying to you at all, of course, but it seems that's not good enough for you. You want me to tell you that I did it because why? That would make your job that much easier? Listen, Serena, I don't know what your game is. But I'm not lying, and, besides, a self-defense justification would be impossible to win in this case. So, even if you get me to confess to something, it wouldn't make the road any easier."

Flashes of intense anger flooded through me, and I closed my eyes. I didn't want to lash out at him, but it was difficult to do. His anger was permeating my pores, and I took a deep breath. I tried to find my center, and, after a few minutes, I did.

So, grief and anger were the two emotions that I was getting from him. So far, no sense of guilt, no sense of remorse. But was he angry because he didn't do it, and felt that I was attacking him? Or was he angry because he did do it, and I was getting too close?

He shook his head. "This interview is over. Now, if you'll excuse me, I need to do a staff meeting so that we can all get ready for the party this evening." At that, he threw his napkin on the table and went into the French doors that led into the rest of the house. I was left at the table, alone, staring at the empty drinking glasses. So far, this wasn't going well at all. I couldn't get a proper read on this guy, and what I was feeling was very difficult to interpret.

One thing was for sure – this guy was closed-off. Aside from the flashes of grief I was feeling from him, and the anger there at the end, I couldn't get anything off of him. It was almost as if he was so guarded that, the second he starts to feel something negative, he brings up a wall so that he doesn't have to access those uncomfortable feelings. Not that he was any different than most of us, because it was human nature to try to cover up and hide from what we really feel. But Slade's tendency to do that was going to make my job that much more complicated.

I went into the house and I found Marina in the kitchen making a pie crust. The kitchen was enormous, the size of a commercial kitchen, with several stoves and ovens, a multitude of pots and pans hanging overhead and as much counter-space as any industrial kitchen. However, the counters weren't metal, like with most commercial kitchens, but were marble. Like everywhere else in this home, the kitchen looked like it was designed by a top-notch interior designer. It was elegant, with a mosaic Italian stone floor and metal appliances that fit in with the décor.

"Mr. Bridgewell is around here somewhere," I said to Marina. "Could you please tell him that I'm going out for the afternoon?"

"Yes," she said in a thick, Russian accent. "I will. Will you be back for the party?"

I shook my head, but then thought better of it. *Get a read on this guy, find out what makes him tick.* I remembered, anew, why I was selected for this job, and observing Slade at a party had to be part of the job description. If he was going to flitting around his guests like a social butterfly, without a care in the world, that would concern me, to say the very least. I did somewhat understand his reasoning for continuing to hold the party. Life did have to go on, and canceling a party where there were a lot of guests – apparently that would be the case with this party – wouldn't necessarily be fair to everyone involved. But hopefully he wasn't going to act like nothing was wrong.

I went to the dog carrier and got the two dogs out of their cages. They were fast asleep when I got there, and when I woke them up, they looked at me with bleary eyes. They both stretched and yawned, with Gigi making a little noise when she yawned. And then, just like that, they sprung to life, their little bodies wriggling excitedly around my feet. I picked up Sadie, and she gave me kisses all over my face. I reveled in her puppy breath and smell, and immediately relaxed. That was what I needed after my stressful interrogation of Slade.

Then I put the carrier in the back of my car and put the two dogs into it.

As I approached the gate of the house, the reporters, hundreds of them, swarmed my car. They beat on the window, asking me to roll down the window and give a comment. I just looked at them and drove right through the phalanx.

And I headed back to San Diego.

Chapter Six

I had no idea why I was heading back to San Diego, except that I needed the drive to clear my head. I was more than confused by Slade. He obviously had many sides to him. He was charming, an animal lover, had discerning taste in décor and was an amazing classical pianist. He seemed to be very kind-hearted. Yet, beneath the surface, there was something there that roiled. I couldn't quite put my finger on it, but it was white-hot. He was a passionate guy, of course. You don't get to where he is without having drive and passion. You don't get your PhD from Stanford in molecular biology at the age of 23, and develop a revolutionary drug shortly thereafter, without passion.

I knew that I shouldn't try to investigate his background until I was done questioning him. I didn't want impassive news articles to color my perception of him. These news articles would probably be glowing, because he had accomplished so very much. I just needed to go with my intuition and not try to let the media color how I saw him, either good or bad. The media filter was not wanted in my world.

So, I didn't bother to do research on him. I had to clear my head some other way, so, when I got back into town, the first thing I did was go to La Jolla cove to watch the sea lions. I couldn't bring the dogs out, unfortunately, because the beaches generally didn't allow animals until after 6 PM in the summertime.

I called Michael on a whim. I hoped that he would be home, because it was his day off. Of course, he probably was surfing.

He answered the phone. "Hey," he said. "What's up?"

"I really need to talk to you. Can you come to the cove?"

"You got me at just the right time. I just got done surfing, and I was scrounging around the house for a bite to eat. You treat me to lunch, and I'll be there."

"Thanks. I'll be where the sea lions are. Not the seals, but the sea lions."

"See you in a few."

I went to the back of my car to check on my girls. I opened the cage and pet them and gave them water, which they eagerly lapped up. "Don't worry, little ones, we'll soon be getting out of here. I just needed to see my sea lion friends for a little bit. They always cheer me up when I'm feeling out of sorts."

Sadie and Gigi both looked like they understood me, and I smiled.

I went back to where the sea lions were, after putting the dogs back in their cage, and I just sat, watching the water. It lapped, wave after wave, on the big rocks. I always craved being near the ocean. It made me feel so very small and insignificant, which I really was, if you think about it. In the course of history, man was very small potatoes. There was no denying that. Our little problems were not only microscopic, but fleeting. A hundred years from now, nobody would even remember who I was, of course. They might remember Slade, but hopefully they would because his drugs would still be in circulation, not because he murdered somebody. He didn't murder that guy.

Did he?

I hated that I had no idea. Slade was way too closed off for me to get a decent read on him. That was why I was there at the beach. Clearing my head was necessary here. It was like a palate cleanser at a fancy restaurant. You had to get the taste of the previous meal out of your mouth before going onto the next course. I was going to approach Slade that evening, and observe him at the party, but I had to do it with a cleared head and no preconceptions.

I closed my eyes and listened to the sounds of the seagulls, who were crying loudly. The distant sounds of sea lions barking on far away rocks also permeated, as well as the excited talking and laughter of the people all around me.

Finally, I heard Michael. I looked up, and he was standing there. "Hey girl," he said to me.

"Hey," I said. "Glad you could make it."

"Of course. I had to, because you don't usually call me like that to meet with you in the middle of the day. I figured you needed to talk to me about something important."

He offered me his hand, and I took it, standing up and dusting myself off. "Let's go to Piatti's. We can sit on the patio, have a glass of wine and talk."

"Cool," he said. "You drive and bring me back here? I got my surfboard, and I'm going to surf after we get done with lunch."

"You got it," I said. I loved Piatti's, because their cauliflower cakes were divine, and the waiters there knew me. They knew not to bring me anything that had animal products in it, and the aioli that was served with the cakes was made with oil, especially for me. I always tipped extremely well, too, so they didn't mind giving me a bit of extra service. Also, their outdoor patio was elegant and beautiful, with white table cloths, wrought iron chairs, umbrellas, lots of shade and large central area that was filled with plants and flowers. I couldn't believe that such an elegant place was dog-friendly, but indeed it was.

We got to the restaurant, I got the dogs out and let them potty on the grass. I picked up their mess and put it into the trash can nearby, and then we headed to the patio, where a waitress was soon there. Sadie and Gigi settled in beneath my feet, and both of them conked out and, almost immediately, started to snore..

"Puppies sure do sleep a lot," I said.

"Dogs do in general. I've noticed that – dogs kind of sleep all day and all night. Guess it's pretty boring to be a dog."

"Yeah."

"So, what's on your mind?"

I took a sip of water. "I have a case. Now, I'd like to bounce some things off of you, but you can't say anything to anyone." I felt that I could trust Michael, even though I really didn't know him all that well.

"What's the case about?"

I took a deep breath. "It's the Slade Bridgewell case."

Michael's eyes lit up. "Seriously? You're working that? You just got on at that firm, and you're already assigned to something like that?"

"No. I mean, I'm on the legal team, but I couldn't imagine I would take the lead on this. I'm doing the preliminaries, though."

"Meaning?"

"Meaning I'm staying there with him all this week. I have to, as Malcolm put it, 'find out what makes him tick.' The translation for that, of course, is that Malcolm feels that I can use my abilities to find the truth of the matter."

"And? Is it working?"

I shook my head. "No. It doesn't seem to be." I sighed. "He's very closed off. I could sense that from the very beginning. He has this affable, friendly demeanor, but it's all a façade. Unfortunately, I'm unable to get anything clear from him. It's like he has this brick wall up."

Michael sat back in his chair. "Ah, I get it. You got the hots for this cat." Then he shrugged. "Not that I blame you. He's pretty smoking." Then he looked at me. "What? I can say a guy is smoking. That doesn't make me gay."

I smiled. "I didn't say that it did. You know that men your age are much more likely to say a guy is attractive than older guys do. That doesn't make any of them gay, either."

"That's cool. So, what's the problem?"

I shook my head. "I do find him extraordinarily attractive. I can't help it. He has this magnetism. He's virile and handsome and….graceful. Discerning. My head is going haywire. So, my attraction to him, combined with the fact that he's closed-off." I shook my head. "I'm worried that I can't do my job. The job that Malcolm wants me to do."

Michael sipped his water, and the waitress came back around. I ordered the cauliflower cakes, "aioli made with oil, not butter," and Michael ordered the grilled salmon.

"I don't understand," Michael said after the waitress left. "Why does Malcolm even care if the guy is guilty or not?"

"Well, he doesn't want to look bad if it turns out that Slade is acquitted, when the whole world knows that he's guilty. Not to mention the fact that he doesn't want to lose this case. And it will help the defense if we know if he's guilty or not. And, really, I'm the perfect person to do the preliminaries if you think about it. We can't put him on the stand if he confesses to his guilt, so we certainly don't want him to admit to anything. Yet I can presumably tell if he's lying. The only problem is, I can't tell at all if he's lying."

"That is a problem," Michael agreed. "What are you going to do about that?"

I took a deep breath. "What do you recommend? Should I try to talk to Malcolm about excusing me from this case, or do I keep going, knowing that I'm probably not going to get a good read on him? Or should I just try to keep getting a solid read? I'm only human, after all. I can't always turn on my psychic abilities on command, as much as Malcolm wants me to. I'm kind of in a dilemma here."

"You are, that's for sure. If you want my opinion, and I think that you surely do, then I say that you need to stick it out. You're not a quitter. And if you don't give Malcolm accurate information, then you don't give him accurate information. You're not a trained monkey. You can't just dance on command. So, don't worry about it. You won't lose your job over it."

"No. But I might lose my reputation. Not to mention the reputation of the firm."

Michael broke open the bread that had just appeared in front of us, and looked at me. "He shouldn't have put you in that position. If you lose your job over something like that, I would think that you would have grounds to sue."

I smiled. "Sue for what? Psychics aren't exactly a protected class under the Civil Rights Act."

"What's that supposed to mean?"

"Race, gender, national origin and disabilities are all protected. You can't fire someone just because they're black or a woman or they're disabled, unless the particular disability interferes with the job description. But I can get fired for not providing an accurate empathic reading."

"Ah, I see. Well, it sounds like you might get fired either way." Then he smiled. "And, Serena, you probably will be fired for sleeping with this guy, so don't go there. Even though I know that you want to. I can see it in your eyes."

"Thanks for the warning," I said. "I'm not stupid. I know that sleeping with him would be a no-no, to say the very least."

"Ummmmkay," he said. "Well, then…" At that, the waitress brought us our food. We dug in with gusto, talking the rest of the time about things that had nothing to do with Slade.

For the first time in days, I truly felt relaxed.

After lunch, I headed back up to Los Angeles. I caught the Pacific Coast Highway when I got north of Del Mar. This was a much more scenic route up the coast, even though it didn't go all the way up to LA. But parts of the PCH went through quaint little coastal towns, the ocean gleaming close by. I loved this part of California, and I wondered how I ever managed to live for so long in New York City, in that cramped brownstone. Not that I didn't love the vibrancy of that city, because I did.

A few hours later, after exiting the PCH and getting on the Five, I was on the road to Malibu. I felt considerable anxiety, and I had no idea why. All that I knew was that there was a prickly, icy-cold feeling that I tried hard to shake. I was getting close, I knew, to getting to the point where I could uncover Slade's demons. They were there, just beneath the surface. I knew it. I could feel it.

Winding my way up the steep hill to his house, I felt a bit calmer. Then, when I approached the gate, and there were more reporters than ever, not to mention a helicopter, I felt the anxiety rising again. I had no clue what awaited me, but it couldn't be good. It was six o'clock, and I didn't know when the party was going to start, but I would imagine it would be soon. I ignored the reporters, of course, and they didn't try to harass me, and I was soon in the gate.

I made my way to his home, and it was completely abuzz. There were waiters in black ties and pants, with tuxedo shirts, everywhere. They were busy setting up tables in the grand room, which was as large as any ballroom. It was filled with tables with white tablecloths, a centerpiece of star lilies and wildflowers, and candles. In the kitchen, there was an entire crew of people back there, preparing lobster and filet mignons, risotto and salads. In the bar area, there were another crew of people who were standing at the ready.

I found Slade, who was busy directing somebody, presumably the head of the wait crew, about everyone's stations. He glanced at me, barely, and then asked the wait crew head to find him the head chef, because he needed to talk to him too.

I waited patiently, and then he turned to me. "What happened to you today?" he asked me.

"I went out." I didn't really want to give him anymore information than that.

"Out where?"

I didn't like his tone of voice. It was accusing, with a hint of bitterness. "Out."

"Well, you probably should check with me before doing that. You're lucky that you weren't followed by a reporter."

"Why should I care if I am?"

He narrowed his eyes. "You're my lawyer. Are you new to this? You obviously are. I can tell that you've never been involved in a case like this one." Then he clicked on the television, and Fox News came on. They were discussing his case. He clicked on another channel. CNN. Also discussing his case. Another channel. MSNBC. Discussing his case.

"Do you get the picture here? You don't want some reporter stalking you. You might give them more information than you should, it you aren't properly trained on what to say. Which I suspect is the case."

I felt my bile roiling. "Mr. Bridgewell, I'll have you know that I'm a professional. I've had plenty of courses on legal ethics, thank you very much, and I know better than to discuss a single word of what you told me. Which wasn't much. But if you think for one second that I would ever, and I mean ever, slip up to a reporter about your case, then I'm disappointed in you. You obviously believe that I'm some kind of green 1L who is seeking the limelight. You couldn't be more wrong about that."

At that, he put his hands on my shoulders, and looked me right in the eye. In spite of my anger, I felt electricity shooting throughout my body where he was touching me. It almost burned. I blinked my eyes, trying to ignore how captivated I suddenly felt. My breathing was shallow as his face got closer to mine.

"I apologize. Of course, you're a professional. It's just that I've had more people selling me up the river than I care to fathom. People I have trusted have talked. None of these people are in my inner circle anymore, of course. I just don't want to lose another one. That's all."

I closed my eyes, feeling his sincerity in my bones. "It's okay, Slade," I said. "You have every right to be angry. From now on, I'll be sure and let you know personally when I leave and what I'll be doing. It was very unprofessional of me to leave like that."

He stared at me for a second. "I think that's the first time you called me by my first name." Then he smiled. "I kinda like it. Lawyers usually don't do that unless I give them permission, which I didn't with you. But it makes me feel that you and I are a bit more than lawyer and client." At that, he seemed to get a devilish look in his eyes.

I then felt the heat between us, and I looked down at the floor. "Maybe we should keep it lawyer-client. After all, I'm staying here with you for the week. It might be weird-"

He put his finger on my chin and lifted up my face. I tried to ignore the weakness in my knees as his face got closer and closer to mine. Then, just like that, he pulled away. "Not weird. It's nice. Please, continue to call me Slade. That's my name, after all."

And, just like that, he turned his back and walked away. I saw him speaking to a guy with a tall chef's hat on, and I had to admit that I had to recover from him touching me so intimately on my chin. For a second, it looked like he wanted to kiss me, and I was embarrassed to admit that I was begging for that.

We were more than lawyer and client. I hated to think about what that might mean to him.

I had to talk myself down, because my heart was pounding out of my chest, and my hands were shaking like leaves in a strong wind. *You're his lawyer, Serena. You can't have him. That would be completely unethical. And, besides, he's not interested in you.*

When I told myself that last part, though, I wasn't so

sure. There was certainly something there in those piercing green eyes of his, while he looked at me so intensely. I could feel it coming from him. He seemed to be as attracted to me as I was to him.

I sighed. I was in trouble, that was for sure. That electrical spark between us was going to cloud my judgment and possibly send my natural intuitive senses completely haywire.

I might never get to the truth about him.

Chapter Seven

At 7 PM, the party was in full swing. Everyone was standing around, eating hors d'oeuvres, which consisted of caviar, salmon puffs, enormous prawn cocktails and beef carpaccio. There was light classical music floating through the air, and I saw a four-piece quartet in the corner. The hall was filled to the brim with people in black tie and evening gowns. It seemed like the crème de la crème was there, from Senators to models and actors. There were quite a few people that I recognized as major film producers and actresses, as well as people that I knew were prominent artists and business people. I didn't recognize everyone there, of course, but I knew that there had to be quite a few billionaires in that room.

And, of course, I noticed that there were a few people in the room taking pictures. I went over to Slade, who was holding court in a tuxedo. I felt underdressed, even though I was wearing a sundress and heels. I didn't think to pack a formal evening gown, of course, never imagining that Slade would have what looked to be a charity ball right when he was under investigation for a brutal murder.

Tone deaf. That was the only word for him at that point.

"Slade," I said.

He put his arm around me and smiled. "Everyone, I would like for you to meet Serena Roberts. She's the person who is going to put this whole sorry affair to bed for me. Serena, this is Senator Johnson, Charlotte Boswell and Max Pierson. Max is an amazing artist who actually just got a showing at the Louvre, of all places. You really should check out some of his pieces – they're amazing, and I have more than one in this home."

I nodded to everyone, and Charlotte, who was a willowy brunette with large breasts, long legs and a perfect face, looked at me suspiciously. "I'm very pleased to meet you," she said. "I'm Slade's girlfriend."

Slade just looked at me, and shook his head. It was then that I recognized her from all the cosmetic ads that she had done. She was a famous runway model who just got a major part in a film coming that fall.

I had to admit, my heart fell when she introduced herself as Slade's girlfriend. I wasn't aware that he had a girlfriend, of course. I thought that he had lots of girl-friends, not just one, although I had to admit that every other girl that I had seen him with were just like this Char-lotte person. Gorgeous, statuesque, without an ounce of fat on them.

Slade looked at the little group of people. "Would you please excuse me," he said. "I believe that Serena needs to talk to me in private. I'll be right back."

At that, he took my hand, and I felt the electricity shoot up through my arm again. Every hair stood on end, and I cursed these involuntary reactions to him. My body was betraying me. It was betraying my mind, too, because all I could think of when I was led through the crowd of people was what it was like to see this magnificent man naked. That image was burned in my brain, and, even though I had tried to let it go, I just couldn't. I craved seeing him naked again, but in bed this time.

We finally got to the den, which was closed off to the party at the moment. However, judging by the way that it was set up, I assumed that there would come a time when the party was going to be heading that way. There were candles and flower arrangements everywhere in that room, where there weren't these things in that room before.

"I can see that you need to talk to me. And, thanks, by the way. Charlotte can't seem to get into her head that we're through. I didn't even invite her. She just showed up, and I didn't want to make a scene, so I just let her stay."

I nodded my head. "I wanted to tell you that there's paparazzi in this place."

"Of course," he said. "There always is. I always invite a few reporters and photographers to my functions. How else can I get publicity for the cause?"

"I'm embarrassed to even ask this, because I guess I should have asked this before. But what is the function for tonight? I guess I didn't realize that it would be so formal."

He smiled. "What, you thought that there would be a host of topless floozies here and men bashing guitars? That's next Saturday night." He wasn't smiling, but I got the joke anyhow. Then he broke into a grin. "Nah, I don't tend to have those other kinds of parties anymore. I go to some, though. But this is a charity ball for the ASPCA. I'm on the board, and it's my pet cause, no pun intended."

I shook my head, feeling ashamed. I berated him for partying while he was under suspicion of murder, and I didn't even bother to ask him what the party was for. ASPCA was a charity that was near and dear to my heart, too, as I annually donated thousands to them. I kind of loved that this was his "pet cause," no pun intended.

He looked at me, and took my hands. "Was that all that you wanted to say to me? That there are photographers here?"

"Yes," I said, feeling my face go white-hot.

He nodded his head. "I love that you're looking out for me, but I got this. It's your job, though, to make sure that my image isn't tarnished while I'm under investigation. Not indictment, though. Hopefully I won't be indicted. But, seriously, I got this. I wouldn't imagine having a charity ball would make me look bad to the public, but you just never know."

He put his hand in my hair. "I forgot to mention, but you have gorgeous hair."

I closed my eyes, reveling in his touch. "Thanks," I finally said. My heart rate was going through the roof, and his fingers were leaving a trail of burning flesh in their wake.

Then, just like that, he dropped his hand. He looked around, because the door was opening. There stood Charlotte, big as life, giving me the stink-eye like nobody had ever given me the stink-eye before. "There you are," she said tightly to Slade. "Senator Feinstein is looking for you. I know that you don't want to keep her waiting, since she's so integral to your cause."

Slade just nodded his head. "Of course." Then he turned to me. "So sorry, Serena. I know that you're looking out for me, but I do have to do a little ring-kissing. There's legislation pending and I need all the congressmen and women I can get on-board this thing. We're trying to end gestation crates for all pigs, and I can't think of anything more important."

He left, and I caught my breath again. He looks like that, *and* he's passionate about animal rights? I shook my head. I was getting way, way over my head on this one. All I could think was that I couldn't possibly do my job correctly.

I had to detach myself. I knew that I had to try to do that, so I closed my eyes and found my center. Sometimes meditation helped me when I was feeling stressed out or out of sorts. I needed to find the calm that I was just starting to find when I was thrust into this man's life. I wished, anew, that I was home, where I felt safe.

Home, where the demons haunted me much less.

The party wore on. The guests were served dinner, and there was a silent auction, and the winners were announced. After the silent auction, the guests dispersed throughout the house. I wondered around, and, everywhere I looked, there was live music, and people laughing, dancing and talking. It seemed that everyone who was in the ballroom earlier was still in the house, enjoying themselves. I went out to the terrace and looked at the pool area below. There were a group of intoxicated people, throwing each other in the pool in their evening gowns and tuxedoes, although one guy was enterprising enough to strip down to his underwear before doing a cannonball into the water. There were peals of laughter as everyone splashed around, and one person after another got pushed in.

I usually liked a good party myself, but I felt out of place with these people.

As I stood on the terrace, a man joined me. Tall and

blonde, fortyish and handsome, he stood next to me, looking out at the people below. "Looks like fun, doesn't it?" he finally said to me in a thick Australian accent. "I'm Dane. I was a friend of Jordan's."

I nodded my head. "Serena."

"I know who you are," he said. "I asked about you, just because I'd never seen you around before." He stood there with his hands at his side, and sipped a glass of champagne. "He did it, you know. He and Jordan had lots of words before Jordan died. He was the only one who would have motive."

I cocked my head at him. "Why are you here? You obviously have no loyalty to Slade. And you should know that I can't discuss his case with you or anyone else."

He looked back at the crowd and shrugged. "I guess he's just keeping his enemies close, as they say. Slade certainly isn't a stupid man. Anyhow, I hope that you don't get him off. A man like him certainly shouldn't be walking free."

At that, Slade himself came out on the terrace. He put his arm around Dane. "Dane, my man. You're being summoned in the great room. I suggest you go in there."

Dane shrugged his shoulders and walked back into the house without another word.

"What did he say to you?" Slade asked when Dane was out of earshot.

"I think you probably know. He has no love for you, that's for sure."

"Of course not. Bastard's been going to the news media, feeding them crap. I'm quite sure that he's one of their many anonymous sources."

"Why is he here?"

He smiled. "I'm quite sure that he probably told you that I'm keeping my enemies close, which is exactly what

I'm trying to do. Believe it or not, there are a lot of people here at this party who would love to see me fry. I'm keeping tabs on every one of them, and I have more than one loyal friend who is reporting to me everything that they're saying about me. That's the best way to know who's a rat, and it's the best way for me to keep on top of things."

Then he smiled. "I hate that they're eating my food and drinking my Dom, though, not to mention all the high-end liquors I always have at these things. Bastards have no shame, really. They'll smile to my face, drink my $20,000 bottle of Scotch, and then spread lies about me to the media. Don't think for a second I don't know exactly who's saying what."

The two of us stood looking at the people below, who were still giggling and throwing each other into the pool. We could also see his hot tub in the woods, and we could just make out the fact that there were three people in that hot tub, all them naked and groping one another. They were two guys and a girl, and the two guys were all over each other as well as all over the woman.

He shook his head. "They'll get what's coming to them, though, once I beat this thing. Ostracized won't be the word. Socially dead is what they're going to be. And I can't wait."

I saw the flash of anger in his eyes, and I felt it in my bones. This guy had a temper, that much was clear, and that worried me. But, really, everyone had a temper. A breaking point. That was just human nature. It would be odd if he wasn't angry with these "friends" of his who were selling his story to the media.

Still, I wondered. How bad was his temper, and could it have led him to do something like what had happened to Jordan?

I hated that I still doubted him, but I couldn't help it. I was having more and more difficulty getting a decent read on him. His emotions were too scattered, and I was getting more confused with each passing moment. One moment, he was unruffled, the next he was intensely angry. And, of course, there were moments that I was feeling pure desire from him. I hoped that wasn't wishful thinking, in spite of myself. Because, even if I couldn't act on it, I could fantasize about him. I could imagine what it would feel like to have those sensuous lips on mine, devouring me. Those green eyes looking through my skin into my soul, drinking me in and twisting my insides like a pretzel. There were so many things that I wanted to do to him, and I wanted to imagine that he felt the same.

Of course, imagining is all that could happen, because I was his lawyer.

He finally smiled at me, and put his hand on my shoulder. "I better get back," he whispered in my ear. The involuntary tingles flushed through my body as his hand lingered on my bare shoulder. "I'll see you later."

Then I saw him go back into the house and go from one group to another.

I sighed. I was really in trouble. Perhaps I needed to call Malcolm and tell him, definitively, that I was the wrong woman for this job.

Then I thought better about that. I was a professional, goddammit. I wasn't going to let this guy derail me. Perhaps that was his MO.

I hated to think that I was yet another victim of his charm.

Chapter Eight

The next day, I stretched and yawned and padded gingerly down the steps. To my surprise, there were still stragglers around, although they were no longer in their evening wear. They were wearing normal clothes, apparently anticipating staying the night. There were about five people in one of the many entertainment rooms, leisurely watching television while eating breakfast. There were more people out by the pool, sunning in their bathing suits.

One of the people was Charlotte, who had a disturbingly perfect body. She was holding court outside by the pool, and she waved at me when she saw me.

I went over to her. I had to remember that I was supposed to learn all that I could about Slade, and I supposed that befriending a woman who was his girlfriend at one time, now appeared to be a stalker, would be a part of that job description.

"Hello, Serena," she said in a friendly manner. "Sorry about last night. I think that I had too much to drink."

I sat down next to her. "Don't worry about it. You weren't rude."

"Of course I was. Listen, I suppose that Slade told you that I'm not his girlfriend anymore. Technically, that's very true. But I think that we're going to be getting back together at any time." Then she smiled sweetly. "I'm very surprised that you're his lawyer. You certainly don't look the part."

"What are lawyers supposed to look like?"

She shrugged her shoulders. "Oh, I don't know. I guess I always imagined Susan Dey. I watched that show when I was a small child and it was on reruns. LA Law. I'm sure that's before your time."

"No, it's not," I said. "I mean, it was pretty much off the air before I was old enough to enjoy something like that, but, like you, I caught reruns. But I'm curious why you would use a show that was on in the eighties and early nineties as your touchstone on how a lawyer should be."

She sipped her mojito daintily. "These are delicious. You should get Slade to make you one."

I closed my eyes, and I felt her vibrations, which were surprisingly strong. She was far from the sunny person she was trying to portray. She was angry, extremely angry, and jealous. Her jealousy was the emotion that I felt most acutely from her.

I opened my eyes, knowing not to trust her. Not that I ever would've trusted her anyhow, considering how much she always seemed to be glomming onto Slade.

"I'm sorry," she said. "What was it that you were just asking me?"

"Nothing," I said. "And lawyers are nothing like on that show. Trust me, most of the work that we do is boring as hell. Very rarely do we get something juicy coming across our desks."

She nodded her head. "And this one is very juicy for you, isn't it?" She narrowed her eyes, and I could feel, imperceptibly, the judgment from her. She was trying to trap me into admitting something, and I thought that I knew what that something was.

She wanted me to admit that I was attracted to Slade, at which point she would go right to my law firm and rat on me. Her motives were becoming more and more clear. She wanted me out of the way.

I guessed that I should've been flattered that she saw me as a romantic rival. I had to compose my face and give nothing, absolutely nothing, away. "Of course," I said. "Murder cases do tend to be more interesting than, say, corporate mergers, although sometimes corporate mergers have a sexiness and an intrigue all their own."

She cocked her head, and then caught a beach ball that was thrown at her. Slade was approaching the pool area, and, with a sly smile, she took off her top, revealing her perfect, and apparently natural, breasts.

Slade approached our chairs and sat on the end of mine. "Serena, I see that you don't have anything to eat, so I brought you some of these vegan brownies and a tofu frittata. Marina made it this morning just for you."

I looked over at Charlotte, who was glaring at me. "Oh, you're one of those," she said. "A vegan." Then she rolled her eyes. "A dime a dozen out here in LA. Probably only doing that because it's the thing, aren't you?"

I opened my mouth, and Slade said "why Serena is a vegan is none of your affair, Charlotte. I'd appreciate it if you'd mind your own business for once in your life."

She said nothing, but turned her attention to the people who were in the pool, and then, with a perfect dive, she was in the water.

I dug into the tofu frittata, which was amazing. I was always impressed when somebody who ordinarily prepared non-vegan food had a deft hand in preparing vegan food as well, and Marina was certainly in that latter group.

He looked at Charlotte, and then back at me. "Sorry about her. She's a beast."

"Yet she's still here." I raised an eyebrow at him. "Either you like the drama, or you really don't mind her presence."

He shook his head. "I'm trying to stop her from going to the media and the police and spreading lies. She's one of the many people who I'm trying to control the best that I can."

It was then that I saw it in his eyes and felt it emanating from his every pore. He was worried. Very worried. I wondered exactly what he was worried about. Was he just worried about all the Benedict Arnolds who were feeding the media crap about him? Was he worried that he couldn't get a fair trial? That he would lose? Or was he worried that I'd catch onto him if I stayed there long enough?

That was the bad thing about being an empath. I could feel others emotions, but their reasons behind their emotions weren't always clear. Sometimes it was, as with Cindy back home. It was clear that she wanted the job that I got, and it was also clear that she had the hots for Slade. But Slade was more of a mystery to me. I was having a difficult time discerning where his various emotions were coming from.

I put my hand on his and tried to get a better handle on him. But, like before, he was apparently able to cover up that negative emotion, because I no longer felt that he was worried. "I'd chase all these people off, but I really don't want to," he said to me. "Believe it or not, I sometimes feel comfortable having a bunch of people around. It's easier to escape that way."

He didn't elaborate on what he meant by "escaping," so I asked him. "What are you trying to escape?"

He looked at me, and I felt like I was going to melt into the chair. "Nothing. It's just a figure of speech." Then he looked down at the chair, and he almost seemed like a young boy. "You look dry," he observed, because I drank the orange juice that he had offered to me. "Let me get you another one."

"My legs work," I said, getting up off the chair. "You don't have to bother."

He grinned. "Oh, I wasn't. I was going to get one of my help to bring you something." Then he looked down again, and I could tell that he was teasing me.

I laughed and made my way up the stairs into the kitchen.

While I was standing in the kitchen, pouring myself a glass of water, I felt Slade come up behind me. He stood there, his chest on my back, and he put his arms on either side of me. "Let me help you," he said, taking the glass of water out of my hand. His breath, hot and moist, was in my ear.

My breath caught as I felt him pressed up against me. It felt uncomfortable, yet completely exhilarating. "I got it," I said. "I know how to get a glass of water."

He ignored me, and turned on the sink, filling the glass to the brim with water. He was still right behind, pressed up against me, his hands on either side of me.

I turned and tried to sneak in underneath one of his arms, but he didn't move. I was now facing him, and he was extremely close to me, his hands on either side of me, gripping the side of the countertop. "You feel it, don't you?"

I swallowed hard. "Feel what?"

"You know what." Then he put his finger underneath my chin again. "You're goddamned beautiful. I hope you know that."

I felt my face flush scarlet. "I-"

Then it happened. He gently put his full and sensuous lips on my own, and I literally lost my breath. I closed my eyes, and got completely and utterly lost as his lips were gliding over, sucking and biting my own. His tongue found mine, and the electricity that I felt before was magnified by a thousand. By a million.

I sighed as he continued to kiss me gently, his hands running through my hair. He leaned into me, and I could feel his erection, enormous and proud, through his shorts. I reared back my head, wanting, longing for him to continue, yet, at the back of my mind, I knew that it was completely, and utterly, wrong.

His lips made their way to my clavicle and neck, his hands gently stroking my hair. His kisses left burning trails all over my skin. I summoned every nerve in my body to tell him to stop, but it was useless. I felt like I was being consumed by him. Consumed by his touch, surprisingly gentle, and his kisses, which were also gentle but were becoming much more heated and passionate with every passing second.

As his hands were making their way to my sides, and then were planted firmly in the curve of my back, I finally managed the strength to push him away. "No," I said. "I'm your lawyer, and, I'm sorry, I really don't want to be another notch on your bedpost."

He looked stricken at my words, and I felt how my sudden rebuke stung him to his core. I sensed that nobody had ever rejected him before, and, at first, I felt that he was hurt. Then, as with the other times before, I didn't feel his hurt anymore. I felt nothingness. His wall had returned.

He simply raised an eyebrow and turned on his heel and walked away.

Once he was safely out of the kitchen, I turned back to the sink, putting my hands on the edge. I was trembling all over, and my mind was going 1000 miles per hour. I had never felt desire like I just felt with him, and that worried me. I was already having problems trying to get a read on him, and this was just complicating matters that much further.

I took a deep breath and tried to gather my thoughts. Every cell in my body, however, was on fire and screaming for him. I wanted him to do things to me that nobody ever had. However complicated it would be to have sex with him, I didn't care. My body didn't care, anyhow, but my mind was still focused on how wrong it would be for so many reasons. Not just the ethical reasons, but also because I wouldn't be able to do the job that I was sent to do. There would be no way I could get a good reading on him if sex complicated the matter.

I had to be a professional. Besides, what I said to him was how I felt – I didn't want to be another notch on his bedpost. Slade was a notorious womanizer. At least that was the story that was always reported to the tabloids. I could think of nothing worse than sacrificing all – my career, my peace of mind – for a fling that would mean zero to him.

I therefore made up my mind. I was going to keep it together. I wasn't going to give into my body, which was still feeling the heat from where Slade had touched it. My body might have been aching for him, but I had to ignore that.

I went out to the pool area, and my mind was made up still further. Slade was sitting on a pool chair, talking to Charlotte, who was still topless. She was giggling and touching him, and he didn't seem to mind.

I sighed, watching him interact with Charlotte, whom he allegedly couldn't stand. It certainly looked like he was into her from my vantage point. I had to stop watching them after a little while. As far as I was concerned, those two deserved one another. They were both fake and superficial and hot as hell.

I then fielded a call from Malcolm, who was calling right at that moment. "Serena," he said. "How are things?"

"Not so good," I said. "I don't think that I'm going to be able to get the information that you're looking for. I can't always get a decent reading, and I feel that maybe my talents aren't going to be on point for this case."

"Why?" he asked me. "Serena, you have to concentrate. It's important."

"Malcolm, I'm not a goddamned trained monkey. I think that I told you this. You're putting an awful lot of pressure on me here, and I don't appreciate that one bit. I tried to warn you that it probably wasn't going to work out." I was, all at once, extremely angry with Malcolm. There was a part of me, though, that started to think that my anger at Malcolm was misplaced. Seeing Slade with the bimbo Charlotte had me seeing red. "I warned you, and you forced me into it, and then what? If I give you wrong information, I'm going to be the one you're going to shove under the bus when it turns out that Slade is as guilty as sin."

Malcolm didn't speak for awhile. Then, after a long pause, he simply said "I'm sorry, Serena, but you have to try. I won't blame you if you're wrong, I promise."

I didn't have words for the real reason why I was so upset. I felt trapped into this situation, and, as attracted as I was to this guy, I could think of nothing worse than having to stay there with him for another six days. To see him drape himself all over any whorish female who came his way was not my idea of a good time.

I was tempted just to tell Malcolm to shove it. I was going to get home, whether he liked it or not, and, if he didn't like it, I'd just quit. There were other jobs. Jobs where my boss wouldn't push me into a situation that made me feel as uncomfortable as this one did.

But I closed my eyes, and tried to find my peaceful center. It was there that I usually made my decisions. They hadn't always been the right ones, but I had found that, ever since I went through intense counseling and hypnosis, my calm center was right more often than not.

I finally was able to reach a place in my conscience that made me realize that I did have to see this whole charade through. It was my inner voice that was telling me that I did need to stay there, for whatever reason. "Okay," I told Malcolm. "But I want your word that I won't be blamed if this whole thing goes south."

"Good," he said, sounding relieved. "I'm really happy that you made that decision, Serena, because, really, we do need you. I realize that your insight isn't always going to be 100%. I've seen enough shows featuring psychics to know that. But, imperfect or not, I believe in you. I think that you can get at the truth. So, I'm happy that you're staying on."

I didn't want to tell him that my scorching attraction to Slade was going to cloud my judgment. That Slade was indiscernible, for the most part, anyhow. That there were a number of factors that made the entire mission that much more complicated.

We got off the phone, and I went into my room, and lay down on the bed and just stared at the ceiling. I imagined Slade and the slutty Charlotte going at it in his bedroom, and I simply cringed.

This was going to be a long, long, long week.

I woke up with a start to find that Slade was laying next to me in my bed. I was fully clothed, I guess because I conked out. He looked at me with my boyishly handsome face and smiled. "Sorry to startle you," he said.

"What are you doing here?" I asked him. "Did Charlotte kick you out of bed?"

He looked perplexed. "Charlotte. No, she didn't kick me out of bed. I didn't give her a chance to. I asked her to leave yesterday afternoon."

"Oh. Well, it looked like you and she were very much into one another." I glared at him. He wasn't invited to join me in my room, let alone in my bed, and I had already told him that I couldn't be intimate with him because I was a professional. So why was he there?

He smoothed my hair out of my eyes. "You must've been tired. I didn't see you after our kiss, so I came to look for you, and you were already out at 3 in the afternoon. I've checked on you every hour, on the hour, since then, and you've been out the entire time."

"What time is it?"

"It's 8 AM."

I shook my head, trying to clear the cobwebs out of my brain. "8 AM. I never sleep this much at one time."

"Well, you probably needed it." At that, he reached over next to him and brought me over a tray of pancakes and orange juice. "Here. This is for you. The pancakes are probably cold, though, because I brought these up over an hour ago."

I looked at him suspiciously but, nonetheless, dug into the pancakes. They were delicious, as they were whole grain and topped with sweet strawberries and a dusting of powdered sugar. I poured some maple syrup on them, and sipped the orange juice. "You certainly do seem to be in a good mood today," I said. "Or maybe you always entertain women by bringing them breakfast in bed."

He looked at me with longing in his eyes. "I don't know why you seem to think that I'm some kind of manwhore," he said. "But, if that's what you think, it's inaccurate."

"Slade," I said. "I admit that I don't know that much about you. That's by design. But I've seen your face on so many supermarket tabloids that it's been impossible to completely avoid you. And the only reason why you're in these tabloids is because you've just about dated every A-list star there is. I'm surprised that Taylor Swift hasn't written a song about you by now. You're the John Mayer of billionaires."

He smiled impishly. "The John Mayer of billionaires. I kinda like that. He does get some gorgeous girlfriends, you have to hand it to him." Then, in a flash, he seemed to get serious. "Listen, I know that my life might look a certain way to you, and that's understandable. I'd think the same damned thing if I were on the outside looking in. But I haven't loved any of those women. They're not what I want."

I shook my head. "What you want, or don't want, from a woman is none of my concern. My only concern is whether or not you bludgeoned your business partner to death in your lab. That piece of information is what I came for, and that's the only reason why I'm here. So, you can date your supermodels, your pop singers and your A-list actresses all you want. I really don't care."

He put his hand on my thigh, which was uncovered by the sheet that was covering the rest of my torso. "Oh, but you do care."

Slade had given me a proper send-off, in my estimation, as he and I ravaged one another late into the night. It started after dinner, as he picked me up, as if I was a feather, and brought me into his bed.

"If you're really going to leave tomorrow," he said, "then we need to get as much fucking in tonight as we possibly can. I want to leave my mark on you, so that you don't feel the need for anyone else. Because you're mine now. You can't possibly belong to anyone else. Not until I release you. And hopefully I never will."

So, we spent the evening and night just consuming one another. I didn't think that anybody could brand me in quite the way Slade did that night. So, I knew that his words were true. I was his, hopelessly his. He possessed me in the way that nobody ever had, and I had no need for anyone else to possess me. His touch scorched me in such a way that I positively felt branded.

So, when I packed up to head back home, I felt sated for the time being. But I knew that there was going to come a time, not so far in the future, where I was going to feel an aching need for him. I hoped against hope that he was right – he would come for me. I was terrified about what I was going to do if he didn't.

He kissed me again, and I felt that I was about to lose myself in him. But my head won out, and I pushed him gently away. "Slade, you need to leave." My breath quickened, and he nodded his head.

"I'm sorry, Serena," he said. "I shouldn't have invaded your privacy like this." At that, he left.

I was confused about my feelings, which were strong for him. I knew that I wasn't going to be able to give Malcolm any accurate reports on Slade. I couldn't sort out my feelings for him, and I really couldn't separate my white-hot passion that was burning inside of me, from the job that I was hired to do.

———————

That night we had dinner on the terrace, which consisted of rice pilaf, beans and veggies for me, and salmon for him, served with the most delicious mimosas on the planet, I broke the news to him.

"Slade, I think that our attraction to one another undermines everything that I was hired to do. I'm acting incredibly unprofessional with you and I really don't have any choice but to call Malcolm and tell him that I need to come home." I hung my head. "I'm really embarrassed that I let it come to this."

He put his hand on mine. "You can't leave," he said, his eyes boring into me. "And you don't want to."

I shook my head. "Of course I don't want to," I said. "That goes without saying. But I need to." My felt the familiar anxiety welling up. "Malcolm is paying me good money to come up here and try to get inside your head. To tease out what you're thinking and feeling, and come up with a narrative about whether or not you're good for your partner's murder. There's no way I can do that job now."

I knew that what I was saying to him was the absolute truth. I was now a biased observer, and any evidence that I gleaned from him was going to be skewed in favor of his absolute innocence. Knowing that, there was no way that I could ethically continue to let Malcolm pay me to get at the truth. That would be not only wrong and deceitful, but also grounds for my dismissal from the firm.

That is, if the fact that I kissed our client twice didn't already doom me.

Chapter Nine

The next day, I packed my bags. I got the dogs out of their yard out back. I harnessed them, leashed them, and brought them to my SUV. Their little bodies were delighted to see me, of course, and they covered my face with kisses. I inhaled them, finding comfort in them. I might never see Slade again. More likely, I'd see him, but in a professional capacity only – assuming that Malcolm didn't fire me when I told him the truth about what happened between Slade and me.

So, what happened between us the past day or so was probably something that wouldn't be repeated. I had to let it go, no matter how much I was possessed by him and attached to him. I knew the reality of the situation, and that was that the odds were against us sustaining anything lasting.

But Sadie and Gigi were two creatures who I knew that I could always count on. They were ready with uncondi-tional love, as only dogs could give, and I found great comfort in that. They weren't prone to vagaries or capriciousness as men like Slade were. They definitely were not full of deception, as humans often were, and as Slade might be. They just were, and that's what I needed more than anything in my life.

I put them in their kennel in the back of the SUV, and I opened the door. Slade wrapped his strong arms around me tightly. "Don't go," he said, as his hands were massaging the back of my head.

"I have to. I can't stay here on Malcolm's dime. That wouldn't be right, and I have to face the music for what I have done." I was going to be strong and invincible. I had the capability of walking away from Slade, of freeing myself from the destructive bond that was starting to form between the two of us. He had an aching need to inflict pain. I sensed that, and I caught fleeting glimpses of it. I had just as aching of a need to suffer pain. He knew that about me.

I had to walk away. My plan was to tell Malcolm, and then suffer the consequences. If he fired me, he fired me. I still had enough money saved up that I could close on a home, although the home was going to be in a less desirable area of San Diego, and it was going to be in worse shape than I had hoped. But I could still get a home, and I could live there until I found something else. In the meantime, I would throw myself into beautifying any home that I would find, and let that occupy my headspace. Drawing up home improvement plans and carrying them out, one board and pipe at a time, would be something that could consume me so that I wouldn't be aching for Slade's touch every minute of every day.

Of course, the ideal situation would be that Malcolm would understand what had happened between Slade and me, and would forgive me.

Then again, that would mean that I would, for sure, have continued contact with this man who had possessed me and branded me, in a matter of days. It would almost assure that I would give in to my own dark desires, because he wanted to fulfill them. The hints that he would be more than willing to fulfill them were sprinkled throughout last night. I would be sucked into something that I swore I was going to leave behind, and there would be no turning back.

As he leaned his head into the car, and kissed me passionately goodbye, I found that I was warring inside. There was a part of me that didn't want to leave, that wanted to shirk all my responsibility to my firm, and just forget the world around me. Forget that Slade was facing a murder charge, and forget that Malcolm would fire me for sure if I continued to stay there without admitting the truth to him.

But the responsible part of me won out. "Thanks for everything," I told him. "Goodbye."

And, at that, I put the car in gear and drove down the winding path, where the familiar hoards of reporters camped out, just beyond the gate. As I made my way through the throng, with the reporters attempting to thrust their microphones into my face, I simply said "no comment."

Just like that, I was free.

Chapter Ten

I got into San Diego in the early afternoon, and I called Malcolm's cell phone. "It's Serena," I said to him. "I need to see you."

"Serena," he said. "I was going to wait until tomorrow to call you. How are things in the city of Angels?"

I took a deep breath. "I wouldn't know."

He was quiet for a long time. "Serena, I don't like the sound of your voice. What's going on?"

"Can we meet somewhere for lunch? I really need to just talk to you."

He sighed. "I guess I can take a long lunch. Meet me at The Fish Market at noon. I'll get a table outside." Then he paused. "It sounds like I'm going to be needing a Bloody Mary for this meeting with you. Why do I have a sneaking suspicion that I'm not going to be in the least bit pleased with what you're going to be telling me?"

I didn't say anything. I had no desire to tell him over the phone what had happened between Slade and me. I had no desire to tell Malcolm, period, but I really didn't want to blurt it out over the phone while I was driving.

"I'll see you at noon," I said. Then I called a dog daycare place and arranged for Sadie and Gigi to be dropped off.

"What time will you be picking them up?" a pleasant-sounding female asked me when I called the place.

"I don't know," I said. I didn't want to explain to her that I might be picking up the dogs very soon. That would be if Malcolm fired me on the spot. Then again, maybe it would all be smoothed over, and I would be returning to work. "It might be around 2, then again, it might be around 7 or 8. I hope that's okay."

"Of course," she said. "But if the dogs stay past 6 PM, we have to charge you for another day."

"Okay," I said.

"It won't be like that if you start bringing your pooches over daily. We try to work with our regular customers who keep irregular hours. We'll talk about that when you drop them off."

I got off the phone, and tried to concentrate on the road. It was difficult to do, though. I had never, in my life, had such satisfying sex as I had with Slade. He just seemed to know exactly how to make me come, and come hard. He was a sensuous lover, yet he injected just enough roughness that it made it exciting for me. I felt my nether parts tingling just thinking about the hours we were ravaging each other.

Then I shook my head. I was going to have to forget about him, and forget about the way that he made me feel. There was a very good chance that I would never see him again, if Malcolm fired me. And, even if I stayed on at the firm, Slade was our client. Our client. A torrid affair with him could get the entire firm in hot water, potentially.

Whatever happened, he was going to be off-limits to me from that point on.

After dropping off the dogs, I headed over to The Fish Market, which was in the harbor. I parked the car and walked past the enormous statue that was modeled on the D-Day kissing couple. The infamous pose of the sailor kissing a random woman, while he bended her over, was made into this statue that stood watch over the restaurant. I loved that statue, and it meant something to this town, that was a naval city for many years. It still was, but it didn't have as large of a base as it did, but the vestiges of the military were still everywhere I looked.

Walking in, there was a large crowd of people who were milling about in the waiting room, looking at the menu. There were fish in aquariums, and also a small place where the restaurant-goers could purchase fresh seafood for themselves. This was an enormous restaurant, and I always enjoyed either sitting in the glass-covered patio or the open patio, because you could look out onto the water and see sailboats passing by.

I headed back to the open-air patio, and found Malcolm who was, just as he said, already nursing a Bloody Mary. He saw me and stood up. "Good to see you," he said. "I got here early so that I could start drinking early."

I smiled, in spite of myself. "I would tell you that my news isn't as bad as all that, but...." I raised my eyebrows and sat down.

"It is as bad as all that." Malcolm stated that as the fact that it was. "Well, Serena, you got me here. Let's have it."

I took a deep breath, and nervously cracked my knuckles.

"Ouch," Malcolm said. "Why do you do that?"

I shook my head. "Bad habit. One of the few bad habits I have left."

The waitress came around and I ordered a gin and tonic. We both ordered our food, too. I got the veggie roll and grilled edamame, and Malcolm ordered the surf and turf. "I know I'm going to regret getting all this food and alcohol for lunch. It's going to put me right to sleep."

I didn't want to say it, but he was absolutely right about that. Heavy food and alcohol usually were a deadly combination in the middle of a work day.

Malcolm and I then just sat there, looking at one another. I felt humiliated and ashamed of what I was going to be telling him. He was going to be livid, absolutely livid. I knew that. I cursed my body, which betrayed me. And, what was worse, it was continuing to betray me. I could still feel the heat on my skin where Slade had touched it. I still could feel the aching in my nether parts for Slade. I swallowed hard, and tried to put all that away. All those feelings, which had come cascading out of me while Slade made love to me, again and again, were not welcome to me anymore.

I finally took a sip of my gin and tonic, which the waitress had just brought, and sighed. "Well. I don't know how I'm going to tell you this, so I guess I just need to tell you. I had sex with Slade." I shook my head, not meeting his judging eyes. "I had sex with him, and, well, I'm useless now. There's no way I can be unbiased on this. I'm so sorry. I didn't mean for that to happen. I didn't want for it to happen, either. But I have strong feelings for him, so, even if he was guilty as the day is long, I wouldn't be able to tell. I'm human."

Malcolm sat there, mulling over my words. He didn't say anything for a long, long time.

I had no idea what he was thinking, and, when I closed my eyes, I got a read on what he was feeling. At first, I felt rage bubbling up. I could feel it, and it flooded over me. My heart started to quicken, and I felt rage as well. I started breathing heavily, willing myself to turn away from the feelings that I was getting from him. That was the worst part of being an empath – when someone close to me was feeling negative feelings, I felt them as well. I felt them just as strongly as that person was feeling them. I closed my eyes, and consciously turned away from his rage. I had learned to do that as a coping mechanism – I could turn off my empathic feelings as quickly as I turned them on.

I blinked my eyes, and Malcolm was still staring at me, but his expression was different. I, once again, tried to tune into how he was feeling, and I no longer felt that he was enraged. Rather, he seemed to be calm and thinking about things.

Finally, he spoke. "Well, Serena, I must say that I'm surprised that you would do that. You weren't up there but a matter of days. I didn't peg you to be somebody who got around like that."

That was an insult, but I let it slide. After what I did, I deserved it. "Malcolm, I'm not like that. Truly, I'm not." I didn't tell him about my past, how I *was* like that at one time. When I was hurting so much, and I had no idea where to put that pain, I was like that. I never sought sex, though, only physical pain. Physical pain which was given to me in various underground clubs. "I haven't had sex in a long time. Not that that's any of your business."

"I don't understand. You don't sleep around, yet you

ended up in the bed of our client, not three days after you arrived there. That doesn't compute."

I sighed. "I know that doesn't compute. Believe me, I know. But I can't explain it, except…"

"You lost all self-control," he said. "Hey, I'm human. I get that. I try to tame my own dark side, but it doesn't always work. But, Serena, there could be serious implications here. I don't just mean the implications that will come from the fact that you won't be able to get a good empathic reading on this guy. But we're going to be open to a bar complaint or malpractice claim if things go south between the two of you."

Malcolm seemed calm, which was weird to me.

"Well," I said, taking a sip of my gin and tonic. "I'm guessing you would like for me to resign. And I totally understand it if you do."

He put his hand on his chin and studied me. "No, Serena, actually, I was thinking the opposite. You're under his skin. That might actually work for us, not against. What's done is done. I'm just trying to figure out how to mitigate the damages and turn this around to a positive. There's always a silver lining."

"What are you thinking?"

He shook his head. "Serena, you could still be valuable. You could remain in a relationship with this guy, and then report to me any kind of pillow talk that might occur."

My eyes got big. "Malcolm, you can't be serious. I'll be committing all kinds of ethical violations by remaining in a relationship with him, and there's no way that I can do that to him. I think that I know what you're getting at, and what you want me to do is exactly the reason why sexual relations between clients and lawyers are frowned upon."

"You know what the rules are. The federal rules, of

course, state that you can't have a sexual relationship with a client, period. But we aren't operating under the federal rules. We're operating in the State of California, and, as you know, in California, sexual relationships between clients and attorneys are only forbidden if you are using the sex in lieu of payment or if you use coercion to enter into the sex."

"It also forbids sexual relationships when the sex might cause the attorney to perform legal services incompetently. And that's a real fear here with me."

"Simple. If you feel that having sex with this guy will make you feel like you're going to commit malpractice, then you have to stop it. But, Serena, just because you're having sex with him doesn't mean that you're going to perform incompetently. And it just might be the best thing, because you're going to make him vulnerable. If he falls in love with you – "

"Whoa, whoa, whoa. Fall in love? I hardly know him." Even as I said that, though, I wasn't convinced that I meant it. I might have just met him, but, there was no doubt about it, there was something there between us. It was an unspoken understanding. I felt that he got me, and I got him. I didn't know exactly why, but that was just what I was feeling.

"Would you let me finish? If he falls in love with you, then he's going to show some vulnerability. There's no better way to get to a truth that somebody is hiding then to make that person fall in love with you. People tend to spill secrets to the person that they care about. It just kind of happens that way with intimacy."

"Malcolm," I began. "First, you send me up there to try to use my psychic powers to get the truth out of him. Now you want me to use sex to do that. Why don't you use, you know, the evidence and things like that to try to get to the bottom of the whole affair. What a concept – an attorney using evidence to get at the truth."

"Because the evidence is ambiguous at best in this case. Let's face it, the guy had motive to kill Jordan. His fingerprints were all over that lab. Granted, it was because he worked in that lab, too, but it doesn't help that his fingerprints were the only fingerprints found, with the exception of Jordan himself. That lab had more security than Fort Knox, so it would be next to impossible for a random person to get in there. And the videotape of the murder is missing. There's video surveillance of that lab, but there's about a half hour missing, and, of course, the missing part of the video was the part where Jordan was murdered. Our guy would have the best access to the video, and he would be able to edit it better than anybody else."

"In other words, it's not looking so good for Slade." Malcolm suspected that Slade was guilty, and that pierced my heart. I knew that I was emotionally invested in Slade, already, and I couldn't possibly provide an unbiased representation of him.

"Listen, of course it's not looking good for him. It hasn't been looking good for him since the beginning. We have to go with a SODDI defense, but the bad part is that we have no idea who that other dude might be."

SODDI meant "some other dude did it," which was always the major way that murder suspects are defended. It was imperative that we find the "other dude" who did this, and I knew that Malcolm had his own investigators on the case. He wasn't going to just let the police do their work, because the police seemed to be fixated on Slade, to the exclusion of all others. That's what happened in high profile cases, unfortunately – the police decide early that a certain person did it, and they look at all the evidence in the light that would support that theory, and dismiss evidence that didn't. It was called "confirmation bias" or "tunnel vision," and, unfortunately, it was just human nature. It was only human to look at evidence with a jaundiced eye, supported by prejudice or some other unconscious process. Unfortunately, the confirmation bias tended to be exacerbated in high-profile cases such as this one, because the cops were dying to bag a big kahuna.

I bit my lip. "I could help with that," I said, and then immediately regretted opening my mouth. I was going to volunteer to do something that was dangerous for me, more than dangerous. It was going to be something that could very well damage my psyche beyond repair, and could plunge me into the darkness that I felt for the first 25 years of my life. I was going to volunteer to try to commune with the dead guy, and, once I did that, I was afraid that the gates would open, and I wouldn't be able to silence the spirits again. They had left me alone for 3 years, and, for 3 years, I was actually able to try to find some peace in my life. It was a hard-fought peace, buoyed by hypno-therapy and constantly trying to fixate on something healthy.

I was going down the rabbit hole. I not only was drawn to Slade for reasons that weren't entirely healthy – I felt that he was a dominant, and I desperately wanted that – but I also, possibly, was going to open up the spiritual floodgates. That would spin me completely off my axis.

But, at the Jordane time, I wanted to do it for Slade. I had no idea why, but I was willing to sacrifice for him. I felt, for some odd reason, that I would go to the ends of the earth for him.

"Oh," Malcolm said. "What do you mean, Serena?"

"I can communicate with Jordan. All that I need would be an item of clothing from him. If you could get that from his widow, I can try to find out what happened to him by communicating with him directly."

Malcolm nodded his head slowly. "That sounds fantastic. But how will I be able to get that from his widow? I can't very well subpoena it. A court would quash that subpoena in a heartbeat. Unless we happened to find a judge who believes in spirit empathic abilities, which would be a long-shot, to say the very least."

"I could always just ask the widow. I could explain to her why I need it."

"You can't just go and ask her. She would think that you were nuts."

"How do you know this? She might believe."

"Listen, his widow is a scientist. A scientist tends not to believe in things like psychics and spirits and all of that. I would be extremely surprised if you get somewhere with this woman."

"I know that, but perhaps she would give me an article of clothing to humor me. Maybe there's a doubt there in her mind that there's no such thing as a psychic or a spiritual empath. She has nothing to lose, after all."

"Well, I suppose. She is coming into the office this week. I can certainly ask her then. She'll laugh at me, and then that will be it. And we'll be back to square one – trying to find out who did this to Jordan. Right now, Slade is the only suspect that the police have. Our investigators are trying to find out more, but this Jordan was a private guy. He was also extremely secretive. He kept almost everything from Slade himself, as far as what he was working on. We've reached a dead-end so far on finding out another suspect for this murder."

"We've got nothing to lose, then." I started to relax. We were getting away from the issue of my continuing a relationship with Slade, and I didn't want to revisit it. We were on a much more comfortable path, talking about the case. "I'll see if I can ask her about the clothing when she comes in to see us."

"Yes," he said. "Now, Serena, you need to tell me the truth about your relationship with Mr. Bridgewell. I would encourage you to keep seeing him romantically. I will not tell anybody at the office about it, of course. That goes without saying. But it could very well lead to us breaking the case."

I shook my head. "I thank you for your permission, but I'm not interested in him anymore." I was lying when I said that, of course. I was lying to him, and I was lying to myself. Truth be told, I craved him. I craved him like I used to crave the feeling of the belt on my back. Like I used to crave the feeling of my nipples being clamped. Like I used to crave the exquisite pain and helplessness of being tied to a St. Andrew's Cross, while being slashed with a cat-o-nine tails. I wanted that feeling of not being in control at all. Of having a total loss of control.

I had to overcome that feeling, though. I knew that.

I had to stay away from Slade, whatever it took. When I saw him again, I would treat him professionally, and wouldn't go there with him ever again.

Chapter Eleven

That evening, when I went home from work, and I picked up my dogs, I got a phone call. I picked up, and Slade's voice was on the other end. "Serena," he said. "Meet me in Del Mar. I have a surprise for you."

I took a deep breath, and closed my eyes. "No, Slade, I can't meet you. I'm sorry. I told you at your house that I can't see you like that anymore."

"Meet me at...." He gave me an address that I didn't recognize. "Be there in an hour. Be there, or suffer the consequences."

I had no idea if he was joking about that last comment. But I was intrigued. "I'll be there," I said.

And then I called Michael. I wanted a buffer when I saw Slade again. If I brought Michael with me, then there could be no chance that I would be in bed with Slade that evening. After all, he invited me to a place that could be a house. I didn't know if Slade owned a house in the San Diego area, but it wouldn't surprise me. And I had no desire to see Slade in a private home. That would be a recipe for disaster. At any rate, I doubted that I could stay out of his bed if I met him in a private home.

"Hey, Serena," he said. "What's up?"

"I was hoping you might be free this evening."

"I'm not, but Donny is. He's just sitting around the house right now, binge-watching *Orange is the New Black*. As usual."

"I'll call him."

"Later."

I then called Donny. "Hey," he said when I called. "When you gonna be home? I'm starving for some vegan nachos. I don't know how you make those, but they're like crack. Not that I know what crack is like from personal experience, of course."

"I'll make those for you special, and I'll do your laundry if you do one thing for me this evening."

"I'm listening."

"Come out with me to meet this guy in Del Mar."

"You need a wing man, or you need a buffer? It's not another Internet date, is it? The last time you dragged me to meet a dude you met on the Internet wasn't exactly the time of my life. No offense."

I laughed in spite of myself. I did drag Donny along to meet a guy, because I wasn't sure about the guy. Turns out I wasn't sure about this guy for a good reason, because that date was total drag. Donny had dinner at a different table, and I called him while my "date" was in the restroom. I told my "date" that I was sick, and then Donny and I high-tailed it out of there and had drinks at a bar in the Gaslamp. The evening started out rotten, but I had to admit that it was fun afterwards. Donny was a funny guy, and I always had a good time with him.

"I need a buffer, but it's not what you think. This guy

is...." I had no words for how I felt about Slade. I barely knew him, yet I felt more strongly for him than I had about anybody ever before. I couldn't explain it, even to myself.

"Is what?"

"I'm just very attracted to him, that's all. And he's a client of our law firm, and I just can't go there. I'll come and get you, but please be ready when I pull up." I felt anxious that I was going to be late meeting Slade, and, for some reason, I knew that he wouldn't be pleased. I wanted to please him. It was imperative to me that I please him.

"Okay," he said. "Why not? I got nothing else going on around here. Buy me dinner tonight, or sometime this week, and I'll be there with bells on."

"Great, thanks," I said.

I picked up Donny, fed the dogs and put them in their kennel, and then we headed up to Del Mar. I had my GPS on, and it was leading me to a nice neighborhood, not that there were any other kind in Del Mar. This was a seaside community where the well-heeled San Diegans lived. It was difficult to find a single-family home that sold for less than a million dollars in this area. Some homes were less than a million, but they tended to be townhomes and condos, and even those were hardly ever found found less than $600,000. It was a highly desirable area of town, that was for sure.

I finally got to the home where Slade was supposed to meet me. It was in a residential neighborhood was was close to the ocean. The home was large, with two stories, and it was a modern stucco home with a Spanish tile roof and was surrounded by palm trees. I walked in with Donny. Slade was in the kitchen of this home, which was empty, making some kind of salad.

I was absolutely confused, but this home was gorgeous inside. Twenty foot ceilings, a skylight, Spanish tile in the foyer, hardwood floors in the living area. Granite counter-tops in the enormous kitchen, which opened up into a sun room, which, in turn, opened up into a large backyard with a pool. It also had a large formal dining room on the main floor.

I looked at Slade, and he saw me, his face lighting up. Then he looked at Donny, and his face fell. He returned to making his salad, without greeting me.

I concentrated on what I was feeling from him, and he was clearly angry. I closed my eyes, and I could feel that anger flashing through me, white-hot. At first I was confused on why he was angry, and then it occurred to me – he was angry that Donny was there with me.

But, to look at him, you wouldn't know that he was that angry. He wasn't looking at either of us, but, to an untrained eye, it simply looked as if he was very into making that salad. He was chopping up a cucumber and an onion, and was sprinkling on herbs, salt and pepper. He was even humming a tune that I didn't recognize at first, but I soon recognized as *Creep* by Radiohead. His knife made quick work of chopping up some more vegetables, including bell pepper, carrots and a tomato.

I finally broke the ice. "Well, well, well. I guess that you're not so helpless. I'm surprised that you didn't get Marina to come down here with you and do this for you."

He looked up at me. "You'd be surprised on what I can do in the kitchen. Granted, I usually have Marina make food for me, but that's only because I work so much that I need help in that area. And, when you were there with me, I was interested in talking with you, not cooking. But I can cook more than you think."

I smiled. "I was only teasing you."

A smile edged around the corners of his eyes. "I know that. Besides, making a salad isn't exactly a huge feat." Then he looked at Donny questioningly.

At that, Donny extended a calloused hand. Slade shook it firmly. "I'm Donny, Serena's roommate for the time being."

I closed my eyes, and still felt the anger that was emanating from Slade. I opened my eyes, and saw Slade shaking Donny's hand with a smile.

That concerned me, to say the least. Slade was an expert at covering up what he was feeling. That wasn't a good sign, because if he could be deceptive about something as simple as this, who was to say that he couldn't be deceptive about everything?

I also felt jealousy coming from Slade, and I smiled. I was flattered that he was jealous, to be honest.

"Well," Slade said. "I made more than enough food, so Donny, you're welcome to join us." That was what his lips were saying, but, inside, he was clearly seething.

"Cool," Donny said. "Whatever it is you're making, it smells fantastic."

Slade shrugged his shoulders. "It's just spaghetti and vegan meatballs. The sauce is authentic, though. My mother is Italian."

It struck me that I had, up until that very moment, known nothing at all about his family. "Tell me about your mother," I said to him.

"Later," he said. "For now, let's eat."

We all went out onto the patio, which had a table and four chairs. It was the only room in the house, however, that had any furniture in it at all. There was a vase of flowers in the middle. Slade brought out a bottle of wine, and he poured each of us a glass.

I sipped the wine, and observed the food. The spaghetti looked scrumptious, to say the very least. He also made garlic bread. "That garlic bread is made with non-dairy butter," he said to me. "I picked it up at Whole Foods."

The food was as wonderful as it looked. "Well, Slade, I think that you mastered the art of making marinara sauce. This dinner is amazing."

"Thanks," he said.

We ate in a strained silence for a little bit, until Donny piped up.. "I don't want to be rude," he said, "but I wanted to give you my sympathy, dude, about you're going through."

Slade glanced at me. "What do you know about me?"

"I don't know that much, but a friend of mine watches Anna Place all the time. She really has it in for you."

Anna Place was a southern blonde woman with a nightly show on CNN. She was loud, aggressive, pushy, and proclaimed guilt until proven innocent. She also was nasty in how she engaged in lurid speculation about her victims, right there on air. She invited "experts" on her show, all of whom engaged in a breathless analysis of the case, all of whom also proclaimed Slade guilty. Anna disgusted me, to be perfectly honest. She hurt people all the time, and was constantly just on the verge of a huge slander lawsuit.

Slade rolled his eyes. "Anna Place has me already on the gurney with a needle in my arm. I don't listen to her."

"Well, even so, I feel for you, dude. I couldn't imagine being put through the ringer like that night after night."

"I appreciate that," Slade said. Then he turned to me.

"You haven't heard what dear old Anna is saying about me, have you?"

I shook my head. "No. I haven't wanted things in my head that might prejudice me. Listening to her would definitely prejudice me. She certainly does tend to go after people she hates, like a dog after a bone, and, even when she turns out to be wrong, she never apologizes. I don't know how she gets away with it. I really don't."

Actually, I did know how she got away with it. She was always on the verge of slander, but never quite crossed it. She engaged in plenty of dirty speculation, and her expert witness guests were careful to tell the audience that they are not connected to whatever case was being discussed, but nobody actually told lies about their subjects.

"Good," he said, as he helped himself to some more spaghetti.

"I wouldn't worry about what she says," Donny said. "She's kind of a stupid bitch."

Slade grinned and nodded his head at that one. "Understatement of the year. Marijuana is being legalized in more and more states, and it's been fun watching her head pop off about that."

Indeed, Anna had been one of the more vocal critics of legalizing marijuana. The fact that Slade was growing marijuana legally on one of his farms was probably one of the reasons why she was so out to get him.

Donny laughed and raised his glass. "Ain't that the truth. Just wait until the federal government legalizes it. She'll really have a Defcon fit."

I finally asked Slade the question that was on my mind. "This house is pretty empty. Is this house yours? Did you just buy it?"

Slade cleared his throat. "Yes, I just bought it," he

simply said. Then he narrowed his eyes. "Dinner is almost over. I need to see you alone." He cocked his head, and his meaning was clear. I knew that he was annoyed that Donny was there, even if he covered it well. Now he wanted me alone so that we could get back to doing what we were doing at his home.

I simply sat up straight, and took a sip of the wine that was in front of me. "I'm sorry, Slade, but when Donny leaves, I have to leave as well. I drove, and Gigi and Sadie are home in their kennel."

At that, Slade disappeared into a different room. He came back in five minutes. "I just solved both of your problems. My driver is coming to give Donny a ride home, and he's been instructed to pick up your dogs when he drops Donny off."

I felt irritated that he would do something like that without asking me. "Slade, I can't stay. I told you this when I left your house this morning. What happened at your home can't happen anymore. I'm sorry."

I closed my eyes after I said that. My body was betraying me again. I felt flush, and my breathing was coming faster and faster, as I thought about what it felt like to be ravaged by Slade. I willed those thoughts away and opened my eyes. Slade was staring at me, his expression indiscernible.

"My driver will be here in twenty minutes," he said. "Donny will be driven home, your dogs will come here, and you'll stay here tonight with me." His cheek twitched imperceptibly, and I could see that he was roiling underneath his calm façade.

I looked at Donny, and he shrugged his shoulders. "It's up to you, Serena. I'm good either way, you know that."

I opened my mouth, but nothing came out. Slade's will,

which was considerable, had an almost hypnotic effect on me. I wanted to protest some more, and tell Slade that he needed to call off his driver, but, somehow, no words of protest came out of my mouth.

Slade smiled. "I thought so."

"You thought what?"

"You want to stay here with me. As much as I want you to stay, you want the Jordane thing."

"No," I said. "Where is there to sleep?"

He raised his eyebrows. "You loved my Vividus mattress, didn't you?"

"Of course. That mattress costs more than my brand-new BMW X5. At that price, it better be goddamned comfortable. At that price, it really should come with men with fans who will peel all my grapes."

Slade smiled. "Glad you love that mattress." He sipped his wine and said no more.

This entire encounter was becoming more and more peculiar. He apparently bought that home, that day, I would guess. There was no furniture to be seen, yet he wanted me to stay there with him, so there was probably at least a bed. A Vividus bed, if his little hints were to be believed.

I tried to calm my breathing, and, I was startled to note, I was yearning to see Donny leave so that I could be alone with Slade. I hated that I felt like I was completely losing control when I was around him, but there was no denying it. I craved him like I had never craved anything.

Finally, the doorbell rang, and Slade went to answer it. "Raphael, this is Donny," he said, as the man shook Donny's hand. "Please take him home, and bring the two dogs who are at the house here. Bring their kennel as well, and don't forget their toys."

The two of them disappeared, and Slade came back to

the kitchen. I was clearing off the dishes and putting them into the dishwasher, and he came up behind me. "Why did you bring him here?" he demanded. He put his hands on either side of me, and he gripped the counter. His breath was hot and moist in my ears.

I turned around. His face was close to mine, and his eyes looked hurt.

"I don't trust myself around you," I said. "When you look at me like that, I can barely remember my own name. I needed a buffer."

"A buffer," he said. "What are you afraid of, Serena? Do you think that I have a dark side, one that's darker than most? Do you think that I'm capable of bludgeoning a man to death? Are you afraid that I'll end up doing the Jordane to you?"

I shook my head, but I felt my entire body shaking. My feelings were so confusing to me. Slade could very well have done it, and I would never know, because my emotions for him were so strong.

"Look me in the eye, Serena. Look me in the eye, and you'll know the truth."

"That doesn't work for me. Not when it comes to you. I can look you in the eyes all day long, and I wouldn't know the truth about you and Jordan. You cloud my judgment, and, because you cloud my judgment, you also cloud my natural intuition. And you're blocking your feelings most of the time. I think that you're the one who's scared, not me."

I looked at him, and I knew that I had touched a nerve. He was blocking his feelings most of the time. He knew it. And, for one brief moment, I did feel something emanating from him. It was brief, but I felt genuine affection and even love coming from him. I cocked my head, not sure if I was feeling what I was feeling. But, before I got a chance to analyze it, that feeling from him was gone.

"What do you think that I'm afraid of?" he whispered to me. He put his finger on my chin and raised my face. He kissed me, gently and slowly, and then looked at me some more. "Huh, Serena? What keeps me awake at night?"

"I don't know. That's the problem. I'm sure that something keeps you awake at night, but I have no clue on what it is. You have to bring down your walls, Slade, or I'm going to have problems getting any genuine readings on you."

"Maybe you can bring down my walls," he said. "You can uncover what's truly bothering me, and I'll give you a hint – it has nothing to do with my guilt over killing Jordan. Because I didn't kill Jordan. I close my eyes, though, and I see his lifeless body, and that's an image that I can never, ever, get out of my mind. It's an image that has been burned into my brain." He shook his head, and I could see the grief in his eyes.

He was still very close to me. He leaned into me, and I could feel his hardness through his pants. He ran one hand through my hair, and then wrapped his arms around me tightly. My arms involuntarily rose, and I ended up gripping his neck. I closed my eyes and willed him to kiss me again. As if he read my mind, he lowered his lips onto mine. I drank him in, trying hard to remain there at the sink, just kissing him, without us leaving the room. I couldn't have sex with him again. I tried to make my body calm down, but it was completely on fire, much to my dismay.

He stopped kissing me, but his face was still close to mine. "I know that you're curious about this house."

At first, I didn't know what he was talking about. My brain was still feeling scrambled, and all that I could think of was how badly I needed Slade to take me to his bed again. How much I yearned for that.

Then it dawned on me that I *was* intensely curious about that house. "Yes," I said. "Tell me about this house. Did you just buy it?"

"Yes. I bought this house for you."

My jaw dropped, and I looked at him, trying to see if he was serious. He was. I could tell by looking into his eyes. He was not sure how I would take that piece of news, and he was bracing for my reaction.

"You're serious," I said to him. "What the hell? I barely know you, and you're already buying a house for me? You're insane." I pushed him away from me and went out to the deck, where we were just eating spaghetti, and looked over the edge. The yard was beautiful, with mature avocado and orange trees, bougainvilleas and enormous date palms. As with most of the homes in that area, there was a gleaming pool and hot tub.

Slade was soon joining me. "You needed a house. Malcolm called me on the day that you came to see me, and he told me that he wasn't sure if you could make it out, because you had your eye on a house that you wanted to close on. You showed up anyhow, so I figured that you didn't get that house."

"So you decided to take matters into your own hands and just buy me something. Not just any house, either, but a house in a housing complex where every house is a million-five and up. What the hell were you thinking?"

"I was thinking that you need a place of your own. You shouldn't be living with those two surfers in that little shack on the beach."

I furled my brows at him. "How the hell did you know

about the fact that I'm living with two surfers in a small house in Ocean Beach, and who are you to tell me where I should and shouldn't be living?"

I shook my head as I looked at him. What a stupid question! He obviously found out information about me by delving into my background without my knowledge. I felt more and more irate as I stood there looking at the beautiful backyard.

He raised an eyebrow. "Answer me this, Serena. What yard do you have for those two dogs?"

"I have a yard."

"Bullshit. I know your neighborhood, and generally where you live. You have a patio, and that's about it."

"I walk my dogs, Jordane as anybody else who's in an apartment. And, when I go to work, I take them to doggie day care. They aren't being neglected, and I have the means to take excellent care of them." Even as I said those words, though, I had to concede the point to him. Sadie and Gigi did deserve to have a nice yard to run around in, and this house had a beautiful one. I imagined the two dogs running around and exploring, and I smiled, in spite of myself.

"Nonetheless, you've been trying to leave that house. You've been looking for something. I just made it easier."

I felt like blowing up at him right then. "Slade, I was looking for a fixer-upper. There's a very specific reason why I wanted a fixer-upper. Basically, I need a project to take my mind off of things. I need a place to focus my energy, and I do a wonderful job when I set about to renovating. I knock out walls and rip up floors, and do all the replacements on my own. I did it on my brownstone in New York, and I was going to do it here as well. You buying me a turnkey ready home has deprived me of doing things on my own."

He put his hands on my shoulders, and I shrugged them off. I was wound up tight, and I felt the need to get out of there.

"I won't apologize," he said. "You needed a new place to stay, and I gave it to you. And I really don't want you living with two men, anyhow. You're mine, Serena, and I'm not willing to share you."

"Share me? Share me? Those two guys are like brothers to me. There has never been anything between the three of us, and there never would be. I would say that you need to examine your need to possess me, but it would be talking to dead air. We barely know one another, and you're already dictating to me who I can and cannot live with."

He put his hands on my shoulders again, and I wasn't able to shake them off. I stood there, my feet rooted to the floor, trying to regain my equilibrium. "You don't want me to possess you? Are you sure of that?"

No. I wasn't sure of that. There was a part of me, a large part of me, that desperately wanted just that - for him to possess me. For him to control me, and make me do things that my body desperately wanted, but my mind kept me from fully enjoying. I wanted him to make me feel like I felt at his home, as he made love to me again and again.

He lightly kissed my neck, and one of his hands grazed my arm. I reared back my head, reveling in feeling his tongue, which was languidly covering my clavicle, neck and shoulders. His lips found my own, and I lost my breath as he kissed me passionately at first, and then more and more gently.

I opened my mouth to tell him that I didn't want him to possess me. I wanted to lie to him while I was lying to myself. As one of his hands touched my breast, I closed my eyes and summoned all my will and strength. With one mighty shove, I pushed him off of me, and he fell backwards against the wooden railing. "Slade, you're going to be my downfall. My life was so controlled, and that's how I wanted it. Ever since I met you, I've been stirred up, and not necessarily in a good way. Now you've bought me my own home, and if you think for a second that I can accept this home, then you have another thing coming. I'm going to go with my original plan of finding my own place and fixing it up."

"Serena," he said. "You're going to keep this place. What's more, I have my eye on the house across the street. I'll be buying that home within a matter of days."

That was too much. Now he was not only trying to force me into staying in this home, but he also wanted to live across the street from me. Why? He wanted to keep an eye on me, that was why. "Why do you want to live across the street?"

"Because, my lawyers are here in San Diego. It would be inconvenient for me to have make that drive down from LA every time I needed to meet with my legal team. Besides, the paparazzi are too concentrated in LA. It's nice to come down here and actually not see reporters hanging around."

"You don't think that the reporters are going to be swarming this street soon? I'm sure. that your neighbors will be thrilled when they look out the window and see hundreds of reporters lining the streets."

"They won't be welcome here," he said. "Obviously. This isn't my LA house, that is pretty secluded, so the reporters can get away with hanging around outside my gate. This is a residential street, where they will be disturbing the peace. It's a different thing. Different ordinances and all of that."

I crossed my arms, annoyed that he was making so much sense. Of course it would be better for him if he lived on a street like this, as opposed to him staying at his beautiful, but relatively secluded, mansion. He was absolutely right – if the reporters started to gather around on this street, the residents would be able to call the police to get rid of them. That was certainly one way to dispose of the paparazzi.

"Well, okay, I guess those are good reasons for you to stay here. Not here, I guess, but in another home around here. But I have no clue on what you're going to do with this house, because I sure as hell am not going to live here." I shook my head. "I don't like feeling indebted to you or to anyone else."

"You're going to be stubborn about this, aren't you?"

I was incredulous by his arrogance. "Seriously? You're going to call me stubborn, just because I won't accept a house from a man that I barely know?"

He took my hand and kissed it lightly. "Oh, but you do know me. You know me very well." He wrapped his arms around me lightly, as if he were trying to dance with me. "You know every inch of me," he whispered to me.

I put my hands on his chest and pushed him away. "I know you in the sexual sense. But I don't really know you at all. I have no idea what makes you tick. I don't even know the first thing about your family." I paused. "I don't know if you're capable of bludgeoning a man to death. If I can't figure out something as fundamental as that about you, then I don't think that we're ready to play house together."

He took a deep breath, as he obviously was trying to keep his temper in check. "We aren't playing house together. I bought you this house, and I'm buying the house across the street. I'm not asking you to move in with me."

"What about everything else that I said? About not knowing your family and not knowing what you're capable of? Those revelations from me aren't sending alarm bells into your head yet?"

"No. I'll tell you about my family in due time. And, as for you not knowing if I'm a murderer, I can't really help that. I've told you one hundred thousand times that I had nothing to do with Jordan's murder. You've chosen not to believe me. That's on you, not me."

I couldn't believe what he was saying to me. "That's on me? I'm telling you that I don't trust that you wouldn't be capable of doing something like that to Jordan, and you're not bothered by that?"

"No. Not bothered by that. Because, if you think about it, anybody is capable of doing anything at any given time. Just for the sake of argument, if I did kill Jordan, it wouldn't be out of character for me. It wouldn't be out of character for anyone, because we all have our breaking point. Even you. If someone pushed you far enough, you would be capable of anything at all as well. Or anyone else. So, no. If you think that it's possibly in my character to do something like that, you're absolutely correct."

I felt a cold chill when he was saying those words. I narrowed my eyes. "What are you saying?"

"I didn't kill Jordan. That hasn't changed. But I'm just trying to say that I'm capable of doing something like that, just like anybody is in this world. Nobody really knows that they're capable of until they're presented with a given situation."

I stepped back from him. "Slade, I think that I better leave."

"Where are you going to go? Your dogs are coming here, and you live here now."

"I don't live here. I live in Ocean Beach with Donny and Michael, and that's where I'm going to live until I can close on a house of my own. Now, I have an idea. You said that you're going to buy the house across the street. Why don't you just transfer the deed for this house into your name, and then you can live here? It's a gorgeous space, very fitting for a man of your means."

He was glowering, and I saw that he was used to getting his way. He crossed his arms, and then made his way over to me again. He narrowed his eyes. "Maybe I should tie you up and force you to stay here. You'd like that, wouldn't you?"

I opened my mouth, and then closed it again. "No," I said weakly. "I wouldn't like that."

"I'm calling shenanigans," he said. "You enjoy that. I know that you do. You like being dominated, and you like pain. I get that, too. I don't judge you for it. I know that you have your reasons for being like you are, and I know that these reasons are good ones."

I turned away. "I suppose you already know what those reasons are? After all, you seem to know so much about me. Must be nice to be able to invade the privacy of anybody that you want."

"No. I have no idea what those reasons are. I hope to get to know what they are, though, eventually." He paused. "I'm interested in you, Serena. I feel that you and I have a lot in common, and I think that we can help each other. I also feel a connection to you, and I felt it from the first time we kissed."

I knew what he was saying, because I felt it the first time that we kissed as well. The connection, the heat, the passion. I felt like I was being consumed by him, and that feeling was there from the first time our lips met. My fingers involuntarily went to my lips, as I was remembering what it felt like the first time we kissed.

I sighed. I could feel my resolve breaking down, in spite of myself. Still, I managed to protest some more. "No. You can't have me. Not like this."

He nodded his head. I could feel that he was defeated, but, as I closed my eyes, I knew that he was feeling that his defeat was only temporary. He recognized that he was possessing me, and that wasn't going to change anytime soon. I might have won that battle, but he was going to win the war.

"Okay," he said. "You can have the bed. I'll sleep on the floor." He shrugged his shoulders as I started to protest. "It's not a problem. I have a sleeping bag." At that, he disappeared into a room and shut the door.

I shook my head and waited for Slade's driver to arrive with my dogs. After he got there, I would take the dogs and go on home. To my home, not this beautiful home that was allegedly mine.

Within fifteen minutes, the driver arrived. He brought the dogs into the house, along with their kennel. Sadie and Gigi excitedly greeted me, their tiny bottles wriggling with delight. I stooped down, and let them kiss my face. I closed my eyes, and thanked the man, Raphael, for bringing the dogs to me. "I would give you a tip," I said. "But I don't have cash."

Raphael nodded his head. "That's fine, Senora. I'm not allowed to accept tips."

I thought that I knew why Raphael couldn't accept tips – probably because Slade paid him so much that tips weren't necessary. Of course, that could be just a hunch, but

Slade struck me as someone who would pay his help handsomely.

Raphael left, and I went out to my SUV. I put the kennel in the back, and the dogs in the kennel. And then, without even telling Slade, I left.

Chapter Twelve

The next day, I got up early for my run. It had been several days since I had gone for my usual run, and I was already feeling rusty. As my feet pounded the pavement, my lungs were burning and my ankles were on fire. I was pushing myself faster than I had ever pushed myself, and it felt amazing. *This is the healthy kind of pain. What Slade represents is the unhealthy kind.*

I had no idea if I could continue to resist him, but I had to. I had to, at least until I was able to get a good handle on whether or not he was good for Jordan's murder. I knew that Jordan's widow was coming into the office that day so that Malcolm and everyone could talk to her about what she knew. I hoped that she wouldn't look at me like I was a total freak when I asked her if I could have an article of Jordan's clothing. That was the only thing that worked for me anymore, as far as speaking with the dead. It used to be that I couldn't get their demands out of my head. But, ever since I'd willfully silenced them, talking to these spirits was difficult for me.

Maybe, just maybe, I'd be able to figure out the truth about Jordan, and that would help me make up my mind about Slade. Malcolm was right that there wasn't a firm rule in California about attorneys having sexual relations with clients. Nevertheless, I couldn't help but be worried that sleeping with Slade would open me up to a malpractice claim, which would, in turn, open me up to an ethics violation.

One thing was for sure – everything was against my relationship with Slade. Not that I had a relationship with him yet, but, if I ever wanted to pursue it, there were just too many hurdles to get over.

I ended my run, and hopped in the shower. After my shower, I walked the dogs and prepared to take them to their day care. As I was putting them into my SUV, I ran into Donny, who was just waking up, and putting his surfboard on top of his car.

"Hey," he said, seeming surprised to see me. "When did you get back?"

"Last night. Don't ask."

He smiled. "I won't, but I have to admit that I'm very curious about last night. What was up with that empty house?"

"He just bought that house and wanted to show it off. He hadn't had time to get furniture in there, though."

"I see." Donny just stood there in the driveway for a few seconds. "Well, I'll see you later."

"I'll be home for dinner."

"I work. But we'll catch to each other soon."

At that, I drove off to drop the dogs off at the day care, and then onto work.

I got into work, and Jordan's widow was already in the conference room, talking to Malcolm and some other lawyers. She was a slight blonde woman, attractive and casually dressed. I knew that she was a scientist, a researcher at the University of California-San Diego, after having gotten her PhD in molecular engineering from Stanford. Presumably, Stanford was where she had met Jordan.

I went to my office and sat down at my desk. I reviewed the files of some of the cases I was working on for the firm, prioritizing all of them. At the moment, I was merely doing the workup for these files, as I couldn't appear in court for any of them until I passed the bar. That exam was going to be in another month, in June.

I was reviewing the file of a mobster who was accused of arson when the meeting with Jane, Jordan's widow, was over. Jane tentatively knocked on my open door. "Serena," she said. "Malcolm told me to stop by your office. He said that you needed to see me."

"Yes, yes," I said as I stood up. I gestured to the chair in front of my desk. "Please have a seat. Can I get you some water? Our firm makes amazing strawberry water."

She smiled and shook her head. "I drank so much water in that meeting with the partners, I'm surprised that I'm not floating away, as my mother would say. But thank you."

I nodded. I felt awkward, as I had no idea how I was going to ask Jane about what I needed.

"Serena," Jane said. "I see your face. I know why you want to talk to me, and it's okay. I mean, I don't necessarily believe in psychic powers. I'm a scientist. I only believe what can be proved. But, at the same time, I don't know how it could possibly hurt. If there's even a tiny chance that giving you an article of Jordan's clothing can help your firm crack the case, then I'm all for it."

I felt relieved. "You mean you don't think that I'm a freak?"

She smiled. "No. Listen, I think that anything is possible. And I know that your firm is going to need all the help it can get to solve Jordan's murder. God knows that police aren't helping out with it. They have their man, Slade. They're dying to put him behind bars, because it'll make their force seem so important." She rolled her eyes. "God forbid they might actually do some work on the case."

"It doesn't help that Slade *is* so important," I said. "And that the tabloids and press have been all over this case from the start. That'll make the police look even better if Slade is convicted, but it certainly won't help us get to the truth."

"No, it won't."

"Now, I won't guarantee that I can get to the truth, either, even if I were somehow able to communicate with Jordan. But, with any luck, we might be able to at least get a lead."

She smiled. "Feel free to come to my house this evening. I'll be home after 6. You can select any article of clothing you wish, although I don't know if I have anything that he's worn that I haven't washed."

"That's okay if you washed the clothes. The energy remains, no matter what." I paused and put my hand on her hand. "I'm so sorry for your loss. I wanted you to know that. I can't imagine what you must be going through."

She bowed her head and wiped away a tear. "It's been difficult. I mean, Jordan had his problems, that was for sure. And he wasn't willing to deal with them. I know about mental illness, and it was frustrating for me to see that he wasn't willing to tackle his. But he didn't deserve what happened to him. Nobody deserves something like that."

I nodded my head. "If there is anything that I can do…."

"Just help your firm find his killer. That's all that I ask."

I took a deep breath and sat back in my chair. "You're sure that Slade didn't do it?"

"No. I'm not sure about anything. He certainly could've done it. Just because he's unusually handsome and wealthy doesn't mean that he's not capable of something like this. But I don't like that the police aren't even trying to find somebody else. I know this case, and I know that they have nothing on Slade except for the fact that he was at the scene when the cops got there. And that he had motive and access to the lab, where nobody else did, except Jordan. And the fact that there is a significant portion of the surveillance recording that's gone."

"When you put it that way, it does look bad for our client."

She nodded her head. "But as a scientist, I know better than to trust my first instinct. There's always multiple explanations for any one thing, and it frustrates me that the police aren't even trying to make other inquiries."

I looked out the window. "Well, they don't know what direction to go in. It's not even a needle in a haystack. It's that there's nothing to go on at all."

"Well, hopefully that'll change, if you can communicate with my husband. Hopefully, you can manage to get something off of him, and then your firm can go in another direction in finding out who really did this."

"Yeah, but will the police go into a different direction as well? They aren't exactly keen on believing psychics most of the time."

"There's the rub, but I guess you'll cross that bridge when you come to it."

I smiled. Jane was certainly a level-headed, nice woman. She was so eager to help, and I appreciated that immensely.

We said our goodbyes, and I arranged to see her at 6 that evening at her house.

In the meantime, I had to work up a mafia case. We were defending Santino Bianchi, who was the high up in one of the most powerful families in the Southern California area. He'd been accused of setting fire to a rival family's place of business, which was a deli in one of the poor areas of town.

The deli was a front, of course, for the illicit business, so Santino did that neighborhood a huge favor. But that wasn't a defense, of course. What complicated matters further was that Santino was good for the arson, and a whole host of other crimes. Our firm was attempting to get him to turn state's evidence against the people above him, but, thus far, he wasn't willing to do that.

It was my job to see him and try to talk to him about the value of turning evidence against his boss. Of course, there was an offer on the table where he could go into the witness protection plan for the duration of his life. But Santino wasn't much for that offer, for a variety of reasons.

I called him at his restaurant, where he spent most of his time.

"Santino's, can I help you?"

"Yes, could I please speak with Mr. Bianchi?"

"Hold please."

A gruff voice was next on the phone. "Santino Bianchi, what can I do for you?"

"Santino, this is Serena Roberts. I'm one of the lawyers working on your case."

"Oh, yeah, yeah. You convince that persecutor to drop those charges yet?"

In spite of everything, I smiled when he referenced the "persecutor." I wasn't at all sure if that was a Freudian slip, or if Santino was trying to be funny. Perhaps he didn't know the difference between the word "prosecutor" and the word "persecutor." I found it funny, though, because that was what defense attorneys often called prosecutors.

"No, of course not. I need to see you about their latest offer."

"Not interested. I'll take this fucking thing to trial. Fuck them if they think that I'm going to risk my life by rolling on Joey or anybody else."

"Joey" was Joseph Bianchi, who was the head of that family.

"Mr. Bianchi, we're working very hard on getting a better offer, but, right now, the prosecutor's office knows that you're good for this arson, and they have you dead to right. We have no leverage here."

"Don't call me again until you have good news." At that, he hung up the phone.

I sighed and put my head on the desk. Sometimes I questioned the wisdom of getting into criminal defense. It was a thankless job, and, unfortunately, with the federal cases, there was very little leeway for our clients. The feds didn't mess around, that was for sure, and they didn't tend to file charges unless they were very, very sure that they would stick.

Santino's case was no different. The feds had done their due diligence on that case, and all the evidence clearly showed that Santino had done this arson. They had DNA evidence at the scene, as well as wire-tapping evidence where Santino admitted to doing that arson to somebody in his organization. The pièce de résistance was a grainy cell phone video that somebody had recorded of the incident. The video unfortunately clearly showed Santino throwing a molotov cocktail at the building and then running away.

With all that evidence, Santino was lucky that he wasn't facing life in prison. Yet he expected that the prosecutors were just going to drop the charges. Not going to happen.

Malcolm came into my office. "What are you working on?"

"The Bianchi case. I've been reviewing this file, and I gave him a call. He's still not willing to sing, though."

Malcolm shrugged. "Can't say that I blame him. We all know what happens to mafia rats, even when they're put into the witness protection program." He paused. "The grand jury returned an indictment against Slade," he said. "That was expected of course, but it does make things more serious."

I nodded. "Am I allowed to watch news coverage of this case now? After all, I don't think that my empathic powers are going to work for him anyhow, so I don't think that news programs prejudicing me is going to be a problem anymore."

"Sure, go ahead, but, fair warning, the news coverage hasn't been pretty. And it's only going to get worse now that the grand jury has returned an indictment. Of course, the old joke about indicting a ham sandwich still holds true for the most part, but that doesn't make our jobs any easier."

I knew that Malcolm was right, having been privy to grand jury proceedings. The district attorneys simply had too much sway over grand juries, and this case, especially, was going to end up with an indictment. It was too bad these proceedings were so secretive, because I would've liked to have seen the evidence against Slade.

I felt nauseated, because, like it or not, I couldn't get Slade out of my mind. He was now formally charged with murder, as the indictment represented the formal prosecution charging document, and yet I couldn't get his touch out of my head.

What the hell was wrong with me?

"Well," Malcolm said, "I just wanted to let you know about Slade's indictment. Carry on."

For the rest of the day, I did client intake interviews, legal research and worked on three appellate briefs. I was able, for the most part, to put Slade out of my head. But I had to admit that I was depressed that he didn't try to contact me all day.

I packed up my things and looked at my watch. The clock read 5:15 PM, and I had to be at Jane's home in La Jolla in forty-five minutes, which was going to be tricky with rush-hour traffic. The traffic wasn't nearly as heavy in San Diego as it was in Los Angeles, but it was heavy enough. So, I headed down the elevator and out the door.

I called the doggy day care and explained that I wasn't going be able to get Sadi and Gigi until later, and they were extremely accommodating. I was grateful for that.

Just before six, I arrived at Jane's home. It was tudor-style, with the pitched roofs and dark trim over white siding. It was surrounded by mature palm trees and was within walking distance from the beach.

I approached the door, and Jane opened it before I even got the chance to knock or ring the doorbell.

"Come in, come in," she said, leading me into the foyer. On the right of the foyer there was a narrow stairway, and on the left, there was a small sitting room with a grand piano, a flat-screen television and a small couch. "Here are some of Jordan's clothes," she said, giving me a garbage sack full of clothing. "I was going to take them to the Goodwill, but I'm really happy that you're going to use them to good effect. At least I hope that you'll use them to good effect."

"Me too," I said. I had to admit, though, that I was feeling extremely nervous about doing this. Perhaps it wouldn't open up the floodgates again, but perhaps it would. I thought about all the torment that I'd gone through before, with the spirits never quite leaving me alone, and I shuddered.

"Would you like a glass of wine?" she asked me, as she opened up her back screen door and let a golden retriever into the house. The dog came up to me and sniffed me, wagging her tail.

I fingered the sack that she'd given me. I was anxious to get started, yet not, all at the same time. "Sure, why not?" I said.

The two of us went out to her deck and she poured a glass of wine for both of us. "I'm happy that you're here," she said, her voice cracking. "Things have been pretty lonely around here without Jordan."

I put my hand on hers. "Believe it or not, I've gone through something that is somewhat similar to what you are."

"Oh?" Her eyes were red-rimmed, and I noticed that she had an open box of Kleenex on the railing of the deck. "What happened with you?"

I shrugged my shoulders. It was still painful to talk about, but not as painful as some of the other things that I'd gone through. "My mother was murdered when I was 18," I said. "By a mass shooter at McDonald's. She died trying to protect my brother, Christopher."

Jane nodded. "I'm so sorry to hear that. I guess you do understand what it's like to have somebody who means so much to you just ripped out of your life senselessly."

"I do. I really do." I wanted to tell her even more about what had happened, but it didn't seem appropriate.

"How did you handle losing your mother like that?"

I bowed my head. "Not very well, I'm afraid. I was already dealing with another major tragedy in my life during this time, and I also had a lot of darkness that came from somewhere that I didn't know. Plus, I was tormented, night after night, by spirits who were constantly trying to contact me. I was losing my mind, and, quite frankly, my mother's death was the final straw."

She nodded. "It sounds like you had a lot on your plate. But you got through it eventually, right?"

"I'm not self-destructive anymore if that's what you were wondering." I felt like I was lying when I said that, though, because my obsession with Slade certainly had the potential to become self-destructive.

"That's good to hear." She sighed. "This house certainly does seem different now. Even Bella has been wondering where her daddy is."

At that, Bella the golden retriever came out onto the patio and put her head on Jane's lap. She patted her dog absent-mindedly while Bella whined softly. "See what I mean? She was never clingy like this before."

I closed my eyes, and felt Bella's vibrations. She did seem distressed, and I felt for her.

"Dogs are resilient," I said. "She'll be wondering about Jordan for awhile, but hopefully she'll get over it."

"I hope that I get over it someday, too." Jane shook her

head sadly. "I certainly hope that these clothes help you find his real killer. I'd hate for Slade to get the death penalty when he had nothing to do with it."

"I'm happy that you haven't rushed to judgment about Slade."

"Well, I know Slade. He's extremely intelligent and doesn't suffer fools gladly, but he's good people underneath his bluster. He's not as cocky and arrogant as these news channels make him out to be, that's for sure."

"I agree."

I finished my glass of wine and rose to my feet. "Well, I thank you for inviting me in for a drink, but I have to get going. I have two little dogs who are waiting for me at a day care place, so I really have to go and get them."

"Of course," she said. "Let me know how this goes." She pointed to the bag of clothes. "I hope that you can get something off of them."

"Me too." I wasn't at all sure, however, that I wanted this reading to be successful. In fact, I was scared to death that it would be. But I had to do it for Slade. There was something inside of me that was screaming that I needed to help him in any way that I could.

Even if Slade never called me again, and I only had contact with him when he visited our firm, that didn't matter. He was under my skin and was a part of me. There was no way that I was going to let him be found guilty if he actually had nothing to do with Jordan's murder.

That was a big "if" of course.

Chapter Thirteen

That night, I lay in my bed, staring at the ceiling. It was 3 AM, and I'd been unable to sleep. No such problems plagued Sadie and Gigi, though, as both dogs were in bed with me, snoring away while laying on their backs. They made quite a sight, and I was happy that I decided to bring them into bed with me and not have them sleep in their kennel.

I hadn't yet had the courage to open that garbage sack full of clothes, but that wasn't what was bothering me. What was really bothering me was that Slade still hadn't called.

Yes, I had become *that* girl. The girl who obsessed about her guy, and let her mind run wild on what was going wrong. I was second-guessing everything at that moment.

I finally decided that sleep wasn't going to happen, so I got up and made myself a sandwich and went into the den and turned on the television. I couldn't help it – I wanted to see if I could catch some of the news coverage on Slade. I was a masochist, after all, even if I hadn't indulged that side of me in quite some time.

I clicked on the television and nibbled on my sandwich, which was made of tofu cheese and oil. It was my version of a grilled cheese, and it always hit the spot.

I found a morning show, which came on at 2 AM my time, as it was an East Coast show. The talking heads were going over some of the usual things on their agenda – politics, a bit of sports and movies, a few interviews. Then they started talking about Slade's indictment.

"We have an update on the Slade Bridgewell case," the blonde lady was saying. "The grand jury returned an indictment against him yesterday. We have our legal analyst, Henry Cantwell, here to tell us what this means."

I shook my head as the panel speculated about Slade's case with the legal analyst, who attempted to assure the audience that Slade hadn't yet been tried, even he'd been tried in the court of public opinion and had been found guilty. The entire panel seemed way too happy to report on Slade's misfortune, and I hated them for it.

I ended up changing the channel after a few minutes, because I was feeling so disgusted by this panel. They might have been preaching "innocent until proven guilty," yet they were talking about the whole affair like it was OJ.

I flipped around the television, finally settling on a movie on HBO. I wished that I could take my mind off of Slade and off of those clothes that I needed to meditate on, but I just couldn't. I was so sucked in by Slade...I disgusted myself.

Finally, it was around 5, which was my usual running time. I went up and changed and put my two little girls in their kennel, after I walked them and let them do their business. I was looking forward to this run, because I really, more than ever before, needed something to take my mind off of my issues.

As I ran, I tried to ignore the voice in my head. *Serena,* the voice said, *if you let Jordan in, you're going to let them all in. You're going to end up not being able to function again. Beware.*

I ran faster, trying not to let that voice win. "Yes," I said out loud to the voice. "I'll be taking a risk. But I'll be able to get through it again."

Not before you self-destruct, the voice said. *And who knows if you'll survive if you do self-destruct again.*

"I have to do it," I said as I ran faster and faster. "I have to. If I don't, Slade might end up getting the death penalty."

What does he mean to you?

"Nothing," I said. "Our firm doesn't want to lose that case, because it'll look bad for our reputation. That's the only reason why I care so much.

Bullshit. You care for him far more than you're letting on, even to yourself.

I shook my head, and kept on running. I ran to the beach, and my legs pounded the sand. I ran up the wooden stairs to the pier, and ran all the way down to the end of it, and then ran back. I paused halfway through to look down at the surfers in the water, and then carried on.

Back on the beach, my legs carried me faster and faster and faster. I shook my head, trying hard to get that voice out of my head, but it just wouldn't be quiet.

"You have to avoid it, you have to avoid it," I chanted to myself again and again.

I ran from the beach to the street, and eventually ended up in front of my house, soaking with sweat. I leaned down and put my hands on my knees, and tried hard to tamp down the feeling that I was going to puke. I guessed that I was feeling sick because I pushed myself harder than I ever had before on my run, but also because my brain was so confused. There were just too many things that were fighting for my attention in my head space.

I showered, changed, got the dogs and headed to the doggie day care place and then onto work.

I was going to avoid those clothes for the time being.

Chapter Fourteen

When I got into work, Malcolm was waiting for me. I knew this because my assistant told me to meet him in his office. So, I went down there to talk to him.

"Come in, come in," he said. "And shut the door behind you."

Crap. Shutting the door behind me was never a good sign. Usually, it was a sign that trouble was brewing. Nevertheless, I shut the heavy door behind me and sat down.

"Don't worry," Malcolm said. "You're not in trouble."

"Good," I said. "So, what's going on?"

He shook his head. "I have no idea why I didn't look into this before, but Jane filed for divorce from Jordan right before he died."

I nodded my head, thinking of how Jane was when I went to see her. She was grieving. That was palpable to anyone. Granted, I didn't try to "read" her, but, nonetheless, anybody in that room would've known that she was grieving. "So, what are you saying? That Jane is the 'other dude?'"

"It's worth looking into. We have our investigators desperately trying to find the missing piece of that surveillance tape, but, thus far, they've come up empty. This wrinkle does make it interesting, though. We're putting together a scenario where Jane and Jordan weren't getting along, so Jane wanted him out of the way. I don't think that a tiny woman like that would be able to bludgeon a man to death, but she very well could've hired somebody to do just that."

"I don't get it. What would she have to gain by having him killed, as opposed to divorcing him?"

"Well...." He leaned in closer to me and lowered his voice. "We've also found things online while we were researching her background. She apparently filed for orders of protection against Jordan at least twice. They were both dismissed. We're requesting those files and they should be in this office this week."

"I see. Perhaps he was violent and threatened to kill her, and she was afraid that if she left him…"

Malcolm sliced his hand across his neck. "Yes. She probably was afraid."

"But why have him killed in such a way? She could've just hired a hit man who could do it clean."

"Because, this way, it would be easier to frame someone else. Someone like Slade. Think about it – if it's a professional hit man, and Jordan is shot and his body disposed of, then the whole thing could very well come back on her. But if Jordan is bludgeoned in his lab, and it's known that one other person had access to that lab, and that person is Slade, then it would be so easy to frame him. They can say that perhaps it was self-defense, but if Jordan was shot, it becomes more difficult. Slade probably wouldn't have brought a gun into that lab."

"But he would bring in a baseball bat?"

Malcolm shrugged. "Perhaps. Listen, this isn't a perfect theory by any means, but it's interesting. We're going to follow it."

"I'm not buying it. She's been so cooperative in giving me Jordan's clothing. She knows that there's at least a chance that I can communicate with Jordan, so why would provide me with the material that would help me do that?"

Malcolm cocked his head. "Have you used those clothes yet to try to talk to Jordan?"

"No. I just got the clothes last night, and, I admit, I haven't had the courage yet to try to communicate with Jordan. You don't know how much communicating with the dead takes out of me."

"Well, we need for you to do that as soon as possible. If it works, then we'll at least have something to go on. Right now, we have nothing at all."

"I'll do that when I get home from work." Then I picked up the paperweight on his desk. It was a crystal prism that Malcolm got from his trip to India. "Is our client going to be coming in this week?" I was ashamed to admit, even to myself, how much I needed to see Slade again.

Malcolm smiled. "No, apparently he's going out of town this week. I'm surprised you haven't heard about that."

My heart sunk. "No. I haven't talked to him for a few days. He didn't mention going out of town." I felt jealous that Malcolm, or somebody close to Malcolm, had apparently talked to Slade recently. "Why did he go out of town?"

"Not sure. I just know that my assistant called him this morning and he said that he was leaving town for a few days. He has that monitor on, and he somehow managed to convince the judge to let him leave."

"I don't understand. How did he get the judge to agree to that? Isn't that your job to make a motion to allow that?"

"It is, which is why the whole thing is surprising to me. He's being monitored, of course, but, as you know, murder suspects aren't usually allowed to travel freely without there being a court order. But I called the judge after Slade called me, and the judge confirmed that Slade was allowed to leave. I'm as surprised as you are."

"Where is he going?"

"To New York, apparently. I have no idea why, though. The judge simply said that it was a family matter. I feel sorry for Judge Samson, though. Once the media finds out about this, he's going to be crucified." Judge Samson was the judge that we drew for this case. He was known to be tough but fair, which was good and bad for us. Since he did have a reputation for toughness, it was going to be difficult to try to get our evidence in and leave the prosecutor's evidence out. But since he was fair, and wasn't necessarily known as a hanging judge, we felt like we had a fighting chance in front of him.

New York. I suddenly felt the need to see Luke and Dalilah. I hadn't seen them in months. They were almost ready to have their baby, and, after that, according to Luke, he and Dalilah were going to be married at her father's place in Montauk. I was going to be invited to the wedding, he assured me.

Then I realized that was just dumb. I was going to go to New York and what? Hope that I just happened to run into him randomly? In a city of 11 million people? That was silly, and besides, I had a lot of work to do right here in San Diego.

"Well, I guess that Slade won't be in this week." My heart was positively in my throat when I said that. What the hell was wrong with me? I was going to see him soon enough, unless he decided to fire our law firm. Which certainly was a possibility now.

"No, he won't. In fact, I don't know when he's going to come in. My assistant is trying to get him in here, but he's pretty elusive. Of course, it's early in the case. Trial is a year away. We have plenty of time to get his case together, but it would be nice if we could get an earlier start."

I felt myself blushing. "I guess that I didn't exactly help. After all, I was the one who was supposed to conduct the preliminary interview, and it didn't go well. To say the very least."

"You're human. Anyhow, what are you working on today?"

"I'm working on the Stallworth appellate brief. It's due in a matter of days."

Malcolm nodded. "You certainly do write excellent briefs. Well, carry on. But if you get the chance, I'd like for you to revisit the Bianchi case. I know that Santino hasn't exactly been reasonable, but, other than the Bridgewell case, the Bianchi case is the most high-profile we got. We shouldn't be taking that one to trial, because the jury will send him up the river for a long, long time. So, Serena, if you could find a way for Santino to take that plea deal, then that would be incredible."

I left the office and tried, hard, to hunker down on the appellate brief. Eric Stallworth was convicted of large scale company theft, as he was convicted of stealing millions of dollars from his employer. But there were a number of errors that were made by the judge in that case, so our firm was angling to get him a new trial. The legal arguments were pretty clear, so this brief was easier to write than most.

But, as I looked up case law and statutes and wrote my

brief, my mind was wandering. I found myself involuntarily thinking about Slade, again and again. I touched my fingers to my lips as I thought about how they burned for Slade. Nobody had ever made me feel quite the way that Slade did, and, in fact, nobody had ever come close. It wasn't just that he was incredibly sexy and was a masterful, absolutely masterful, lover. It was more than that. I really did feel that he had the power to heal me. To forget all that happened to me. Certainly, it was wonderful that I had ways of trying to push my pain down – running, renovating houses – but these other things were stop-gap at best. They were band-aids.

Slade held the key to making me whole, which I hadn't been in a long, long time.

He wasn't coming in that week. And, he wasn't calling me, either.

I worked for the rest of that day on my brief, and then I made an appointment to go and see Santino. He wasn't changing his mind, of course, about taking the deal, but I hoped that I could work with him.

But I went home, after picking up the dogs. I fully intended to be brave enough to try to communicate with Jordan. It needed to be done, sooner rather than later, so that our firm might be able to get a lead on who was really responsible for Jordan's death. I hoped that Slade wasn't good for the death, and I couldn't imagine Jane was, either. So, there had to be somebody else.

I got home, fed the dogs and put them out, and then let them on my lap as I sat in the easy chair in the living room. I clicked on the television, and then realized, about halfway through the program, that I wasn't interested in watching tv. I was only procrastinating, and I had to stop that. Soon.

With a sigh, I pet the dogs' heads, and went over to the

garbage sack that was full of Jordan's clothes. I dreaded doing this, but it was going to be done, sooner or later. I would've done absolutely anything to guarantee Slade's freedom.

I selected something, a golf shirt, and sat back down in the easy chair. The two dogs leaped back on my lap, and I pet their heads absent-mindedly. They whined a little, their little ears perking up.

I considered the dogs' reaction to be a good sign. Animals were known to have a sixth sense, much more than humans, so if there was a spirit around in my home, the dogs would be the first to sense it.

"What is it, Sadie?" I asked the little dog, who was still looking alert, her ears pointing straight up in the air. "Do you sense that Jordan is around?"

She didn't answer, of course, but she continued to look as if she was on high alert. Gigi whined a little bit, and she jumped off my lap and went to the door. She barked and started to run around, her little body wriggling.

I let her outside, and she took off. Sadie, for her part, followed Gigi out the door.

I shook my head, not certain about why the dogs were acting weird. I hoped that they had felt the presence of a spirit, but, most likely, there was a bunny or a possum outside.

Then, when the dogs came back to the sliding glass door, I smelled it. A skunk. I smelled both of the dogs, and neither smelled like skunk, thank God. "Come on in," I said to them. "Here I was all excited, thinking that you guys were sensing Jordan."

I got back in my chair, and the dogs got back with me. They both put their heads down, and I soon heard them snoring.

So much for them sensing Jordan. It was clear that neither dog was sensing anything, and I wondered if this whole thing was going to be fruitful.

I took a deep breath, and nervously fingered the shirt. Then I closed my eyes and put the shirt to my face and breathed in deep. It was laundered, and smelled of Tide detergent. I felt my heart racing, as I concentrated on the article of clothing.

So far, nothing. But that was okay. Sometimes it took awhile.

Then, all at once, I felt it. I was there in the lab. I was looking through Jordan's eyes. It was weird, being in his body, because I got a sense for how his brain was working. Jordan's mind was feverish, dreamy, and chaotic. I felt all of these things. As Jordan, my thoughts were racing a million miles an hour, but I was able to concentrate on something.

I looked around the lab. There wasn't anyone there, but there seemed to be a number of top-secret concoctions that were in various tubes.

I suddenly had a flash, and I knew what Jordan had been working on before he died.

And I wondered if that had anything to do with why he was killed.

Too soon, I was out of the lab and back in my chair. I knew that Jordan was showing me just what he wanted to show me, so I knew that what I saw in that lab had to be significant.

My heart was pounding. I had to talk to Malcolm, because, while the "tour" of Jordan's lab didn't exactly show me who killed him, it did, possibly, show me why he was killed. Not that what I saw exonerated Slade, or Jane, for that matter. But it was something to go on.

I looked at the clock, and it read 9 PM. It wasn't exactly early, but it wasn't that late, either. I knew that Malcolm had a wife and two children, but it was early summer, and school was out. So, I decided to give him a call.

"Serena," he said after he picked up on the third ring. "What's happening?"

"I need to talk to you. I got a very brief reading off of Jordan's things, and Jordan showed me something that he obviously felt was significant. Unfortunately, though, I was brought back to reality a little too soon to understand what was the significance of this finding, though."

"Well, what was it?" he asked me. "I'm waiting here with bated breath."

"Jordan was working on something before he died. Slade made reference to it, but he said that he had no idea what Jordan was working on, only that he knew that Jordan was hard at work on something that would revolutionize the drug industry. I now know what it was."

"I'm listening."

"Jordan was apparently working on a marijuana pill."

Malcolm was silent for a few minutes. "And?" he finally said.

I shook my head. "A marijuana pill. That has to be behind the whole murder, somehow, someway."

"That's ridiculous," Malcolm said. "There are already marijuana pills on the market. They aren't common, but they've been developed. I don't see how that could get him killed."

"I don't know why, either, but let me try to do a bit of research on this. I'm telling you, Jordan showed me this scene for a reason. That's how spirits work, at least with me

– they show me what they need to show me, and I have to interpret why I'm being shown that particular thing."

Malcolm sighed. "Serena, I don't want to pressure you, but please try again. Hopefully Jordan will show you who actually did this, instead of leading you down a path that might or might not bear fruit."

I shook my head. If only spirits were that direct with their messages. "Let me do some research," I said. "And maybe I can start to figure this whole puzzle out."

We hung up, and I put my head in my hands. Slade had a farm in Oregon, and this farm grew, among other things, marijuana. What did that mean? It was a $10 million a year "side business," and Slade had mentioned the whole thing only in passing to me, so it certainly didn't seem like a venture that he spent a lot of time or mental energy on.

Was Slade's marijuana business significant? Perhaps it would be, but then again, that wouldn't make sense. If Slade was growing marijuana, and Jordan was developing a way to put this marijuana into pill form, then Slade's business would be even more lucrative. Therefore, I couldn't imagine a scenario where Slade would want to kill Jordan just because Jordan was working on a marijuana pill.

I decided to do some research on the current marijuana pills on the market. Truth be told, I'd never even heard of such a thing, but, when I did a quick Google search, I discovered that there were, in fact, marijuana pills that could be obtained for certain patients. But, after doing a bit of reading, I also discovered that these pills weren't desirable because they took too long to hit the bloodstream. Because of that, smoking the drug was still preferable for those patients who needed marijuana as a medication. It was apparently too difficult to dose because of the delayed reaction.

I bit my lip. I needed to find out more about Jordan's marijuana pill that he was developing, but I had no idea how to do that. Our law firm could subpoena the records for the lab, but would that particular drug show up? After all, it was top secret, to the point where Slade apparently didn't even know that Jordan was developing it. It could very well be "off the books."

I drummed my fingers on the desk, trying to figure out why this particular drug was so significant. It wasn't immediately obvious.

I decided just to get some sleep and try to parse it all out with fresh eyes. That often helped me – to take a bit of a break. Do something else, and then come back to the problem. And I would get back to the problem the next day.

Chapter Fifteen

The next day, I got into work, after going through my usual run and dropping off the dogs, and went to see Malcolm.

"Well?" he asked me. "Did you get any more readings off of Jordan?"

I shook my head. "No. I'm going to try to go with the lead that he gave me yesterday."

"The lead? It wasn't much of a lead, was it? He just showed you a pill that he was working on. That doesn't seem very significant to me."

"Well, it *is* significant, otherwise Jordan wouldn't have chosen that one thing to do show me. How it is significant, I don't know yet. I only know that it is."

Malcolm merely grunted. He seemed to be in a foul mood. "Okay. Listen, you have to visit Santino today. He's talking about jumping bail and disappearing."

"I'll talk to him, but he's such a loose cannon. I have no idea how we're supposed to get him to take that deal if he doesn't want it."

"Well, figure it out, or we're not going to have a client. I know that he has a monitor on his ankle, but he knows people who can take that off of him. He also knows plenty of people over in Italy, and he knows people who have private planes. You have to get over there ASAP and talk to him. Try to convince him not to jump."

"Okay, I'll go there after I put the finishing touches on the appellate brief. It's due tomorrow before five."

"Forget about the brief for now. You have to get on this Santino thing. I'm telling you, he's thisclose to jumping. Get over there now."

I sighed. "Okay, but the brief is due. That would mean...."

"You're going to have to work on it this evening or later on today. I'm sorry, Serena, but I really have no choice here."

"Can't somebody else talk to Santino?"

"No. You've been assigned the work up on this case, so it's all on you. Besides, you're the one he trusts."

"With all due respect, sir, he doesn't trust me that much. He hung up on me yesterday. He's not at all getting close to taking the deal."

"Use your charm," Malcolm said. "Call me when you get to his place of business."

I groaned, feeling used. Apparently, Malcolm was just fine with the prospect of me spending the entire evening, and probably into the morning, on the Stallwell brief. That brief was looming, and I hadn't worked on it nearly enough. I had intended to have finished it at Slade's, assuming that I spent the entire week with him. I didn't, of course, so that was the one thing that was on my agenda.

But, then again, Santino jumping wouldn't be great for the firm, either. Malcolm didn't say as much, but I had the feeling that Malcolm's main concern was not that Santino would be in trouble if he jumped bail, but that the firm wouldn't get paid if that happened.

I felt totally cynical for thinking that way, though.

I went to my office, packed up my briefcase, and prepared to go to Santino's restaurant in Little Italy.

I got to Little Italy, and found parking. I loved this part of town. Trees lined the streets, and there were random houses here and there that were from the Victorian age. It was fascinating to me that there were still these residential homes in the middle of the city, even if these homes weren't necessarily residences anymore. Also lining the street were pictures of famous Italians. Despite the fact that this was "Little Italy," there weren't only Italian restaurants in this area, although there were quite a few of these restaurants. There also were shops, sushi restaurants, pubs, and hamburger joints.

Perhaps the most interesting part of this area were the airplanes. They flew so low over some of the buildings that I often wondered how they didn't crash onto some of the roofs. I sometimes felt that, if I stood on my car, I could touch the plane as it came in, although I knew that this was impossible.

After I found parking, I walked to Santino's restaurant. It was a newish place with a patio outside. People were chatting and eating, as it was 11 AM. I felt bad that I was going to be bothering Santino during his busy time, and, indeed, I wouldn't be surprised if he threw me right out.

I went into the place. It had high ceilings, exposed brick and exposed large pipes in the ceiling. Despite the exposure of the pipes, this place was attractive and cozy, and the pipes actually added to the décor.

"How many will be in your party?" a lithe hostess asked me without looking up.

"I'm not eating. I have to see Santino."

"He's busy." She seemed annoyed. "You need to come back after the lunch rush, which will be around 3."

"I need to speak with him now." That said, I patted my briefcase. I had brought my legal brief with me, just in case I was stalled in talking to Santino. All I needed was a place to sit and research, because I also brought my tablet with me, so I didn't even need Wi-Fi.

"That's not possible," she said, and then she looked behind me. "Now, if you would please step aside, there is a line of people behind you."

I raised an eyebrow. "I don't care about the people behind me. I need to see Santino now. Tell him that Serena is here to see him."

She opened her mouth to protest, but, just then, Santino showed up. He put his hands on her shoulders. "Serena," he said. "I'm busy. You're going to have to come back later."

"I won't. I need to talk to you."

"I'm not going to talk to you, so just give up."

"Listen-"

"No, you listen. I have a business to run here. If I don't run my business, then I don't have money. If I don't have money, then your firm won't get paid. Now, if you'll excuse me, I have hungry people who need to get a seat and eat some of my delicious pasta."

I wasn't going to get anywhere with him, that was clear.

Santino's face softened. "Listen, I'll talk to you later. Maybe I can come to your house?"

"No. I don't feel comfortable with that."

"Okay. But I know why Malcolm sent you down here, and, I'll be honest, he's not far off. If you allow me to come to your house this evening, we can sit down and talk about things. Otherwise..." He shook his head.

My heart started to quicken. I didn't want this goombah in my house. I didn't even want him to know where I lived. But, at the same time, perhaps I could keep him in town if he was looking forward to seeing me at my home that evening. And, if I got a chance to sit down with him, perhaps I could also get him to take the deal.

"All right," I finally said. "Be at my home at 6 this evening."

He nodded and winked. "See you then."

I walked out of the restaurant feeling apprehensive about what I'd just agreed to do. I ordinarily wouldn't have agreed to such a thing, but I felt that Santino had left me no choice. If I could keep him from running by letting him come to my house, then that's what I had to do.

I decided to go on home and work on my appellate brief and wait for Santino. So, I got the dogs and headed home. I called Malcolm to tell him what I was doing, explaining that I needed to concentrate.

"As long as you convince Santino to stay in town, I don't care what you do," he said. "I'll see you tomorrow."

So, that was what I did. I went home and sat in the sun room and researched and wrote my brief.

Chapter Sixteen

Right at 6, there was a knock on door. I put Sadie and Gigi in their kennel and went to open the door. There was Santino, a bottle of red wine in his arms. I inwardly groaned, because it looked like he was coming over for a romantic evening. His hair was freshly combed and he was wearing a nice pair of brown slacks and a button-down top. He really cleaned up well, as he was a handsome Italian man, but he was absolutely hulking. He was at least 6'4" and a good 225 pounds of solid muscle.

"Hello there, Miss Serena," he said. "I brought this bottle of wine from my restaurant."

I shook my head. "Come on in. I wasn't prepared for this to be a night of alcohol." I felt annoyed because I really wanted Slade to be there with a bottle of wine, not Santino the would-be felon.

"Thank you." He looked around. "Cute place you got here."

"Thanks." I wasn't going to tell him that I was looking to move as soon as I could. That wasn't his business.

"You like living near the beach?"

"Love it. I take the dogs to the beach after 6, and it's nice to be able just to walk there. God knows parking isn't so great in this town, although it's better than where I came from."

"New York, right?"

"Right. You remember."

"I got people in New York." Then he looked sad. "Where do you want this bottle of wine?"

I got out a couple of glasses. "Come on, let's sit in the sun room and talk."

I poured the wine into the glasses and took a sip. It was smoother than red wines usually were. "Tasty," I said. "Now, let's get down to business."

"Miss Serena," he said, "I can't take that deal. I'm sorry. There's just no way that I can roll on my family like that. Joey would literally kill me."

I almost felt a bit sorry for him. "Santino, there's nothing that can be done, here. The prosecutors won't give you any deal at all unless you cooperate with them. So, basically, you're looking at spending a great deal of your life in prison."

"So be it, but I'm not rolling. If I roll, then I won't survive. At least if I go to prison, I have a chance of walking out of there someday. I know that you're talking many years, but maybe you can get the sentence down to a few years. Five years, and I walk out of there in two."

I shook my head. "Not with the feds. It's pretty much five years and you walk out of there in five years. And the prosecutor's not offering that. They're offering 20 years. You're, what, 32? You'll be in your fifties before you ever see the outside of a prison cell."

"Okay, I understand."

This was strange. Santino had hung up on me because I wasn't able to get the "persecutors" to drop the charges against him. Yet, here he was, as relaxed as you please, telling me basically that he didn't care about the fact that he was facing twenty years in prison.

"Santino, listen, I know what you're thinking about doing, and I'd advise against it. You might not think that Italy will extradite you if you flee there, but I'm here to tell you that they will. And, when you get brought back here, you'll be facing the rest of your life in prison, not just twenty years."

He cocked his head, and I closed my eyes. I could feel his emotions, and I knew that I was right. This guy was planning on fleeing the country, and I had zero idea what to do about it.

Then he asked me something that shocked me. "How are things going with the Slade Bridgewell case?"

I furrowed my brows. "I can't talk about that with you, but why do you ask?"

"I know something about that case. I might be able to help you."

"Help in what way?"

"Listen, I know people. You're my lawyer, and I can give you information that you can't get anywhere else, and hopefully people won't know it was me who told you."

I involuntarily leaned forward in my chair. I had no idea what Santino knew about Slade's case, or if he knew anything at all. What I did know was that it was suddenly very important that I was able to persuade him not to jump. "I'm listening."

"What are you going to give me in exchange for this information?"

"I'll…"

At that, he was on top of me in one fell swoop. He took me by surprise, and I turned my head when he tried to kiss me.

"No, stop," I said. "Stop."

He did stop, but he looked chastised. "I'm sorry, Miss Serena, but you're a beautiful woman. And I'd like to see you in a social manner. That's what I want, and I'll give you the information that you need."

I shook my head. I wanted to solve the Slade case, more than anything in the world, but not if it meant that I'd have to sleep with this guy. I doubted that he even knew anything, but I had to admit that I was surprised that he would've even brought Slade's case up.

"No," I said. "Forget it." I hoped that I wouldn't regret telling him that, because, on the off-chance that Santino did know something, I might never know.

"Okay. Well, I guess we're done here."

"Santino, I know that you're going to jump, and...."

"Miss Serena, you know what I want. If you want me not to jump and tell you what I know about Mr. Bridgewell's case, then you know where to find me. Or, maybe not. Perhaps I might be in Italy the next time you talk to me."

"Let me show you out," I said, feeling like I wanted to get him out of my house as soon as humanly possible.

We walked out, and when we got to the porch, Santino turned and planted another kiss on me. He held me tightly against his body, and I turned my head. "Santino, I thought that I said..."

And then, just like that, Slade was on the porch with us. He put his hand in Santino's hair, and dragged him off of me. Even though Santino was imposing, and stood a good two inches above Slade and probably had 40 lbs on him, Slade didn't back down when Santino threw a punch at him. Slade was lightning quick, and he ducked when Santino tried to punch him. Then Slade threw a punch at Santino, right in the gut.

The two men were then wrestling, right there on my porch. Santino hit Slade in the face, and Slade came back with an upper-cut to Santino's jaw. Punches were thrown on both sides, as I stood there, not sure what to do. I certainly couldn't call the police – both men were out on bail, and there was a chance that their bonds would be revoked if they were caught assaulting one another. But Santino started to punch Slade, again and again, and I screamed. Nevertheless, Slade ended up, somehow, getting the better of Santino, and Slade was all fists. He gripped Santino's collar, and he hit him several times. Santino finally put his hands up in surrender.

"I don't know who the hell you are," Santino was saying. "But you can throw a good punch." At that, the two men stood up, and Santino held out his hand for Slade to shake. With a nod, Slade shook Santino's hand, and I let out a sigh of relief.

Santino was rubbing his jaw. "Man, I hope you didn't mess up my good looks." Then he smiled at Slade. "But it looks like I might have messed up yours."

He headed to his car. I felt mixed emotions as I watched him drive off, because I wasn't at all sure what was going to happen. Did he really have information that might help us with Slade's case? Was he really going to jump?

But those mixed emotions were soon forgotten as I looked at Slade. He'd sat down on the porch swing, and I could already see that a shiner was forming on his right eye. He looked like a truck had run over him, and I went inside to get a bag of peas for his eye, which I gently placed on his right eye.

He lay back with a small groan.

I was thrilled to see him, of course, but, at the same time, I didn't necessarily know what to say. He'd disappeared on me several days prior and went out of town without a word. Now, here he was, and I'd no idea why he was here.

After wrestling with the matter, I decided to not tell Slade anything at all about what Santino said to me. For one, I was Santino's attorney, and I really couldn't say anything that was protected by privilege. And, for another, I felt that I had to get Santino on more neutral territory and then ask him more about what he was talking about.

I sat next to him as he lay there on the porch swing, groaning a little in pain.

"So, what brings you here?" I finally asked him.

He shook his head. "I wanted to see you. I've had a rough week, and you were the first person that I wanted to see. Of course, I didn't exactly expect you to be on your porch with a tattooed goombah."

"How do you know that he has tattoos?"

"I know the type. Listen, I don't know what that guy was doing here at your house, but I can't believe that you'd be so incredibly stupid as to have him here after dark like that."

"A guy like what?" I was incredulous. Santino showed up looking respectable, yet Slade had already decided that he was a tatooed goombah who was somehow suspect. I knew the truth about Santino, of course – he *was* a tatooed goombah who was suspect. But how did Slade know this just by looking at him?

"A guy like him." That was all he said, and that was all he as going to say, apparently.

"I never asked you to come over here, guns blazing. I could've handled that guy by myself."

Slade scoffed lightly. "Bullshit. He had 100 pounds on you."

"He was leaving. He was on my porch, remember? He's harmless."

"Harmless my ass. Listen, Serena, I don't want another man's hands on you like that. Ever."

"I'm sorry, Slade, but I don't remember the part where you put a ring on my finger. I hardly know you, and we had a few days of bliss together. Yet you're suddenly treating me as if we're in a monogamous relationship." I crossed my arms in front of me. "And if you're going to go gallivanting up to New York doing God-knows-what, then I can't see how you can possibly be acting this possessive."

He furled his eyebrows. "I wasn't going to New York City doing God-knows-what. I had a family emergency."

"So you said. So you told the judge."

He hung his head. "Why I went to New York is none of your concern."

"Oh no. You're not going to pull that bullshit. You can't come in here like the Incredible Hulk and try to tell me that I can't have another man's hands on me, and then try to tell me that what you do is none of my concern. You can't have it both ways, Slade."

He narrowed his eyes, but he didn't say anything for a long, long time. Finally, he spoke…"My mom is sick, okay? She has pancreatic cancer. She found out a few days ago, and I rushed up to see her. She's literally the only family I have." Small tears came to his eyes.

I closed my eyes, and felt his overwhelming grief. I realized that he was very close to his mother, and I felt horrible. I put my hand on his stomach and rubbed it lightly. "I'm so sorry."

He shook his head. "It's okay. I mean, it's not, but what

can I really do? I made sure that she had the top doctors, and that's what we did while I was there. Looked for the most world-class doctors. It doesn't look good. It never does with this particular kind of cancer, but if anybody can beat it, mom certainly could. She's one tough, tough, tough lady."

"Where is she? Is she still in New York?"

"No, I'm actually bringing her here. I found a cancer specialist that came highly recommended specifically for pancreatic cancer. That kind of cancer generally only has a 2% survival rate, but this guy has more like 20%. The odds are still not great, but they're something." He shook his head and smile ruefully. "She's going through a lot. Her only child is accused of a brutal murder and now this. And she's pretty young, too. She just turned 43."

I quickly did the math in my head. His mother was only 15 when she gave birth to him.

"Listen," he said. "I didn't come here to talk about my mother. I came here to see you." At that, he sat up, and his hands ran through my hair. Even though he was roughed up, and his eyes looked like they were both going to turn black, I felt my body start to flush as he touched me. I started to tremble, and I took a deep breath.

I closed my eyes as his lips met mine. His hands were on my face, and his tongue parted my lips and interlocked with my own. I drank him in, tasting him and biting his lips. He breathed heavily, and I felt intoxicated by his scent. It was clean soap, spicy aftershave and pure, pure man.

"What are you doing to me?" I said to him in a whisper. "I've thought of little else but you for the past few days."

He smiled. "I'm surprised. After all, you left that house that I bought for you without saying a word to me."

"Come on," I said as teasingly as I could. "You couldn't

have surprised me more. It's not every day that a man buys me an entire house, let alone a house in Del Mar."

He looked at the door of the house. "Are you going to invite me in? Or are you afraid that, once I'm in there, I'm going to urge you more than ever to take that house over as your own?"

"This place is just fine."

"Perhaps. But you deserve better, and so do your dogs."

"I know. I'm looking at homes this weekend. They're in Solana Beach and La Jolla, and they're in my price range. I'm going to buy a house like a normal person, with a mortgage and a down payment. And, as I told you before, I want something that needs some work. I need that."

"Why do you need that?"

"I need that because I need a project. I need something that can take my mind off of things. I don't want to self-destruct anymore."

He lightly raised my hand, and tenderly stroked my scars on my wrists. "I thought, at first, that perhaps you'd slashed your wrists because you wanted to kill yourself. But I know that your wrist scars haven't come from any kind of suicide attempt. You either cut, or you enjoy others giving you pain."

My breathing started to increase. "That's none of your business."

He got closer to me, and his breath was warm on my face. "It *is* my business. It is if I am going to help you heal."

"How are you-" I was going to ask him how he was going to help me heal, but I soon found that I didn't have words. And, in the silence that followed my aborted statement, Slade took the opportunity to once again put his soft lips on mine.

We kissed for several minutes. After our lips parted,

Slade said "okay. Perhaps I overstepped my bounds in buying you that home. But I can compromise. I'd like to come along with you when you look at those homes that you're interested in."

I nodded my head, actually feeling excited that Slade was going to be coming with me to see these homes. The excitement came from the fact that I was going to be seeing him, period. I hated that I felt like I had to be with him at all times, but I was increasingly feeling consumed.

"That would be wonderful."

"Well, are you going to invite me in or aren't you?"

I felt embarrassed, truth be told, to have Slade come into my bungalow. It was small and cramped, even though it did have a lovely sunroom. After having been in Slade's beautiful home, I was afraid that he'd run from my place screaming.

"Why don't we go down to the beach instead?"

He raised an eyebrow. "Is there a place where I can ravage your beautiful body on the beach?"

I shook my head. "No, there's not." I stood up and took his hand. "Come on, let's go down there. The ravaging will have to wait." It was almost impossible for me to turn him down, because I was craving him just like I was craving him at his home. But I had to slow him down. I suddenly knew that I didn't want my relationship with him to be all about sex, so I felt that I had to get him out of the house with me and into the world.

He smiled and gripped my hand tighter. "Sounds like fun. Let's go."

Chapter Seventeen

We got down to the beach. Even though it was 8 o'clock, or sometime thereafter, there still were hundreds of people around. They were huddling under umbrellas and tents, and there were more in the water. People were throwing balls to one another, and others were walking dogs. The sun was setting, and, as sunsets over the water go, this sunset was gorgeous. I took off my shoes, and Slade did the same.

"I bring my dogs down here usually," I said. "After 6."

"We should've brought them now."

"I know. But I wanted to be alone with you." I felt selfish, even as I said that, and mentally made a note that I'd bring Sadie and Gigi next time for sure.

We walked to the shore, dodging footballs and small children who were running around without looking. The waves were coming up, but they were small and light.

"Come out here when there's a full moon," he said. "The tide acts dramatically different."

"Oh, I know. I also like coming out here when there's a storm. The waves are violent."

We walked along, the water gently lapping at our ankles and feet. I noticed a sand dollar on the beach, and I picked it up.

He put his arm around my waist, and he clutched it with his strong hand. I handed him the sand dollar, and he looked at it, evidently impressed. "I love finding these things," he said. "When I was a kid, I used to look for these high and low. It was like trying to find a four leaf clover or something."

He gave the sand dollar back to me.

"Keep it," I said. "It's yours."

"No. I didn't find it, so it's yours." He put his hand up for emphasis when I started to protest.

We walked all the way down to the end of Ocean Beach, and then headed back. By then, the sun had completely set, so we were in the dark. Even so, there were still hundreds of people who were milling about, and there were several bonfires that were being set in the fire pits.

We sat on the sea wall, and Slade put his arm around me protectively. "You know how you told me that you've thought about me a lot over the past few days?"

"Yes."

"It's been the same with me. I can't seem to get you out of my head, no matter how hard I try. But I haven't exactly tried hard to stop thinking about you."

"I must confess that I'm surprised. After all, you always have no shortage of female attention." Then I smiled. "It must be the forbidden thing. We can't really be together, openly, so that makes it more of a challenge for you. I know how men like you love challenges."

"Don't all men love challenges?" He brought my hand up to his lips, and kissed it lightly. "But, no, it's not that with you. You are a bit of a challenge, I have to admit, but I can't get you out of my head for other reasons. I don't quite know what they are, though, so don't ask me. I only know that I get a feeling with you that I haven't quite experienced before."

"Not even with your actresses and supermodels?"

He laughed. "Especially not with them. Women like Charlotte hold no interest for me. They never really did, and they really don't now. I'm more into beautiful brunettes with brains. I don't suppose you know any of those types of women, do you?"

I felt myself blushing. My hand gripped his tighter. "I can't lose myself in you," I said. "Being with you is like trying to breathe underwater. I feel like I lose all control of my faculties when I'm with you, and that's not a good thing. In fact, with my history and background, it's a really, really bad thing."

"What kind of history and background are you talking about?"

I shook my head. "I can't talk about that."

He looked at the water and kept gripping my hand. "That bad?"

"Yes." I took a deep breath. "Let's change the subject. I now know what Jordan was working on before he was killed."

"Oh?"

"Yes. He was developing a marijuana pill. It apparently is one that's quick acting, and that would change the industry."

He nodded his head. "I know all about that. He was getting close, for sure, to perfecting something. Why do you bring that up?"

"Oh. I'm sorry. I thought that was what was secret. I'm surprised that you know about that."

"Of course I do. Jordan and I were talking about how perfect it would be if I supplied some of the weed from the Oregon farm for the pill that he was developing. If you think that I'd be left out of something like that, then you don't have a very good sense of my business acumen."

I shook my head. I was more confused than ever. "Now, why would Jordan show me that?"

"Come again?"

"Jordan. I got an article of clothing from Jane, Jordan's widow, and he showed me that marijuana pill. He took me into the lab and showed me that pill, specifically."

Slade put his hand on his chin. "I'm sorry, but I really don't believe in all that."

"You don't believe that I can talk to spirits?"

"I don't believe in spirits, period. It's mumbo jumbo. We're born, we die, we decompose into the earth, unless we're cremated, and that's pretty much that."

"Oh, I see. You're an atheist."

"You make that sound so wrong somehow. Stephen Hawking definitively said the exact same thing. Do you look down on him as well?"

"Who said anything about my looking down on you? You have your ideas, and I have mine. I can definitively say that I can speak with the dead, though, so I don't believe that there are no such thing as spirits and possibly heaven and hell. Although reincarnation is also a distinct possibility. At any rate, I don't think that our physical bodies are all that there is in this world."

He bit his lip and said nothing.

"So," I said. "If you think that I can't talk to spirits, then you must think that I'm crazy. Because, pretty much all my life, I've heard them. They've shown me things and told me things, things that turned out to be true." I felt tears coming to my eyes. "I could've saved my mother if I just would've listened."

He put his arm around me protectively, and I put my head on his shoulder. I felt comforted, incredibly comforted, just sitting there on that seawall with Slade's arm around me. Even if he didn't believe in what made me me.

"How could you have saved your mother?" he asked me after a few minutes.

I suddenly didn't have words for him. Plus, he thought that I was crazy for being able to talk to spirits at all. I didn't feel comfortable talking about this with him. "Nothing. Forget I said anything."

He put his finger under my chin, a gesture that I loved, and brought my face to him. He kissed me passionately for a few minutes. "Hey," he finally said after our lips parted. "Don't do this to me. I might not believe, but you do. So, tell me what you were talking about. How could you have prevented your mother's death?"

I sighed. "It was that McDonald's shooting about 10 years ago or so. I'm sure that you remember it. Everybody remembers it. I was dealing with the spirits even then. I was actively trying to block all that out, though, because I couldn't stand it. But that day, I got a message. Spirits don't tell you things clearly, though, unfortunately. They're pretty cryptic, and give you puzzles that you have to try to figure out. But this message was strong. I saw the gunman, I saw the gun, and I saw the place. I had no idea that my mother was involved, though."

"I guess I don't understand. How was a spirit communicating with you before those people were killed? Wouldn't you have been haunted after the massacre, not before?"

I sighed. The memory of that day was flooding through me, and I felt as if I was falling apart. That day was all too much. I had been running, so far and so fast, from not only the spirits, but also from something that I didn't quite understand.

"The gunman killed his wife before he tore into that McDonald's that day. I don't know exactly who contacted me about what was about to happen, but I can only assume that it was her. She showed me a perfect picture of the gunman, Chester Woods, and she clearly showed where he was going to be."

"I see. And what did you do about it?"

"Nothing. I was so tired of fielding messages from beyond, and I was dealing with a personal issue that was horrible. I pretty much took several shots of alcohol, which usually was enough to get those voices out of my head, but this message was so strong, that even nine shots of tequila wouldn't silence it." I felt my breathing coming faster and faster. "It was horrible. Then I saw the massacre on the news, but I had no idea that my mother was one of the ones who was killed. The media didn't release the names of the victims until the families were notified, of course. But just seeing the shooting on the news...." I shook my head. "I couldn't believe it, and the guilt was overwhelming. I'm not at all sure what I could've done to prevent it, but that spirit evidently wanted me to. And then when I found out that my mother was the last person killed..."

I focused on the waves that I couldn't really see anymore, as it was dark out, but I could hear them. They were usually very calming for me, but, at that moment, nothing could've been calming.

"That must have been hard. But you can't blame yourself."

"Yes I can. I can. I saw where that gunman was going."

"And, what? What? Did the ghost want you to call the police? They would've hung up on you."

"I could've done something. And I could have gotten my mom, at least, out of there. She didn't quite understand me, and she didn't believe in what I could sense and feel. None of my family ever did. But, I don't know, I could've done something. I could've called her and told her that I needed to see her immediately. I could've faked a serious injury. I could've done something to make sure that she and Christopher were not at that McDonald's."

Slade shook his head. "Serena, the ghost didn't show you the fact that your mother was going to be involved. So, how would you have known?"

"I could've called her to ask her what she was up to. If she would've told me that she was taking Christopher to McDonald's, then I could've distracted her. I didn't do any of that, though. I just ignored the spirit's message, and my mom died because of it."

Slade put his arm around me tighter, and I put my face into the soft fabric of his shirt. Hot tears were gushing out of my eyes, even though I had no desire to cry in front of him. I couldn't help it, though. That was the first time that I had ever verbalized the guilt that I felt over my mother's death. I never told anyone how I felt about that, even my therapists. Yet I was spilling these feelings to Slade, who didn't even believe in spirits, let alone messages from beyond the grave.

"I don't know what to say, Serena," Slade said. "As I said, I don't believe in spirits. So, it's difficult for me to give you advice on what you could've done about your mother. I don't doubt that you thought that you got a message, though, but…."

"I did get a message. I did. You can believe me or not,

but I did. I could've saved my mother if I just would have heeded it."

He lifted my chin, and commanded me to look at him. I did, and I almost melted into his beautiful green eyes. "You can't blame yourself," he said. "You can't. The only person to blame is that deranged man, Chester Woods."

I nodded my head, but I didn't believe him. I always felt that the whole thing was my fault, which was why I covered up so much, and my behavior was always so self-destructive. My therapist told me that I was continually punishing myself, and maybe I was. All that I knew was that physical pain felt right to me. It was the only right thing for me in the years after my mother's shooting.

"You're not picking up what I'm putting down," Slade said. "I'm trying to tell you that you need to let all of that go. I understand what you think happened, but, come on. If that spirit would've just told you, point blank, that your mother was at McDonald's, I'm quite sure that you would've done something."

I couldn't tell if he was humoring me, or if I was changing his mind about spiritual messages. I assumed it was the former, though, and I felt like he was condescending to me. I closed my eyes and tried to pick up his vibrations, and I felt that he was grieving with me and was concerned. But I didn't quite feel that he was believing the words that I was telling him.

The wind picked up, and I felt a slight chill. It was early summer, after all, so the oppressive heat had not yet settled onto the city. In place of the heat, that was sure to come in July and August, we were still in the middle of "May Grey," which referred to the relentless days of over-cast that resulted in cool evenings. Slade was wearing a light dress jacket, and he took it off and put it on my shoulders. I clutched the lapels, wrapping the jacket tighter around me.

"Let's go back," I said. "It's getting late, and I'm going to have to get up super early to get this appellate brief done. It's almost there, but not quite."

We walked back, Slade holding my hand. It felt absolutely right for him to hold my hand, even more right than the physical pain that I had always sought.

We got back to my place, and I asked him to come in with me, on a whim.

"I thought you'd never ask," he said.

I let the dogs out of their kennel, and put them in my little backyard to do their business. As I was standing at my backdoor, Slade came up behind me and wrapped himself around me. "You smell amazing," he said, as he bit my neck lightly. His hands roamed down my stomach, and his fingers gently pushed aside my panties and found my soft inner folds. I put my hands on the wall to steady myself and moaned lightly.

"My roommates might be home at any second," I said. I'd just given up trying to resist Slade. There was no resisting him anymore. My body had officially taken over and silenced my brain.

"Oh?" he asked. "Let's take this into your bedroom, then."

I stood there for a few minutes more, calling the dogs to come in. All the while, Slade was behind me, his fingers lightly tickling my clit. Slade lips were on my neck, and one of his hands was deftly making its way underneath my shirt. With a flick, my bra was loosened, and I felt his hand lightly rubbing my breast.

The dogs finally made their way inside, and I put them back in their kennel. "I'm sorry, little girls, I know that you sleep with me usually, but tonight, you'll have to sleep right there in your little cage." Sadie and Gigi seemed to understand, for they both yawned and curled up together.

Slade then picked me up effortlessly, and took me into my little bedroom. He laid me down on the bed, and covered me in kisses. "I know that this sounds crazy," he said. "But I missed you these past few days. Nuts, huh?"

I shook my head. "Not nuts. I felt the same way." I spread my legs underneath him, and he lay down on top of me. He piled my hair on top of my head, and put his legs in the crook of my own. He was still wearing his clothes, and so was I, but he unzipped my skirt and pulled it off me while I unbuttoned my own shirt and exposed my chest to him. He brought my shirt down and off of me, while he lightly kissed and tickled my breasts with his tongue. His scent was spicy and sweet, with just a hint of natural man. My legs shook beneath his weight, and I reared back my head.

Slade raised my arms over my head, as he buried his face in my chest. With his free hand, he undid his pants and slipped them off, although he still had his ironed and pressed dress shirt on his magnificent chest. His other hand was firmly placed on my two wrists, which were suspended above my head. "You like a little pain, don't you, Serena?" he asked me in a whisper.

I said nothing, but just nodded my head. I wanted to feel him dominating me. I needed for him to immobilize me, make me submit. Make me lose control.

"I'm not going to hurt you yet," he said to me. "Not like this. I will later, as much as you want. But not like this."

I nodded my head, feeling profoundly disappointed. But I knew why he wasn't going to hurt me. A relationship based upon domination and pain wasn't just something that two people begin without talking about it first. There needed to be conversations about safe words and hard limits and what I wanted from him. I was disappointed, yet grateful that he respected me enough to not go there without talking to me.

He took off his shirt, and I looked at his hard chest and abs. He was sheer perfection, from head to toe. From his sinewy, hard pecs to his eight pack abs and on down to his muscular legs, he was a beautiful sight to behold. His manhood, which was thick and long, was something that felt amazing to me as he entered me. I was dying for him to sheath himself, so that I could feel his glorious cock inside of me, but he was more interested in teasing me.

He brought his belt out, and wrapped my wrists in it. As he tightened the belt, so that there was a slight pain on my wrists, I practically orgasmed. Just that little hint of what was to come, this very subtle pain, excited my imagination on what would happen in the future. It tripped my pleasure sensors, so that I felt that I was going to be begging for it soon. Begging for him to take me rough, to cover my body in bites and stings, to take his belt and crack it savagely on my back and ass.

I hated that I was going to have to wait for that, but what he was doing to me felt amazing anyhow.

He tightened the belt even more, and I felt even more pain. A jolt of electricity ran through my spine, and I moaned. "Please, please, please give me more," I said to him.

He shook his head. "No. This is as far as I'm going to go right now. I'm going to give it to you nice and slow, and very, very vanilla. But it gives you something to look forward to."

At that, he kissed me slow and deep. He raised my wrists

above my head again, and secured them by wrapping the belt around the bed post behind me. That feeling of being helpless, and now knowing what he was going to do next, was intoxicating to me. I felt the white-hot feeling of lustful tingles that started in my vagina and quickly, like wildfire, ran all the way through my body.

If I was already feeling powerful orgasms, what was going to happen when we really got going? When we really had sex the way that I wanted to? The way that I *needed* to? I didn't know what was going to happen, but I did start to feel as if I was on a different planet. That I was floating effortlessly above the bed, watching this beautiful man, down below, ravaging me.

With my hands secured behind me on the bed, I was helpless to do anything but lay there and let him take me. He was gentle, though, more gentle than I wanted him to be, yet it still felt amazing all the same. His tongue was making circular motions down my belly, and he soon was between my legs. He nibbled, sucked and licked that area, his skillful tongue darting in and out of my private folds. I felt that I was on fire, because my body continued to burn with desire with every stroke and lick of his sensuous lips and tongue. He put two fingers in my ass, and I felt the familiar pleasure tingles that made me cry out his name, over and over.

"Are you ready for me, Serena?" he asked me as he put his wrist over my own, which were still completely bound to the bed.

I said nothing, but just nodded my head. I didn't have words for him, because I felt that desire, complete and overwhelming desire, had blocked my speech. I could hear the words in my head, though – words that were begging him to put his glorious and enormous cock deeply inside of me.

"I'm more than ready."

At that, he sheathed his manhood, and, in no time, he was deeply inside of me. I cried out in ecstasy as I clawed his back. He lightly pinched each of my nipples, and I felt the sweet feeling of surrender to him.

"Do that again, and do it harder," I commanded him.

He shook his head. "I'm in control, and I'll do what I want to you. If I do what you tell me, you won't be surprised."

I nodded my head, but I was desperate for him to make me feel pain.

He continued to stroke in and out of me, and, to my immense pleasure, he tightened the belt around my wrists still tighter. I could feel the circulation in my wrists starting to wane, and they tingled as my hands filled up with blood. I reared back my head, concentrating on the pain that I was feeling in my wrists, and then, when Slade savagely bit my breast, I cried out in ecstasy and pain.

Control me, control me. I couldn't stop thinking those words in my head.

Finally, after I orgasmed several more times, Slade apparently did the same. He closed his eyes and lay down on top of me, his breathing heavy and labored. I wrapped my arms around him, and stroked his hair. He kissed me lightly on my lips and around my face, his tongue gently grazing my lips. "Tell me what your fantasies are?"

I felt embarrassed to be telling him, for some reason. "Um…" I took a deep breath. "As you know, as you have suspected, I have some issues in my life. My therapist has told me that I feel that I need to be punished because of what happened with my mother. And my issues also are rooted in something deeper. Something that I never under-stood until just recently."

"I'm listening."

I wasn't ready to tell him, just yet, about my deep-seated issue, so I stuck to more firm ground. I'd already told him about my guilt regarding my mother, so I decided just to relate my dark desires to that. "I have overwhelming guilt, so I used to seek out pain. I went to underground clubs, but not to have sex. I went there because I needed people to hurt me physically. I can't explain it, except when I feel physical pain, it helps me. I feel that I deserve it, and the physical pain takes my mind off of my emotional issues. I'm trying to work through that in therapy. At least I was, when I lived in New York. I haven't found a therapist here yet."

"Sounds familiar." Then he narrowed his eyes.

He didn't elaborate on his statement, and he didn't go into whether or not he was a dominant, although I had the feeling that he was.

I felt shy to talk to him all of a sudden. It was difficult for me to admit to these things with somebody that I was interested in. The people in the underground club didn't judge me, of course, because that was what that club was for. Even though I had the feeling, the strong feeling, that Slade was into that just as much as I was, I somehow couldn't talk to him about that openly.

He kissed my knuckles. "You don't want that anymore, though, do you?"

I felt myself blush. "Why do you say that?"

"You've said enough to me to make me think that the intentional infliction of pain is something that you're trying to stay away from. You've talked about making sure that you don't lose control over your life and your routine, and you've talked about how you use running to cope. What does your therapist say?"

I shook my head. "She says that, for me, it's a mental

disorder, but that's only because it's distressing for me. If it didn't cause me mental issues, then it would be fine that I'm a masochist. But it does, so my therapist has been treating me for that and...."

I couldn't believe that I was telling him so much about me. My hidden desires, and my hidden issues, which nobody knew about until recently – yet I was telling him as if I had known him all my life.

"And what?" he said. "What are you afraid of, Serena?"

"Nothing. I'm not afraid of anything. I just have to continue with a new therapist and keep trying to figure everything out."

Slade smiled. "Serena, it's okay to not be right with yourself. Most of us have something. I'm really no exception. If you scratch the surface with most people in the world, you'll find all kinds of different dysfunctions. You can talk to me. I'm more understanding than you might think."

It was crazy to me how this conversation was evolving. I thought that Slade and I would talk more about negotiating a BDSM relationship between us, yet he was getting me to open up and admit how much I really didn't want that anymore. I had to admit to myself that I felt that pain was an addiction, more than anything else, which meant that I needed to stay away from it because it wasn't healthy for me.

I closed my eyes, but not because I wanted to tune into Slade's vibrations. I was trying, hard, to tamp down my rising panic that Slade himself might become an addiction for me. A dangerous addiction, because what if he ended up in prison? What if he didn't want from me the same thing that I wanted from him? Would I end up self-destructing again?

"I'm tired," I finally said. "And I have to get up really

early to get this appellate brief done. I'd ask you to stay, but that would be disrespectful to Donny and Michael." That was an excuse, of course. I really just wanted him to leave, because he was getting too close. I couldn't trust myself around him, and that was really scary for me.

Slade raised an eyebrow. "I'll leave, of course, because you evidently want me to, for whatever reason. I'm not buying that your roommates could give shit less if you have a man spend the night with you, so I'm thinking that there's another reason why you want me to leave. And that's fine."

I felt tears come to my eyes as Slade silently dressed and put on his shoes. I wrapped my sheet around me and sat up in the bed. "I'll get dressed and walk you out," I said.

"That would be great, but, really, you don't have to bother." He was fully dressed, and he came over to me and kissed me on the forehead. "Night, Serena. I'll see you soon."

And, just like that, he was gone.

I immediately felt empty.

Chapter Eighteen

The next day, after I went for my run and spent several hours at home working on the appellate brief, I went into work. I was eager to find out what our firm was doing on Slade's case, more than ever, because I decided that it would be positively devastating for me if our firm lost this case. I could think of nothing worse than Slade going to prison.

I couldn't believe how invested I had become in this outcome.

I went into Malcolm's office. "I just wanted to get an update on the Bridgewell case," I said to him.

"Well, today we're going to interview his sister. We're hoping that she can be a character witness for us."

I cocked my head, remembering that Slade had told me that he was an only child. "Excuse me?" I said. "I'm so sorry, I thought that you just said that we would be interviewing his sister."

"Yes. His sister. She lives in San Francisco, but she arrived last night. We're putting her up in a hotel. Why do you seem surprised? We need character witnesses in case this whole thing goes south and we end up in the sentencing phase. God forbid."

I shuddered to think about the prospect that this case would end up with sentencing. The possibility of Slade getting the death penalty was all too real.

I walked into my office, feeling beyond confused. Slade's voice from the night before was ringing in my ears. *Her only child is accused of a brutal murder and now this.* I picked up the phone and called Malcolm.

"Serena, what can I do for you?"

"Slade's mother. Have you been in contact with her? Can she come in as well?"

"Yes. She's on the schedule for next week. Why do you ask?"

"Where does she live?"

"In Monterey. Why?"

I closed my eyes, trying to block out the sinking feeling that Slade flat-out lied to me about where he was those few days. He told me that his mother had pancreatic cancer and that he was her only child. Now, here was Malcolm, telling me that not only did Slade have a sister, but that his mother lived in Monterey, not New York.

"Well, I'm surprised that she's coming in. I thought that she'd be starting cancer treatment soon."

"Cancer treatment? I know nothing about that. She certainly didn't mention it when I talked to her."

"I guess I misunderstood," I said. "I need to put the finishing touches on the brief. Thanks for the information."

I turned back to my brief, but I really couldn't concentrate. Slade had a sister? His mother lived in Monterey? What was going on, and why would he lie to me about something like that?

He lied because he had something else going on in New

York. Maybe he was seeing a woman. What was he really doing in New York?

I sighed. I was just starting to think about letting my guard down and let Slade get close to me. Now I felt that I couldn't trust him at all. Of course, I had no idea how Slade was able to convince his judge that he could go out of town like that if there wasn't something else going on, something serious.

I knew that this was going to happen. Slade was occupying my headspace like nobody had ever before. I needed to do my job, and I needed to live my life. I couldn't worry about him, especially if he lied to me.

I finally finished the brief, plus all elements that had to go with it, by the end of that day. I sent it to a courier to file, and I packed up to go home. I had no idea what I was going to do that evening, because Slade was inscrutable. He didn't mention going out when I saw him last night. In fact, he didn't mention seeing me again, period.

I decided to make an appointment with a lady that I learned was showing a house in Pacific Beach. PB, as the locals called it, wasn't as upscale as Del Mar, Solana Beach or La Jolla, but this place was still close to the beach. The house wasn't as nice as the other homes that I had my eye on, of course, but that was a plus for me. The more run down the house, the better, as far as I was concerned.

So, I packed up my briefcase, called the doggie daycare place, and headed out to Pacific Beach to see my new home. At least, I hoped it would be my new home.

I got to the house, and, from the outside, it was exactly what I was looking for. It was a smallish bungalow that was evidently built in the 1940s, for, from the outside, this house looked like all the homes in the area that were built during that particular decade. I had been inside homes like this, and they were always larger than they looked from the street. This house was baby blue with white trim, and there was a well-kept flower garden that lined the outside of the home.

The real estate agent was waiting for me outside the door. She was a fiftyish woman with black hair that was tightly tied in a low ponytail.

"You must be Serena," she said, giving me her hand. "My name is Bobbi Dunne."

I shook her hand, and the two of us went inside the home. It was exactly how I pictured it. Hardwood floors that were slightly worn, an old-school kitchen with old-school appliances and a vinyl floor, and a bathroom that was small and had an older bathtub – complete with claw feet – and an older toilet, plus a pedestal sink. The tile floor in the bathroom was light blue and looked to be at least 20 years old.

Still, this was a cute place, and I could see the potential in it. It was two bedrooms, and it also had a sun room that I absolutely fell in love with. I could picture myself in that sun room on a lazy Sunday afternoon, reading a book while the dogs rested at my feet. It also had two bathrooms, one of which was attached to the "master" bedroom, that really was about as big as the other bedroom. Meaning that it was very small. Well, cozy. That was a better word. Every room was hardwood, which was a no-brainer for me with my two dogs, and there was also crown molding throughout the house.

I knew what to look for in a decent house, of course, and I examined the plumbing, the floors and the walls. I concluded that the house had excellent bones, and, with some cosmetic changes, I could have a beautiful little home.

The only problem was that the yard was extremely small, and that was the way it was in the beach communities such as this one. There was little that I could do with my financial constraints. Sadie and Gigi were small dogs, though, so they would be able to still have enough room to run and play a little bit. Granted, this tiny house was nothing like the beautiful mansion that Slade tried to give to me, but that was okay. It would be mine, and I wouldn't owe anybody anything for it.

Well, I wouldn't owe anyone anything except for the mortgage holder, of course. I had the 20% down payment, but would have to finance the rest. Which was actually just fine, because I knew that I had excellent credit and would be able to get a really good rate.

"What do you think?" Bobbi asked me.

"I love it. I love the location and the price couldn't be better. I'd like to talk about possibly closing on this house within the next 10 days."

Bobbi beamed. "I knew that you'd like this. And you're right — the owner is motivated to unload this home. He's looking to move to Arizona to be close to his children. Unfortunately, he doesn't have a lot of time left. He's been diagnosed with Stage 4 lung cancer."

Hearing about the owner's cancer reminded me of Slade's mother, who allegedly also had cancer and lived in New York. New York, not Monterey.

It was so bizarre. It was a small thing, really, but if he could lie about something like that so glibly, he could lie about anything. Including lying about killing Jordan. I hated that I doubted him like that, and I hated that I was unable to get an accurate reading on Slade and his emotions. He apparently was lying to me, and he got in under my radar. That made him dangerous to me, because I literally had no idea when he wasn't telling me the truth..

"That's a tragedy about the owner. I feel bad trying to take advantage of that."

Bobbi smiled. "It's a horrible thing, of course, but it's good for you. You won't find a home around this neighborhood for this price. I know that it needs some work, though."

"That's what I love about this house. It has amazing bones, and I'm so looking forward to renovating it."

Bobbi put her arm around me. "Okay, well, let's get started with the paperwork as soon as possible. I assume you have a lender lined up?"

"Yes. I'll be using a conventional lender."

We walked outside, and then I noticed a red Porsche hybrid. It occurred to me that I didn't know what kind of car Slade drove, because I didn't pay attention when he came to my house, but the car did look familiar. It looked like a car that might've been on Slade's property when I went to visit him.

Sure enough, Slade emerged from the front seat of that car. I felt happy to see him, but also alarmed. How did he know that I was there?

And he didn't look happy in the least.

Bobbi looked at him, and then back at me. "Do you know him?" she asked me. Then she squinted at him. "Oh, my. That's Slade Bridgewell. He's even more handsome in person than he is on the TV." She nudged me a little. "Do you think that he did it?" she whispered.

"Uh…" I didn't want to tell her that I was on Slade's legal team. I didn't want her to ask too many questions about the case. "I can't talk about that. I mean, I don't know."

"Well," Bobbi said. "This is where I leave you. But I'll be in touch within the next few days. You need to get with your lender and see what we can work out."

"Thanks for meeting me," I said. "I'll talk to you soon."

Bobbi took off in her Toyota Corolla, and I approached Slade. "Hello," I said. "I have no idea how you managed to know where I was."

Slade raised a single eyebrow and crossed his beautiful arms in front of him. "I tracked your phone. I figured that you might be coming here to see another man, but it seems to be even worse than that."

"I'm sorry?" I had no idea why he was angry, and, to be honest, I was put off by him tracking me down like that. If anybody should've been angry, it was me. "Listen, Slade, even if I was coming here to see another man, that's none of your damned business. Despite what you keep saying, you don't own me. Tracking me down by my cell phone strikes me as stalker behavior at best."

Slade said nothing but just continued to glare at me. "Serena, you're going to buy that house, aren't you? After you told me that you'd include me in your decision, you went ahead and left me out of it, didn't you?"

I hung my head. I *did* tell him that he could come with me to see houses. Yet, that didn't excuse what he did. He shouldn't have stalked me like that.

"I'm sorry for not inviting you, but, Slade, I found out that you lied to me about New York, and, quite frankly, I didn't really want to talk to you until I was able to cool off."

"What are you talking about?"

"You and New York. It's rich, you know, that you're so scared that I might be seeing another man – so scared that you suddenly are stalking me through my phone – yet you're going to New York to see God-knows-who and you're doing God-knows-what. Yet I can't peacefully see my real estate agent without you showing up here out of the blue."

"I told you what I was doing in New York. I wasn't lying about that, either."

"Bullshit. Listen, you never said that you had a sister. In fact, you said that you were an only child. And, for the record, Malcolm said that he's asked your mother to come into the office next week. Your mother who lives in Monterey. Not New York. So, let me just say that I've caught you in a lie, and who knows what the hell else you've lied about."

Slade's eyebrows furled and he shook his head. "Okay. If that's how you want to play it, then, okay. Have a nice fucking life."

At that, he got into his Porsche and drove off in a fury.

Chapter Nineteen

A week went by, and I hadn't heard hide nor hair from Slade. I did get to meet his mother, though. She was a doyenne type with helmet hair and long fingernails which were perfectly manicured. She wore a dark-colored dress, which was unusual for people in San Diego during the day, and carried a very expensive bag. She reeked of expensive perfume, and when she spoke, her very voice communicated that she was very wealthy. And, although she was very lean, probably didn't weigh more than 110 lbs, she hardly looked sick. In fact, she looked like she worked out a lot, as her tanned arms were lean and muscular, and her posture was very straight. Her calves also looked extremely solid.

I sat in on the interview, at Malcolm's request, because he took one look at her and told me that this woman probably was not to be trusted. "So I need you to try to tune into her vibrations," he said.

It turned out that wasn't really necessary. She told us nothing but good things about Slade, her "little boy" who she knew could never have done something like bludgeon a man to death. "He always got the best grades, he was always polite," she said. "He has never been in trouble."

I tuned into her vibrations, as Malcolm asked me to do, and I felt that she was telling the truth. Of course, I doubted that she knew her son as well as she should. She seemed the type who would let the nanny raise her children. But she wasn't lying. She did seem to have genuine affection for Slade.

I thought, however, about Slade's words. About how absolutely anybody in the world is capable of absolutely anything. It just depended upon the circumstance and how far a person was pushed. It was like that movie, *In the Bedroom*, with Sissy Spacek and Tom Wilkinson. They played the most normal suburban couple ever, who were pushed to their breaking point when their daughter was murdered by her deranged boyfriend. When the boyfriend beat his murder rap, Tom Wilkinson's character killed the boyfriend in cold blood, with the full knowledge of his wife. That movie made it clear that we all have it in us to kill, every one of us.

So, even though Slade was a "good boy" who had "never been in trouble," that didn't mean jack. Slade still could be guilty, and I knew that.

There was one other thing that bothered me about his mother. Slade told me that his mother was only 43 years old. This woman looked to be in her sixties, and she certainly didn't look the type who would have a child at the age of 15.

I so wanted to ask her how old she was, did she ever live in New York, and if she was sick with cancer, but I kept my mouth shut. It wasn't my job to ask questions, but, rather, to listen and tune into whether or not this woman was deceptive.

When the mother left, I decided to have a talk with Malcolm about Slade's case. "Where are we as far as finding another suspect?"

Malcolm shut the door. "I hate to say this, but Jane is looking good for it. She had the code to the lab, even though she told us that she didn't. And she's intelligent enough to be able to edit that surveillance tape so that there's nothing on there that shows anything."

I shook my head. "That doesn't sound right at all. Listen, I didn't get a single bad vibration off of her, and she was more than happy to give me those clothes. She wasn't standing in my way at all. Plus, Jordan showed me that marijuana pill. I can't imagine that she had anything to do with that."

"Regardless, she had motive, means and opportunity. Of course she gave you the clothes. She's a scientist, I can't imagine that she believed that you could've done anything with those clothes. You didn't get a bad vibration from her, but you've admitted to me that you can't turn your psychic powers off and on. It's possible that she just has a wall up. As for Jordan showing you that marijuana pill, it's possible that the spirit put up some misdirection. That happens, doesn't it? If Jordan wanted to protect Jane, he could've showed you something that was irrelevant, and would cause you to go on a wild goose chase. Right?"

I had to admit he had a point. If Jordan loved Jane, he very well could've been putting me on the wrong path deliberately.

"Okay. Now, you said that Jane had the code to the lab, but she told you that she didn't? How did you find out that she did?"

"We subpoenaed her computer records, and it was on there. I didn't think that it sounded right that she wouldn't have the code to her husband's lab, and I was right about that."

"Maybe somebody put that code on her computer. Maybe somebody is trying to frame her."

Malcolm shook his head. "This isn't the movies. Who would do something like that?"

"The real killer. He hacks into her computer, puts that code in there, and voila! Jane looks like a big liar."

"You've been watching too many movies. At any rate, we're following that lead."

I shook my head. Jane killing her husband seemed wrong to me. She was a tiny woman, and Jordan was a big guy. Not a huge guy, but 200 lbs at the very least. Granted, the killer used a baseball bat, but she would've had to have superhuman strength to do all the damage that happened to poor Jordan.

I went back to my office, and put my head on my desk. Sometimes I hated my job. I hated that I was privy to the very worst of human nature, and I hated not really knowing if the people we were defending were guilty or not. And I really hated having to deal with good people like Jane being ensnared in all this nonsense. The poor woman was grieving, yet we were piling on.

I felt cheered, though, later on that day, when I talked to my lender and found out that I was approved for the loan. The house was $500,000, I had $100,000 in the bank for the down payment, and the closing costs were to be paid by the lender. I'd be able to move into the home as early as next week.

That piece of information – that I soon would have my

own home – put me into a better mood than I'd been in awhile. I was still upset beyond belief about Slade's deception about his mother, and I was more than sad that Malcolm was going to be pursuing Jane as the alternative killer for Jordan. But at least I was going to finally have a place of my own. Not just any place, either, but a cute little place that would occupy my time and was close to the beach. I craved that, because I craved being near water at all times.

So, I got home and Donny was sitting in the living room, watching television and smoking out of a bong. He greeted me with his usual nod when I walked through the door. "Hey, baby," he said. "What's going on?"

"Well, I found a house in PB. I'm going to be moving in next week."

"Ah, dude, I'm going to miss you. But I'm glad that you're getting a place of your own. Those two little rugrats are going to be happy, too."

As if on cue, Sadie and Gigi bounded into the living room and hopped up on Donny's lap. Donny laughed as they covered his face in doggie kisses.

I smiled. "They're going to miss you, and I will too. But you'll have to come and visit me."

"You know I will. I get bored surfing around here all the time. Maybe I can find a new scene in PB and meet some other people. Expand my horizons, you know."

"There you go."

"So," Donny said as he sucked on the bong some more. "What's been going on with that Slade Bridgewell case?"

I shrugged. "It's coming along. We're interviewing character witnesses right now, but we're soon going to be going into serious depositions. Why do you ask?"

"Dunno. The news people are reporting something new on the case, and I wondered if you had heard about it."

"I haven't heard about it. You know I stay away from these news reports. They're so slimy and so inaccurate most of the time."

"Yeah, I know, they're bullshit. Especially that cunt Anna Place. That woman really needs to join Isis or something." He smiled.

Still I was curious. "Well, I don't really care, but what did you hear?"

"Man, I don't know if this is true or not. It sounds pretty bogus. But they're reporting that Slade's mother is terminal, and that gives him motive. They're saying something about Slade killing Jordan because Jordan refused to finalize development on a drug that could cure her. That they got into a fight about that, and Slade beat him up."

That sounded like crap to me, but my ears perked up when Donny mentioned Slade's mother being terminal. "That's ridiculous. I could imagine getting into a fist fight over something like that, but, come on. Nobody would have done something like what happened to Jordan just because of a disagreement."

Donny sucked on his bong again and blew the smoke out. He laid down on the couch, and invited the dogs up with him. They eagerly got on the sofa with him, and Sadie laid her head down on Donny's bare torso. "Yeah, that new theory does sound like crap to me too, but you never know. Something like that could make you pretty angry, I'd imagine, especially if Slade was feeling desperate to save his mother."

I shook my head, and heard Slade's voice in my ears.

Anybody is capable of doing anything under the right circumstances. Would these be the right circumstances? Saving his mother?

And what was going on with the mother anyhow? That woman who came into that office didn't seem like a cancer patient, that was for sure.

"Listen, that doesn't even seem right. Even if Slade were desperate for a drug to cure her, he certainly wouldn't get the drug at all if Jordan were dead, now would she?"

Donny shrugged. "You're not rational when you're really, really angry. Perhaps Slade went outer limits."

I opened my mouth to say something, but nothing came out. I hated that Donny was starting to make sense, and I really hated that I still had suspicions about Slade.

I wanted to call Slade to ask him about all of this information coming out, but I didn't. I figured that he would eventually show up as he has a habit of doing.

Chapter Twenty

It turned out I was right about that. I closed on the new house, and arranged for movers. Everything was happening super fast, lightning fast, but that was fine with me. As long as I had something to look forward to in life, such as a brand new house, my mind was taken off of things that I simply couldn't control. Like Slade.

On moving day, I went to the new house and unlocked the door. It had a musty smell, so I opened all the windows and looked around. It was empty, of course, but it wasn't before. The emptiness made me look at it in a whole new light. I made a list of all the things that I was going to need right away, and then went around the house and made a list of my long-term projects. It always helped me to make lists, because, if I didn't, I would always be going on a wild goose chase.

As I was making my list of things that needed to be repaired – broken cabinet doors, a screen door that wasn't shutting properly, a light fixture that didn't seem to want to turn on – I turned around, and Slade was standing right there in the front door. He had a bottle of champagne in his hands, along with a dozen red roses.

I smiled at him. I wanted him to know that I wasn't angry anymore, and that I really didn't mind him stalking me, as he apparently was still doing. Otherwise, how would he have ever known that I was moving in that very day?

"You certainly do know how to make an entrance," I said as he tentatively stepped forward.

"Well, I wanted to help you christen your new house. And I also wanted to tell you that I'm sorry for showing up before. It was wrong of me to do that. I don't want you seeing other men, of course, but I guess I just have to trust that you're not."

I bit my bottom lip. I didn't want to go off on him and his double standards. Not until I got a better explanation on what exactly he was doing in New York. I was quite sure that there was a reasonable explanation for his trip there, and for the fact that the woman who was in the office was clearly not 42 and didn't seem to be a cancer patient. I just had to figure it all out.

"Don't just stand there," I said with a smile. "Help me clean this place up." I gave him a broom and a dustpan, and he took them both with a grin.

"I can't remember the last time I actually cleaned anything," he said.

"Oh, I know. You have Magdelena or whomever do that, right?"

"I'm joking. Listen, I know how to clean. I haven't always been so reliant on the help. But you have to admit that my house in LA is huge. If I had to clean that place myself, that would literally be all that I'd have time for. But this little place is right up my alley."

Slade swept the entire place, while I worked on cleaning

the bathrooms and the kitchen, and then he came to me for rags and cleaner. "Your windowsills are filthy. I'm surprised that the real estate agent didn't do a better job of making sure this place was more turnkey."

"I don't want turnkey. I've told you that before. This place is lived in, and it's just how I like it. It's going to be gorgeous when I get done with it, I can assure you."

"I know, I was just teasing you. Really, this house is very nice, and you're right. It needs a lot of work, but you could really make something out of it." He paused. "And I hope that you might let me help you make something out of it. I'm pretty handy with floor sanders and refinishing myself."

I smiled. Slade certainly did seem to have a different attitude now. Instead of demanding, he was inquiring in a hopeful manner. *Maybe he really has been chastised.*

As we worked, I tried to think of how to broach the topic of what I really needed to know. I had to find out about his mother and about New York, but it didn't go so well the last time I brought all of that up, so I was hesitant to do so again.

I knew that it was my delivery about it last time, though, so I made a vow that this time I would make sure that I asked him in a more polite way. When things were calm.

Evening fell, and we ordered two pizzas – one with cheese and one without. "The movers will be here in the morning," I told him. "So tonight, I guess I'll be staying in a hotel."

"You can come to my house."

"Your house? You mean the one that you tried to make me live in?"

"The very one. When you turned that down, I decided just to keep it for myself." He helped himself to a slice of pizza, and took a swig of the Pale Ale that I bought at the liquor store around the corner. "But, I don't know. It might be kinda romantic to just stay here tonight. Just you and me, no lights, no television, no distractions."

"Well, I did bring a sleeping bag and a pillow because I figured that I'd be staying here tonight. I also have a blanket. If you don't mind sharing the pillow, I can lay the sleeping bag out on the floor and we can cuddle up." I hoped that he didn't mind doing that, because he was right – staying there that night *would* be romantic.

But before I even thought about anything sexual, I needed answers.

So, while we ate our pizza and drank our beer on the floor, I decided just to ask him what I needed to know. "Slade," I began. "Listen, I'm sorry about what I said before. When I accused you of lying to me about New York. But help me understand." I took a deep breath. "Your mother came into the office this week, and she didn't look sick and she certainly didn't look to be in her early forties. And your sister came into the office as well. You told me that you're an only child. I'm totally confused."

Slade looked stricken and didn't say anything for a long time. I sat there, in silence, willing him to speak and tell me what was going on. But I didn't push him. He looked like whatever it was he was about to say was going to be very difficult for him.

Finally, he spoke. "The woman you saw is my adoptive mother. My sister is my adoptive sister. She's the biological daughter of Helen, though, who is the mother that I've spent most of my life with. Well, with the nannies that she hired for me, that is. I didn't spend all that much time with her though."

I nodded. It was becoming clear, although I didn't

necessarily know why Slade was still in contact with his biological mother. "I see. And your biological mother…"

I closed my eyes and tuned into him. He was open at that time, emotionally, and I felt a range of things – grief, anger, despair. It was as if he was letting loose with something that he had bottled up all these years.

He sighed. "My biological mother's name is Margot. Margot Facinelli. I didn't lie when I told you that she's Italian. Helen isn't, though. She's French Canadian. But I lived with my biological mother for the first seven years of my life. She taught me how to cook, and she was always making sure that I had skills. Life skills. I'm guessing that maybe she was foretelling what was going to happen. That maybe those life skills would come in handy for me one day."

"Margot," I said. "That's a lovely name."

"Yes. And she's a lovely woman." He paused for a long time, while he stared at the wall. "She served time in prison for killing my father."

He said that so matter-of-factly that I had to take some time to process it. I closed my eyes and I felt his vibrations. He was devastated beyond measure, but you'd never know it by looking at him. He was perfectly calm and was eating his pizza.

Something told me that he had to learn how to tell this story without breaking down, because he was a master at doing just that.

"She killed your father?" I asked him. "Why?"

"He was abusive. Extremely abusive, to both her and me. He beat both of us so badly that we ended up in the hospital on a regular basis. It was always difficult to explain, though, and the doctors just thought that we were unfortunate enough to be in many car accidents. I hated her as much as I hated him, because I felt that she was just letting him do this to us. I was extremely young, though, so I didn't necessarily know what she could've done to get us out of that situation."

I put my hand on his shoulder and closed my eyes. I wanted to somehow communicate to him how much I cared for him, and how much I was grieving right along with him. He seemed to understand, because he put his hand on top of my own and squeezed tightly.

"Anyhow, she finally had enough, I guess, because she shot him one night in cold blood. He wasn't abusing her at that time, nor was he laying a hand on me. He was sleeping. Because he wasn't threatening her or me at the time that she killed him, she couldn't claim self-defense. Her defense attorney tried to get her off on the battered woman syndrome, but that didn't work. The good news was that the jury didn't convict her of first degree murder or even second degree murder. She was convicted of involuntary manslaughter and served seven years in prison."

"And Helen?"

"She adopted me out of foster care. That was the last thing that I wanted. I wanted so much to stay with my mother, even if I had to go with her to prison. I remember thinking that I was going to ask the judge if I could live in that prison with her. She was all that I knew, all that I loved. She was just ripped from me, and I had to live with a family that I knew nothing about. Not that they were a bad family, but my father, Scott, was a very busy person. Very important. Was a CEO of a tech company. And Helen, well, let's just say that I doubt that it was her idea that she adopt me. She had no use for me, nor for my sister, Alice. She had use for her tennis buddies and her drinking buddies – she played cards during the day and they all would get sloshed on gin. But she had very little maternal bones in her skinny body, and the nanny, Vera, was who I knew the best."

I took his hand and kissed it lightly. "I'm so sorry."

He shrugged his shoulders, but I knew that he was grieving beyond measure. "Yeah, me too. I got my mother back, when she got out of prison, and we repaired our relationship. I didn't see her the entire time she was in prison, because Helen refused to take me to see her, no matter how much I begged. So, I didn't see my mother at all in between the ages of 7 and 14. Then she contacted me the day that she was sprung, and she made sure that she and I kept in contact." He took a deep breath. "And now this. I'd do anything for her, to help her beat this hideous disease. As much as I know that the odds are against her, I also know that I at least have to try."

I tried to bite my tongue to prevent myself from asking him another question, yet I felt that I had to. I had to clear the air.

"Slade, do you know what the news channels are saying now? About your mother and your possible motives for killing Jordan?"

He shook his head. "Yes, I've heard, and it's the dumbest thing that they could've ever come up with. Why would I kill Jordan if he was in the middle of developing a drug that could cure my mother? Wouldn't that prevent him from developing said drug? I mean, come on. That doesn't even make sense at all."

"That's what I thought, and I figured that they were just going on random speculation like they always do. But I had to ask you and clear the air."

He took another swig of his beer and opened up another. "You didn't believe that, did you?"

"No, of course not."

"But you still, deep down, believe that I did it. Or you don't really know if I did it or not. Right?"

"No." Even as I said that, I knew that I was lying. I was 90% sure that he didn't do it. But there was 10% of me that was doubting him.

Slade narrowed his eyes. "Listen, Serena, if you and I are going to make a go of this, then you have to trust me. You have to. And if there is even 1% of you that still believes that I'm good for Jordan's murder, then you don't trust me at all. So, tell me the truth. Is there even a small part of you that still thinks that I did this?"

I wanted to lie, but I was an awful liar. I used to be a much better liar, but since I had turned over a new leaf, and I stopped lying, I found that I simply couldn't do it anymore. "Yes," I said quietly. "But only a small part."

Slade shook his head. I tuned into his vibrations and found that he was really, really angry. And, unlike all the times before, he didn't try to cover it up with a wall. "Serena, I don't know what to say to you. If you can't trust me more than this, then I think that there's really no hope for us. As pained as it is for me to admit to that."

"Slade, hear me out. You were the one who told me that absolutely anybody is capable of absolutely anything. Right?"

"Yes, and I believe that. As wonderful as you are, you're capable of killing somebody too. But that doesn't mean that I did it. And that's absolute crap that you believe that I did."

I opened my mouth, but I had no words. Inside, though, I was panicking. Was this going to be the end for us? How could we sustain a relationship, if that was the right word for what we had at the moment, if I thought that he could do something like this?

Finally, he sighed. "Serena, you're right. You can't be

sure that I didn't do something like this, although I wish that you would use your so-called psychic powers to discover that I didn't. And I really don't blame you. The facts certainly are against me. But you certainly seem to believe, in your heart of hearts, that I'm a decent person, otherwise I doubt that I'd be here right now in your new living room. You'll soon find out that it wasn't me, though. When you do, then things between us can get serious. I'd like that, too, Serena – to get serious with you."

I felt relieved that he was saying these words. And he was right – there was only a small part of me that believed that he did this. It was the part of me that was logical, as opposed to emotional, and that was just because our firm was having problems coming up with the "other dude" that allegedly did it. If there was just something, anything, that would lead our firm into another direction, I believed that I would have such a burden lifted off of me in my budding relationship with Slade.

He kissed me lightly on the forehead. "It's dark, and there's a light chill in the air. What do you say that we build a little fire in your fireplace and cozy up next to it with this champagne I brought?"

I smiled. "That sounds amazing. I have no firewood, though."

"We can go down to the beach and see if there's any lying around next to fire pits. We usually can find something down there." He paused. "By the way, I forgot to ask you where your two little rugrats are?"

"They're at a doggie hotel, living it up in style. I knew that I was going to have to focus on moving in, so I arranged a stay for them for the next few days at least. They're going to be thrilled to live in this place. I know that the backyard is small, but I plan on running them down on the beach every evening."

"You take such good care of them," he said to me, with a kiss on the forehead. He kissed my lips. "You know that I'm falling for you hard, don't you?"

"How could I not know? I'm feeling the exact same way. As scary as it is."

He took my hands. "Don't be afraid. I know that you might have a certain image of me because of how the media portrays me, but it's not exactly accurate. I mean, it *is* accurate, in the sense that I really did date all those celebrity women. But I have no desire to end up with women like Charlotte or people like that."

"Well, Charlotte does give you some celebrity cache."

"She does, but who cares? She's not real, not in the least. Her breasts are though, surprisingly enough." He smiled and raised his eyebrows, and I lightly nudged him in a joking manner.

"Let's go down to the beach and try to find some firewood," I said to him.

At that, we walked to the beach, hand in hand, and went from one fire pit to another. Some of the fire pits had people standing around them, of course, but there were others that were abandoned. One of them still had twigs and logs that weren't burned, and Slade and I scooped them up and brought them back to my house.

We got in, and I brought out the lighter that I somehow remembered to bring, and I put the tinder into the fireplace and lit it. It soon had a warm, orange glow, and I reveled in the scent of burning wood. It was always something that was heavenly for me, that scent – it was like the pipe that my uncle used to smoke when I was young.

"I love that smell," I said, as Slade poured the glasses of champagne.

"I do too. But most people do. Are there any scents that you like that people might find strange?"

I smiled. "Believe it or not, gasoline. I know that it's dangerous to smell gasoline, but I can't help it. I've always loved it."

"I'd wear a gasoline-scented cologne to get you going, but I don't think that they've invented that just yet."

"What about you?"

He looked wistful. "Garlic. It reminds me of all those sauces that my mother made when I was growing up. And onions, too. Onions always made me cry, of course, as it does anyone, but that was a good thing for me. My father demanded that I be a man at all times, which meant that I couldn't cry, at least not in front of him. If I did, he gave me something to cry about. But when I cut up onions, I could cry without getting into trouble."

I cocked my head, as I looked at his face. He was staring at the fire, looking very lost in it. I could sense that he was really wrapped up in the memory of his mother and his father, and I felt for him. He was just a little boy, and apparently was getting beat just for tears.

"He didn't mind you helping your mother cook? Most misogynistic men don't want their sons doing such sissy work." I air-quoted the words "sissy work."

He smiled. "Surprisingly, no. I guess because he himself was a pretty mean cook, so he didn't necessarily think of it as women's work. So, yeah, cutting up onions gave me an outlet for my emotions, because, in those days, I always had plenty to cry about."

I stroked the back of his neck, and he closed his eyes while he sipped his champagne. I tuned into his vibrations, and I felt only pleasure. He might've been thinking back to his past, but he seemed to still be very much in the present. "I'm sorry all that happened to you," I told him. "Sometimes I just don't know what gets into people, to say the very least."

He shrugged. "It happens. I guess I should be happy, really, considering. I managed to get into Stanford, and, since my adoptive family was so well-off, I never had to take out any loans or anything like that. If I would've stayed with my biological mom and dad, who knows? I probably could've qualified for scholarships and grants and all of that, but I still probably would've graduated with some debt. Maybe a lot of debt. Who knows if I would have been able to get my company off the ground?"

"I guess that's one way of looking at it." I paused for awhile, rubbing his back while he lay on his stomach, watching the fire. "How is your mom? Your biological mom?"

He smiled. "I call my biological mom, mom, and my adoptive mom, Helen. So perhaps that would be easiest for you as well. And she's….sick. Very sick. I hate this disease so much. I've never known anyone who has had it up until now, but what it's doing to my mother.,.." He shook his head. "She's lost so much weight, and she's already turning a bit yellow, which is panicking me. The doctors are trying to cure her with radiation and all of that, but even they tell her that there's not really a cure. There's a stop-gap, which buys her a few months, but that's really about it. It just makes me angry because I feel so helpless. I'm not used to feeling helpless. And it's ironic that I'm a pharmaceutical scientist, and developing drugs is what I do."

I lay down on my back, my hair spread out behind me. It occurred to me that I was completely, and totally, relaxed, maybe for the first time in a long, long time. Being with Slade like this was like heaven. He was open, vulnerable, and so very sweet. I could feel that his walls, his carefully constructed walls, were coming down at a rapid rate, and I loved that.

"I know how you feel, losing somebody that you love very much."

"I know you do." He paused for a long time and then started to sing softly. "All the king's horses and all the king's men…." He shook his head. "That's how you feel when you can't help the person who means the most to you. My mother used to tell me that nursery rhyme all the time."

"Mine too. I had a book of nursery rhymes, *Mother Goose.* It had a black and white border, I think, and I think that it had a woman with a tall witch's hat on top of a goose on the front."

"I think that all kids had that one growing up," Slade said with a smile.

He lay down next to me, and we were facing each other on the floor. He has his hand under his head, and he lightly rubbed my arm and my shoulder. "So. I'm sorry to change gears on you, but…" And then he kissed me, slowly and deliberately. I breathed in, and tried to drink in his essence. He was such a beautiful, beautiful man, inside and out, I was finding. I was feeling less apprehensive about my strong feelings for him. When he opened up to me the way that he did, it meant a lot to me. He was giving himself to me, in a way, and I loved that.

He opened up his shirt, and I rubbed his hard pecs. My finger trailed down his stomach, and he closed his eyes and lay back. I straddled him, and put my hands on his shoulders. I closed my eyes, and I found that he was totally relaxed. "Do you still want to be in control?" I whispered to him.

"Always," he said. "But I like the way this feels all the same."

"Good." My fingers trailed the light patch of hair that was on his chest, and I removed his shirt, and took a good look at him. He truly was a beautiful man. Every muscle in his chest and his abs was sinewy and defined, and, when I removed his jeans, I marveled again at his powerful, and muscular, legs, and his extremely large manhood, which was already standing at attention. It was as if I was seeing him for the very first time.

He closed his eyes. "This is the first time that I've really let a woman do this. Take control like this. I have no idea why I feel this way about you, but I know that I do."

I smiled as I made my way down his chest with my lips and tongue, while Slade lightly groaned. I got to his cock, and I gently put my lips on the tip. It was really thick, but I managed to suck him, my fingers going up and down with my mouth on his long shaft. I looked up at him, at his face, and his eyes were closed and he had an enormous grin on his face. "That feels amazing, keep doing it just like that."

"As you wish," I said, and continued on. I grabbed his jewels, and my fingers lightly played with his rear. I squeezed his impossibly hard ass, and he groaned some more.

"I need to be inside of you," he said to me. And, at that, he sat up, and rolled me over on my back. He removed my shirt and my jeans, and his fingers found my wetness, and they were inside of me in an instant. I raised up my legs, and he sheathed himself, and even though his motions were sudden up until this point, when he finally entered me, he took his time. He was softly stroking in and out, kissing my lips the entire time. I put my hands on his back, and I gripped him tightly.

We were like this for the better part of the hour, with him slowly and deliberately making love to me. Surprisingly, perhaps for the first time in a long time, I didn't miss the pain. I didn't want him to hurt me. I only wanted to feel him like this with me. Just feeling his enormous cock rooted inside of me was enough.

He came with a mighty rush, after I orgasmed several times, and he lay down on top of me, his elbows on either side of my head. He slipped the condom off, and discreetly disposed of it, and then lay back down next to me. "You're amazing," he said.

"You too." I closed my eyes. I was so close to him, right at that moment, as close as I could possibly be to another human being.

For the first time in a long, long, long time, I actually felt safe.

Chapter Twenty-One

After Slade and I had our breakthrough at my house, I finally felt that we were becoming an actual couple. Which was weird, because I saw Slade almost every evening, as he came to my house and helped me renovate and move in every evening, and, during the day, I was immersed in his case. It was becoming increasingly important to me that we win this case. Losing it was not an option for me, not in the least.

Slade was a tremendous help, really, in helping me move and settle in. Before the movers got to my house, we worked together to sand the floors and refinish them, and he was right about one thing – he *was* handy with a sander. He did the living room, while I did the bedrooms, and it took us no time at all. By the time we were finished, the floors had gone from looking worn and old to being beautiful. They were dark brown and had a gorgeous natural sheen. I admired our handy work, feeling so accomplished.

Then we painted every room. So, by the time the movers arrived with my furniture, I was feeling that they were bringing the stuff to a brand new, beautiful home. Of course, the kitchen and the bathroom needed to be updated as well, and Slade and I made a date to go to Home Depot to pick out all new appliances, back splashes and countertops.

I was really having the time of my life with him, and I was starting to see, more and more, that we could actually make a go of it.

Of course, there was always this nagging voice in my head that told me to not get too far ahead. Slade wasn't out of the woods, not by a long shot. In fact, I felt that our firm was no further ahead in his case than when we started. Yes, depositions were scheduled, and boxes of discovery were brought into our firm every single day. Witnesses were lined up, and our investigators were looking into every single lead. But, even so, we still had nobody other than Jane as an alternative suspect, even though she didn't know that she was, of course, and I still felt that she was a weak "other dude." I didn't think for one second that we could convince the jury that Jane was good for Jordan's murder, and that frightened me. If we truly couldn't find another suspect, how could we win Slade's case?

It was winnable, of course, even without another suspect. We just had to put reasonable doubt in the jury's mind, and that worked before in high profile cases. OJ, Casey Anthony...but then there was Scott Peterson, on death row. I shuddered to think that Slade might suffer that same fate.

That just couldn't happen. I needed to work overtime to follow every lead.

And then I remembered, suddenly, something – Santino had told me that he knew something about Slade's case. I couldn't believe that I'd forgotten that fact, but it just came to me one day when Malcolm asked me to give him a call.

"He's still around, he hasn't jumped yet," Malcolm said. "But he's still being stubborn and wants his day in court. The prosecutor is getting antsy, and they're going to revoke the deal if he doesn't take it soon. Once they have to start preparing for trial, all bets are off."

I groaned, at first, not wanting to go and see him. The last encounter wasn't exactly great. But that's when it hit me that he said something about Slade's case. *He* brought Slade up to *me*. That had to mean something.

So, even though I knew that it was all a long shot, I felt that I had to talk to him.

"I'll go and see him," I told Malcolm. "I'll go and see him today."

"Good. By the way, how is the bar studying going?"

"It's not. But it's all good. I got this."

"I told you that. When is it, next weekend?"

"Yeah. In Sacramento. Two straight days of hell. Oh, joy."

"Well, carry on."

And, at that, I made an appointment to see Santino.

I got to Santino's restaurant, and I arrived at a time when I knew that it wouldn't be busy. Well, not as busy as his lunch rush. It was 3 PM, and, even though the restaurant was filled, there weren't a lot of people waiting, and it seemed to be a relaxed atmosphere.

The same hostess was there, even though she appeared not to remember me.

"Table for one?" she asked me.

"Yes. And please bring Santino out to my table. Tell him that Serena Roberts is here to see him."

She looked annoyed, but she sat me, and, within ten minutes, Santino appeared at my table.

"Well, if it's not the beautiful Serena Roberts," he said, kissing my hand. "To what do I owe this pleasure? I'm assuming that the persecutor has come to her senses?"

"No. The deal is the same, but it's going to be expiring soon," I said. "But listen, I'm here for another reason as well."

Santino looked defeated, but he sat down across from me anyhow. "I'm listening."

I took a sip of my water nervously. "You said something to me about Slade Bridgewell. That maybe you had something for me on his case. A lead."

"Yeah, I do. What are you going to do for me if I give it to you?"

I knew that this was coming. I was going to have to sing for my supper. Guys like Santino never bothered to give things away for nothing, especially when they were facing a lot of time in prison, as Santino was at the moment.

"Listen, I know your prosecutor well. If you're able to give up somebody important in this Slade case, then I can probably get a better deal for you. Prosecutors love to get information on mobsters, information that will put one of them behind bars for a long time. If we're able to bag a big kahuna, thanks to you, I would imagine that would be valuable information for them."

"I like the way that you're talking, but I ain't gonna sing unless there's a better deal on the table in exchange for my testimony. I won't roll on Joey for my case, because he's family, but I can give you somebody else. Somebody who might be good for your guy's case. You just gotta get me a better deal, and then we'll talk."

I took a deep breath. I had no idea how all of this would even work. I wasn't lying, of course – these federal prosecutors were always dying to nail mobsters, and, if one of them was responsible for Jordan's death, then that would be very valuable information indeed.

Would it be valuable enough for Santino's prosecutor to cut him a better deal? It might. It very well might. It would be getting the feds involved in Slade's case, and that would be a better prospect than what was happening at the state level. They would have to work out the jurisdictional issues, of course, which would be complex. But I wanted to cross that bridge when I came to it. I first wanted to see what the prosecutor might do for Santino in exchange for his tip and eventual testimony in Slade's case.

"Okay," I said. "I'll see what the prosecutor can do, but you have to give some kind of hint on what you're thinking. I would imagine that this would be a huge coup for them if this tip pans out, because they're going to be getting in the middle of the most high profile case in the country right now. Are you sure that you're comfortable doing this?"

"Yeah," he said. "I am. I mean, I don't want you to think that my tip is a slam-dunk, but it does involve a rival family, so I'm not scared. Joey will protect my ass, especially since I ain't rolling on him for my case, and nobody messes with Joey. Nobody. But I ain't saying nothin' until you tell me that there will be a deal for me."

"Of course. But you do know that any deal that this prosecutor makes on your behalf is going to be something that is contingent on how good your tip is."

"I know that. I can't just pull a theory out of my ass and

expect the persecutor to suddenly lay down at my feet. I'm no dummy. I know how this works."

I closed my eyes, and I felt that Santino was sincere. He really did seem like somebody who did have a piece of information about Slade's case and Jordan's murder.

"Okay. Well, let me go the prosecutor and float this to her and see what she says. Hopefully, she'll be interested enough to talk to you, and she can tell me ahead of time what she can give you if your information is sound."

At that, we said our goodbyes, with Santino giving me a hug. "I'm sorry about that last time at your house," he said. "That was a dick move."

"Well, it was, but that's okay. Bygones."

"Take care, Miss Serena, and I'll see you soon. Hopefully, you'll have some good information for me the next time I see you."

"I will. At least, I hope I will."

And, at that, I left. I really had no idea what the future would bring, but, for some reason, for the first time, I was actually starting to see some daylight.

Chapter Twenty-Two

I saw Slade that evening at my home. All my furniture was in, and the place looked amazing. I had all my stuff in storage when I lived with Donny and Michael, all the stuff that I had at my brownstone in the Village in New York. It was all brought in, and Slade and I spent days unpacking and straightening everything, and I finally felt that I was home.

So, Slade brought over a bottle of good scotch, and we celebrated. I also finally was able to bring my girls in, and they were excited about their new place as well. All of us wanted to celebrate, and that was such an important thing to me.

"So," Slade said, as he poured the scotch into two glasses. "This place looks amazing."

As well it did. Aside from the kitchen and the bathroom, of course, my place looked like something that you would see in a magazine. I really felt that Slade had the eye of a decorator, really, because he was able to help me arrange all my things in such a way that it all seemed to fit. I was impressed with how much he seemed to know about where to put the furniture, the fixtures, and the little knick-knacks, so that the small house didn't seem cluttered, but, rather, seemed cozy.

We clinked glasses and I took a sip. The scotch was smooth as silk, which told me that it was very high dollar. Indeed, I looked at the label, and recognized it as being a bottle that was worth many thousands of dollars.

"Such a fancy scotch for such an unfancy place," I said with a smile.

"Oh, I don't know. I think that this place is pretty goddamned fancy if you ask me."

"Now it is, thanks to you."

"I didn't do much. And, by the way, I'm sorry for giving you such a hard time about buying this place without my input. It really is a great place, and you can't beat the location, even if it is close to restaurant and bar central."

Indeed it was. It was walking distance to the boardwalk, which was lined with bars, restaurants and large hotels. As a result, there were crowds of people every evening on that part of the beach and boardwalk. Still, it was nice to be so close to so many things, and I wasn't bothered by the crowds. Slade was, for obvious reasons, but even he didn't mind going out there with me in the evenings, holding my hand and stealing kisses whenever he could.

People inevitably stared at him and pointed, but he just shrugged it off. "I'm used to the attention, and I always have been. Well, I mean, the media has been interested in me for several years, long before all this happened. So, it's no big deal, even if the scrutiny is that much heightened."

"I like it." I took a deep breath, not quite knowing what to tell him about Santino and his claim that he knew something about Slade's case. It was clear that there was no love lost between the two men, or, at least it was clear that evening that Slade kicked Santino's ass. I had no idea what kind of reaction I was going to get when I told him. "Listen, I might have a lead on your case. I don't know yet, though."

"Oh?"

"Yes. Santino Bianchi has hinted that he might know who's good for your case." I didn't tell him any more about it, though, because that might be a violation of attorney-client privilege. In fact, just telling Slade that Santino knew something might also be a violation, but telling Slade that Santino was trying to secure a better deal in exchange for his information would be at least crossing the line. I felt fairly secure, though, that simply telling Slade that Santino had some information would not be privileged, because it didn't concern Santino's case *per se.*

Slade's face paled, and I immediately felt that I told him the wrong thing. I closed my eyes and I felt anger and jealousy coming from him. I shook off the feeling and opened my eyes. Slade was staring at his glass of scotch, not saying a word, but his hand was shaking ever-so-slightly.

"I thought I told you to stay away from that goombah."

I bristled. "No, you never told me that, and that would be difficult to do, considering he's my client and all."

He narrowed his eyes. "You should've gotten yourself removed from his case when he came over to your house and tried something with you. In fact, that's what I want you to do. I want you to remove yourself from his case. Yesterday."

"I will not. Listen, Slade, if this man has information on your case, then I'm going to pursue that. And you can't tell me who can be my client and who can't be. Besides, he's not really my client, exactly, because I haven't taken the bar. I can't represent him in court just yet, so I'm just doing the preliminaries."

Slade shook his head. "You need to get off his case and you need to stay away from him."

"Why? Because he tried to kiss me? I can handle myself."

"Yes, because he tried to kiss you, but also because he's a dangerous man. He burned down that deli, and his family is known to be one of the most powerful in the area. You don't want to be involved with all of that, trust me."

"What is it that you think that I do? Listen, I'm a criminal defense attorney for one of the largest firms in the area. We represent mobsters. That's one of our most lucrative areas. We also represent all manner of white collar criminals, as well as gang-bangers who can afford our fee. And, may I remind you, we also represent plenty of men and women who are accused of murder."

He shook his head. "No. I don't want you being involved with that case. If you don't think that attorneys are never targets of hits, then you're naïve. What happens to you if something goes south with this? Let me guess, Santino wants to give up somebody who's not a part of his organization. Am I right? What do you think is going to happen to you once you get that information from Santino? Answer me that."

"I can hold my own," I said, although I felt doubtful even as I said that. "How is this other mobster going to find out that I know something?"

"Again, you're naïve if you think that this other mobster, whomever he is, isn't going to find out what you know and what you're about to give to the prosecutor. This Santino doesn't have to worry about giving you this information. I'm quite sure that his family will protect him. But who will protect you?"

"I'm taking my chances with this, and that's that. If there is even a slight chance that this information can exonerate you…"

"No. I'd rather go to prison than to see you in danger. I'll take my lumps, but I don't want you to go anywhere near that Santino guy again. Get yourself taken off that case, and don't go and meet with him. I'm serious, Serena. You tell that man that you changed your mind about talking to the prosecutor about him in exchange for this information to you, and shut that door. I mean it."

I crossed my arms. I was going to talk to the prosecutor, and I was going to find out what Santino knew. Slade wasn't going to stop me. "Let's just change the subject."

"No. I won't change the subject. I need you to tell me that you're not going anywhere near that guy again."

"And then what? What? As soon as I pass the bar, I'm going to have mob clients of my very own. I'm going to have murderers, rapists, drug dealers, sex traders, you name it. You can't just put a restriction on what kind of client I'm going to represent. They're not all going to be handsome billionaires. Most of them are rough. That's the name of the game, here – representing men who are not exactly the pillars of their communities. If you want me to be completely safe, then perhaps I need to get into estate planning."

"I know that you're going to have rough clients, but this is something different entirely. If you're a mob lawyer, fine. Your clients won't put a hit on you. But you're talking about giving up a guy who hasn't hired you for anything, so that means that he has no loyalty to you or anyone at your firm.

That's dangerous, Serena, too dangerous. I mean it – I'd rather go to prison for life than to see you in danger."

Slade was evidently determined that I wasn't going to talk to Santino, and I was just as determined that I was. I finally decided just to lie to him just to get him off my back about this.

"Okay, then, you've convinced me. I'll tell Santino that I'm not interested in his information. Okay?"

"No. You're lying to me. Serena, I'll find out if you do something like that. Don't think that you can go behind my back and go ahead and talk to him about my case."

"I know."

At that, Santino narrowed his eyes. Sadie and Gigi woke up from their nap and came over to the two of us and looked at us with expectant eyes. Slade slapped his lap, and the two dogs got on it, and licked his face.

"Serena, I'm not feeling it tonight. I'm sorry, I know that you made dinner, but I have to go."

I nodded my head. Slade was obviously not believing me when I told him that I wouldn't talk to Santino about this case, and I had to admit that he had good reason for that.

But, no matter, if this meeting with Santino led me to another suspect, one who might be good for Jordan's murder, it would all be worth it.

"I understand," I said, not meeting his eyes.

He nodded his head. "It's come to this, hasn't it? Serena, I don't know what to say to you. I'm falling in love with you, but if you go behind my back and do this…." He shook his head. "Don't do it, Serena. I'm warning you."

I had to admit that my eyes got wide when he confessed that he was falling in love with me. I had to admit, right at that moment, that I was increasingly feeling the same.

Which was why it was more important than ever, for me, that I talk to Santino. Slade might've said that he was willing to go down for Jordan's murder, but I wasn't. Perhaps he was right, and I'd be putting myself in danger for talking to Santino about this.

So be it. I was determined that I was going to do all that I could to keep Slade out of prison, and if it involved a mob snitch, it involved a mob snitch.

Slade left without another word, and I drew a breath. My heart was pounding and I was shaking. I knew that I was risking it all by talking to Santino.

But I didn't care.

Slade was going to stay out of prison, and that was that.

Chapter Twenty-Three

The next day, I paid a visit to Santino's prosecutor. "Serena," the prosecutor, Hillary White said to me when I showed up at her office. "How are things?"

"They're fine. How are things with you?"

She shook her head. "Just look at this stack of files I have, and you tell me. Life on the hamster wheel."

"I know how that goes. Listen, I need to talk to you about Santino Bianchi."

"Yes. Listen, I'm going to start preparing for trial on his case today. We're scheduling depositions. So, once those wheels start turning, our rather generous offer goes off the table."

I took a deep breath. "Santino isn't going to give up Joey, but he apparently has information about another case that might be a huge win for this office."

She narrowed her eyes. "I'm listening."

"He says that he has information on Slade Bridgewell's case. I don't have any more information than that, though.

He wanted me to first find out if I can make a deal on his case in exchange for this information."

She pursed her lips. "You don't have any idea what or who he's talking about here? Are you sure that this would even be a federal case at all?"

"I don't know. I believe that it would be, because I believe that it involves another mobster. I'm so sorry, I don't have more information than that. He didn't tell me much. He wants a tentative deal on the table first."

I could tell that the wheels were turning. Hillary was human, and I knew that the prospect of getting into the middle of such a high-profile case appealed to her.

"Okay. Let me talk to your guy, and I'll find out what he knows. If it checks out, I'll work a deal with him. I'll offer the same deal that I was offering in exchange for his testimony against Joey Bianchi."

I was excited. If this all worked out, Slade might be in the clear, *and* Santino would be able to avoid prison. He would be on probation for five years, a probation that I doubted he could walk down, but he at least wouldn't be put in prison for this particular crime.

"I'll bring him in," I said. "Tomorrow or maybe even today."

"Okay. Now, I really have to make this deal tentative. He can't just throw a name and a theory at me and expect me to give him this deal. If his story checks out, I'll give him that deal. I'll make that clear to him when he comes in here."

"Thanks. I'll give Santino a call."

I got out into the hallway and called Santino. "Miss Serena," he said when he answered the phone. "What can I do for you?"

"I talked to your prosecutor. She's willing to talk to you,

and to give you the deal that she offered you in exchange for testimony against Joey if your story checks out."

"When can I talk to her?"

"Today if you can. I'll let you know."

At that, I went back in to talk to Hillary. "What time do you have open today to talk to Santino?"

"2 PM would be great."

At that, I went back into the hallway to tell Santino to meet me in Hillary's office at 2.

Then, we said our goodbyes, and I left for my office.

Slade called me in my car. "You were at the federal prosecutor's office just now. I hope that you were telling Santino's prosecutor that you're withdrawing from his case."

I groaned. "I told you that I'm not the attorney of record, so there's not a need for me to withdraw from his case."

"Regardless, I want you off that case. I'm serious, Serena."

"I can't talk to you about that right now."

"Serena…." he started to say, but I just hung up on him. I didn't want to deal with him right at that moment. It was more important, much more important, that I get this whole Santino thing squared away. I knew that there was a good chance that Slade would be so angry with me that he might break up with me, but, considering the alternative – Slade gets convicted of murder and ends up with the death penalty – it was worth it to me.

I got into the office, and I talked to Malcolm about what was going on. "I need you come with me to Hillary's office, because she's offering another deal to Santino in exchange for some information that he possibly has about another mobster who might be good for Jordan's murder."

"What time?"

"2. I know that you don't have any court appearances or depositions at that time, so I hope that you can go with me." I knew that, since I wasn't officially a California attorney, I was going to have to have Malcolm, or another licensed attorney, along when the deal was being made.

"Tell me about this information you have."

"Santino just says that another mobster he knows might be good for Jordan. He hasn't told me much, though. He's waiting for a deal to be more solidified before he is willing to go into detail."

Malcolm furled his brow. "I have to admit that I'm intrigued. Okay. I'll rearrange my schedule to be there with you."

Everything was scheduled, then. It was just a matter of getting it all together.

I would deal with Slade later. I had a feeling that it wasn't going to be pretty, either.

Chapter Twenty-Four

At 2, everyone got together in Hillary's office. Santino, Malcolm and I all sat across from Hillary, who was ready and waiting for Santino's story to be told.

"Okay, Santino," Hillary said to him. "I understand that you might have some information that might shed some light on the Slade Bridgewell case." She turned to me and Malcolm. "And the two of you know that, even if this lead bears fruit, that doesn't mean that the prosecutors will necessarily drop Slade's case. We can try each of these men simultaneously, but whether the state prosecutor on Mr. Bridgewell's case decides to dismiss the case is up to him."

"I understand," I said, but thought that the state prosecutor probably would drop the case against Slade if the evidence against this "other dude" that was going to be offered up by Santino was compelling enough.

Hillary looked at Santino expectantly. "What do you know about this case?"

Santino looked at me and Malcolm, and we both gave him the non-verbal cue to speak. "Okay, yeah," he began.

"There's this guy, his name is Michael Garancino. You probably have heard of him. Most people have, especially people in law enforcement. He was Jordan's dealer."

Hillary was nodding her head. "His dealer. Meaning drugs?"

"Yes, drugs."

That made sense to me, as I remembered Slade talking about how Jordan would stay up for days. While it certainly sounded like a person in the throes of mania, it also sounded like somebody who was on stimulant drugs. And it was well-known that people with bi-polar disorder tended to self-medicate. That Jordan was apparently on drugs therefore came as little surprise to me.

Santino twiddled his fingers and looked down at them. "Now, this is all stuff that I've heard from Joey, but he's very much in the know. Michael and Jordan apparently made a deal for this marijuana pill that Jordan was creating."

My ears perked up when Santino talked about the marijuana pill. I glanced at Malcolm as if to say *see I told you it something to do with that marijuana pill*. Now, of course, it was always a possibility that the spirit was deliberately trying to throw me off, but Santino's testimony was making more and more sense.

"Michael was to supply the drugs for the pill, and he was going to get a serious cut of the profits when the pill came to market. Now, I don't know much about the drug business, but I know that you can't generally patent weed. But, from what I understood, Jordan was trying to get a patent for this drug because of the way that it was processed made it different. So, there was going to be a lot of money in it."

Hillary was furiously making notes while Santino was talking.

"At the last second, Michael got cut out. I guess that Jordan was having problems getting a patent approved for the pill, and I heard that Michael was pissed."

Hillary nodded her head. "So you believe that Michael was angry enough to kill Jordan?"

Santino shrugged his shoulders. "I guess. Listen, I'm not telling you that Michael is good for that murder, but I thought that it might help if you got another lead."

Hillary glanced at me, and my heart sunk. I had this feeling that this might be yet another brick wall. Maybe. But, then again, Santino was offering us one "other dude," so it was better than the needle in the haystack we were faced with before. I just hoped that Hillary decided to go ahead and give Santino a better deal for this information. After all, Santino was sticking his neck out to give us this.

"Okay," Hillary said. "I need to check this Michael out. I understand that you're risking a lot to come here and speak with me, so I want you to know that your contribution isn't lost on me."

Santino looked agitated. "What's that supposed to mean? It sounds like that deal is off the table."

"No, no, it's not off the table. But I need to check this Michael out. What you've given me is circumstantial. At the same time, I know that you're taking a risk in coming here with this information." She looked at Malcolm and me. "Can I speak to the two of you alone?"

I looked at Santino and nodded my head. He looked pissed, but he got up and went out the door.

"Okay," Hillary said to us when Santino was safely out the door. "I appreciate your client coming forth with this, and it does give me something to investigate. I'm sure that your firm will also do the same. I know of Michael Garancino, he's been on our radar for years. So…." Her voice trailed off, and she took a deep breath. "I'm sure that I'm going to regret this, but your client has provided us somebody who had motive and means to kill Jordan. That piece of information is valuable. So, I will go ahead and offer Santino what I promised I would. Even if this information comes to nothing, it gives us something to go on, and something to nail Mr. Garancino on."

I let out a breath of relief. "Thank you so much, Hillary."

She shook her head. "Your client needs to keep his nose clean, though. The terms of probation are going to be extremely strict, and he's going to be watched. Make sure that you let him know that."

We all stood up, and said our goodbyes. I was anxious to talk to Santino out in the hallway. Yet, I also felt disappointed. This deal was good for Santino, excellent even, but this flimsy information was bound to steer us into another brick wall. I doubted that Michael could be prosecuted for this.

Then again, as Hillary said, Michael had motive and means to kill Jordan. After all, if Michael was closely working with Jordan, then it stood to reason that he probably had a code to get into the lab, or that Jordan would've actually invited him into the lab. That got around the whole problem about how few people had access to that particular lab. He probably had the opportunity to kill him, too. So, while it was weak, it was better than a sharp poke in the eye.

Then it hit me. Slade was going to be infuriated when he found out that I went behind his back to meet with the prosecutor. So, if this piece of information went nowhere, it was entirely possible that Slade was going to break up with me for something that wasn't worth it after all.

Santino was out in the hallway. He stood up when he saw the two of us approaching. "Well?"

"Good news. Apparently your information was valuable enough to Hillary that she's going to go ahead and give you the deal that we talked about."

"So, probation? Five years, right?"

"Yes. But you need to make sure that you keep your nose clean. I'm serious, Santino. You need to get out of the racket."

Santino smiled and put his arm around me. "Maybe. Or maybe I just need to not be stupid enough to do things that are on video."

I shook my head. Santino was a mobster. That was what he did. Crime was literally his life. He was dodging a bullet in not having to go to prison this time, but, in the future, he might not be so lucky.

"Listen, are you sure that you're going to be okay? You don't need some kind of protection, do you?" I said.

"No, I told you. Joey protects me. He knows that I'm loyal, so I don't need to worry. Our family is more powerful than the Garancinos, and everyone knows it. So, no. I'll be fine. I'm just happy that I'm staying out of the joint this time."

I rolled my eyes when he said the words *this time*. But we both knew what he was thinking. Santino, unfortunately, was more of a soldier with his organization than a leader, so he had to do the dirty work. Sooner or later, he was going to get caught. But, for now, he was free, and he looked very relieved about that.

We got out into the street, and Santino gave me a hug.

I turned around, and Slade was standing right there. His arms were crossed, and he looked absolutely pissed.

"Mr. Bridgewell," Malcolm said to him, extending his hand. "It's good to see you."

Slade looked at Malcolm and said nothing. Then he turned his focus back to me. I felt like he was burning a hole in my skin while he stared at me.

I glanced at Malcolm, and he gave me a mystified look and shrugged his shoulders. "I'll see you back at the office, Serena."

"See you."

I then turned back to Slade, who was still staring at me and not saying a single word. I didn't have to close my eyes to know what he was feeling. It was written all over his face.

He narrowed his eyes and finally spoke. "Get in," he said, opening the door of his car. "Now."

"I have to get back to work."

He raised an eyebrow and picked up his phone. "Malcolm, this is Slade," he said. "Serena will be gone for the day." He looked at me and nodded his head. "I understand, but you're just going to have to find somebody else to take over her duties." After a pause, he looked at me. "I knew that you would understand. Thank you."

It was my turn to cross my arms. "You can't order me around like that."

"Like hell I can't. Now, get in my car. We need to talk, and I really don't want to do it right here in the street like this."

I swallowed hard. I didn't like his tone, I didn't like the way that he was looking at me, and I didn't like his body language. Nevertheless, despite my misgivings, I got into his car. I buckled my seat belt, and the two of us sped off to parts unknown.

"Where are we going?"

"To my house."

"All the way to LA?"

"No. My house in Del Mar. Remember? The house that you so rudely refused."

"I wasn't rude in refusing that house. I wasn't about to let you just buy me a house. But we talked about that, so I don't want to go back to it."

Slade didn't answer. He was staring at the road, but his hands were gripping the steering wheel tightly. He looked like he was about to explode.

We got on the highway, and he drove so fast that he was weaving in and out of cars. "What's the big hurry?"

Slade said nothing at all.

In no time, we were in his neighborhood. He parked the car in his driveway, and he got out of the car without a word. I reluctantly followed him into his home.

The two of us ended up on his back patio, and he didn't say anything for a long, long time. I felt uncomfortable watching him, and I felt just a little bit panicky. I had no idea what was in his mind. I closed my eyes, and I felt the white-hot anger, but I didn't know if he was going to break up with me or if the whole thing was just going to blow over.

Finally, he spoke. "I don't know what to say to you, Serena. I made my wishes very clear, and you ignored me. Not only that, but you lied to me."

I sighed. "Slade, I...."

"You didn't get what you wanted, did you?"

"I did. I got a lead, and I got an excellent deal for Santino. Everybody wins."

"Everyone but you. Who did Santino give up?"

"Michael Garancino. He's a mobster-"

"I know who he is. He was Jordan's dealer."

I blinked my eyes, astounded. "You knew that Jordan was on drugs? And you didn't tell me?"

"Yes. I knew. I didn't tell you, because I knew that you would start sniffing around that angle, and I didn't want you to go there. Michael is a very dangerous man, much more dangerous than Santino ever could be. Or he was, anyhow."

"He was?"

"Yes. He's dead. He's been dead for a couple of weeks. Santino knew this, of course. I mean, I don't know that Santino knew this fact, but I would imagine he did. He's no dummy. He'll give up a dead mobster in exchange for a better deal. Word to the wise - you better plea him soon before the prosecutor finds out what he did."

I furled my eyebrows. "Santino didn't pressure me to plead him out soon."

"He probably doesn't know that the prosecutor can withdraw her agreement when she finds out that Santino gave up a dead guy."

"How do you know that this Michael is dead?"

He sighed. "Because Michael was killed before Jordan was. What Santino told you, what I imagine he told you, was right, of course. Michael and Jordan did have an agreement, and Jordan did threaten to cut Michael out because of patent issues. But Michael disappeared, and Jordan found out that he died. Two days later, Jordan was dead as well."

I shook my head. "And you never told me this?"

He crossed his arms in front of him. "No. It's not relevant, not anymore. Michael is dead."

"And Jordan didn't have other dealers? Any one of them might've done it."

"No. He didn't have other dealers. Michael was the only one."

"Then why were you so upset about Santino and the information that he might have had? None of this is a surprise to you. You had to have known that Santino was going to give up Michael. That's if Michael was the only dealer."

"He was."

"Well, then, we'll find out about that, won't we? Now that we know that Jordan had a drug problem, that gives our investigators something to work with, so thanks for that."

I was sarcastic, because I couldn't believe that Slade left out something as pertinent as the fact that Jordan had a drug problem and a mobster drug dealer. Perhaps Slade didn't find the information relevant, because Michael was dead, but that certainly didn't make the issue dead. On the contrary, the issue was very much alive, and we finally had something to go on. No thanks to Slade.

"Go right ahead and investigate. You're not going to find anything. Michael was his only dealer."

"How would you know? You said that he was secretive, and that you didn't know what he was doing in that lab. He could have had 10 different dealers, and you wouldn't have known it."

"I would have. Jordan was very open to me about his drug issues, and he only talked about Michael."

"Then why would you keep Jordan's drug issues secret? Please help me understand, Slade. That piece of information is so important to finding out who really did this."

I asked that question, and Slade got very quiet. Too quiet.

"Slade? Answer that question."

He finally took a deep breath. "Do you believe in love at first sight?"

230

I shook my head, but not because I didn't believe in it. But that question gave me whiplash, coming from him. "I believe in lust at first sight."

"Have you ever met somebody who you knew, you just knew, you would do anything to protect? Somebody who you would sacrifice yourself, completely and totally, so that person would be safe?"

I had to admit to myself that I didn't have that kind of experience, at least not regarding somebody that I just met. I had no idea what he was driving at. "I do want to protect the people that I love, and I would do anything to make sure that happens."

He took my hand. "When I met you, I knew. I knew that you were going to be somebody who was worth protecting. I'm not going to say that I fell in love with you at first sight, although maybe I did. But I knew, from the moment you were standing in front of me with those two dogs, that..." He shook his head. "Well, I knew that I'd never let anything bad happen to you. So, yes. I didn't tell you about the mobster, because I didn't want you getting involved with that. Even if Michael was dead, I didn't want you going there. I didn't tell you about Jordan's drug issues for that reason alone."

I felt stunned about his confession. "Slade, I had no idea. But, listen, I'm not some shrinking violet who needs the protection of a man. I can hold my own."

Those were my words, but my emotions were getting away from me again. When Slade confessed to me that he might have fallen in love with me at first sight, it allowed me to admit to myself that I felt the same way about him.

"Nobody can hold their own against something like that. Don't ever think that you can. So, please, Serena, stop. Stop going down that path. There's nothing there for you, and you might end up in trouble or worse."

"Slade if this lead ends up helping you get acquitted, then that's all that matters to me."

"Find another path."

"We'll look for another path. Believe me when I tell you this. But we have to turn over every stone."

"No, Serena. Either your team lays off this line, or I'll fire your firm from my case."

I couldn't quite believe what I was hearing from him. "It's that important to you?"

"Yes. I'd sooner go to the death chamber than to see you get involved with elements such as the Garancinos."

"I can't ask Malcolm to not go down that road. Your legal team is bound by the Sixth Amendment right to counsel, which means that we're bound to give you a vigorous defense. That means that we must, ethically, follow every lead wherever it might go."

"You work for me. Malcolm works for me. I call the shots. I'm telling you not to go there. That supersedes any kind of theoretical concerns about the Sixth Amendment, and you know this. You know this, as an attorney, Serena. Now, I'm telling you, I'm ordering you, to quit on this. If you don't, then I'll have no choice but to find another firm. You might be stubborn about this, but Malcolm won't be. He needs my millions, and he needs the exposure that he's getting. My case has put your firm on the map. Malcolm won't give that up for all the oil fields in the Middle East."

I couldn't believe what I was hearing, but, by looking at Slade's determined jaw, I knew that this was a battle of wills that I was bound to lose.

"Okay. I'll call Malcolm and tell him to stop going down

this road. But the prosecutor is already on it, and she's not going to be bound by your wishes."

"The prosecutor will find nothing. She'll find a cold path. Michael is dead, and he was acting alone. Even if he weren't acting alone, but he was acting on behalf of the other Garancinos, that doesn't matter. The prosecutor won't find the thread. She can try all she wants, but she won't get anywhere with this."

I shook my head. "Why are you so adamant about this?"

"I just told you. I'm in love with you."

I involuntarily parted my lips, and I touched them. I remembered what it felt like to have Slade kiss me, and I admitted to myself, finally, that I did feel the same about him as he did about me.

"I don't know what to say."

"I do. You're in love with me too. You know it, and I know it. I really can't stand the fact that I might lose you violently to a mobster."

"You're not. I told you, I defend mobsters all the time. All the time. Mobsters make up a great deal of our business."

"And I told you that mobsters aren't going to hit their own attorneys. But they will hit people who are behind giving them up."

I felt like I was losing my breath as he continued to look at me with those penetrating eyes. I wasn't ready, though, to admit to him how I was feeling about him.

He then kissed me, and, for some reason, his kiss burned even more than usual. There was something different about the feeling of his lips on mine, compared to what it felt like before. There was emotion behind his actions, feelings that I didn't know were there before. I'd felt like I was falling for him, crazy-head-over-heels for him, before, but I had no idea that it might've been reciprocated. Now that I knew that it was, his kiss was that much more meaningful.

"Slade," I finally said when our lips parted. "I can't do this. I can't just sit idly by while there possibly is a good lead on who did Jordan, not when your life is literally on the line. I can't, and you can't ask me to."

"I'm not asking you to. I'm ordering you to." Then his hand came up to my face and he kissed my forehead. He held me close, and I could feel his hard-on. "I don't want to talk about this anymore. The subject is closed. I just need to feel your skin on mine."

In spite of myself, I felt that I was losing to him. My body was, once again, betraying me. I felt my heart start to race as his hand gently, yet firmly, made its way from my shoulder and down my breast. He cupped my breast, and I parted my legs, almost involuntarily.

In no time, it seemed, he had carried me to his bed, our clothes were off, and we were devouring each other with our lips and tongue. I felt hungry, like I needed to be sated. My earlier irritation about the fact that Slade was trying to control me was soon forgotten as his masterful lips and tongue made their way to my vagina, and he lightly, yet aggressively, licked and sucked and stroked that area. I reared back my head as I came, again and again. Then Slade sheathed his enormous manhood, and plunged it into me, which sent electricity all the way through my body. I never knew that sex, without pain, would be so glorious, and I thought that maybe I was healed from my previous addiction.

After awhile, Slade groaned and laid down on top of me, and then rolled next to me. While he stroked my hair, he said "you have no idea what you do to me. The thought of losing you at this point…" He shook his head. "I don't want to go there. I'm sorry, Serena, but this is for your own good."

I opened my mouth, determined that I was going to talk him out of his plan to fire our firm if we didn't do what he wanted.

"I understand, Slade, I really do. I know that I'm chasing a dangerous path by trying to find out more about whether or not Jordan had other dealers. But, Slade, I couldn't imagine what would happen if we lose your case. And that's a real possibility. Unless we get a decent lead on who else would've done this, then we're stuck with pursuing the drug dealer angle."

Slade said nothing, but I could tell that he was pissed. He turned away. "It's late, and I need to get some sleep. I'm conducting business from here, even though I can't be at the lab, obviously. So, I have a long day ahead of me tomorrow."

I felt disappointed, but I nodded my head. I closed my eyes, and I knew that Slade was trying to get rid of me. He was obviously angry and frustrated that I persisted in pursuing something that he didn't want me to pursue.

"I'll see you soon?"

He shrugged his shoulders. "Maybe." His brick wall was definitely up, and I knew why. He didn't want to continue to have feelings for me if there was a possibility that something might happen to me. Not that I blamed him – he had dealt with a lot of loss in his life, and, apparently, he was going to eminently be dealing with the loss of his mother. I knew how he felt. That was the reason why I always tried to not get too close to people. I never wanted to feel the devastating hole that I felt when my mother was ripped from me. It was easier, far easier, to just not have deep feelings for anyone, and, that way, you never had to feel that kind of devastation.

I nodded my head. "Okay, then, I guess…"

He looked at me, and his eyes pierced into me. He took my hand. "Please be careful."

"I will."

And, at that, I made my way out of his house and then promptly realized that my car wasn't there. I went back in, feeling embarrassed that I didn't think of that.

Slade was on the phone. "Thanks, I'll see you soon." He looked at me. "I'm having my driver come and get you. Sorry about that. Just wait for him in the living room."

I shook my head. Slade wasn't even going to drive me to my car. That wasn't a good sign.

That wasn't a good sign at all.

Chapter Twenty-Five

The next day, I called Hilary. I was concerned, of course, that she was going to find out that Michael Garancino was dead. If she found that out, she would naturally want to withdraw Santino's plea agreement.

"Hello, this is Hilary," she said as she answered the phone.

"Hilary, Serena Roberts," I said tentatively.

"Yes. I was just going to call you. Listen, the guy that your guy gave up is deceased. I know that I told your guy that I would go ahead with the plea agreement, and I still might. Our office has some leads on some other elements that might have been involved with the transactions between Michael and Jordan. I'll see if they check out, and in the meantime, tell your client to sit tight."

I gulped. Slade's voice was in my ears. *There was nobody else who was dealing to Jordan, just Michael.* I couldn't help but think that this was also a lie, and Hilary was all but confirming this.

"That's great. Our investigators are looking into it as

well. Hopefully, between our office and yours, we can start to unearth something."

"I'll let you know. At first, I was furious when I found out that Michael was dead, but then when our investigators found that there might've been others involved, I wasn't so angry anymore."

"Your office does work fast."

"We do sometimes. This is an important case, as you know, so I put a rush on finding out information."

"Take care, and keep me posted."

"You do the same."

We hung up, and then I called Santino. "Miss Serena," he said. "What's up?"

"You know that Michael is dead, don't you?"

He paused on the phone. "Does this mean that the deal is off?"

"No. Apparently there might've been others who were involved in the Michael and Jordan deal. The prosecutor is investigating these other leads. We'll see where it goes, but, for now, the offer is suspended."

To my surprise, Santino was non-plussed about this. "Okay, Miss Serena. Call me when you find out more."

"I will."

We hung up, and I had to resist the urge to call Slade. It seemed like our relationship, such as it was, was too up and down. I felt like I was getting whiplash all the time.

Yet he said that he was in love with me. I hated to admit it, even to myself, but I felt the same about him. And that scared me to death. I was too attached, too close. He was a bit of a manwhore, or, at least, he used to be. Plus, he was facing life in prison or even the death sentence.

And I still wasn't entirely sure that he didn't kill Jordan.

Chapter Twenty-Six

That night, I had a dream. I was in the control room of Jordan's lab. I had no idea how I knew that I was in this control room, as I hadn't been there in my life, but I looked out and I saw that there was clearly a lab. I looked on the screen, and I was able to see that everything that was happening on that lab was being recorded. There were the images, surprisingly clear, of all that was happening in that room. At the moment when I was being shown the images, there was nobody in the lab working. It was quiet, as it apparently was after hours.

Then I noticed it. It was Jordan's body, lying on the ground in a pool of blood. He had been beaten very badly, and he was obviously dead. I didn't see anybody around, however. It was just Jordan.

It was like I was a ghost, though, because I soon saw somebody come into the control room, and this person didn't notice that I was there. The newcomer in the control room was a man, and he was dressed in a black hoody and jeans. He was tall, about 6 foot, and lean. He sat down at the controls, and he pushed some buttons on the keyboard. He went through the video, frame by frame, until he got to the part where Jordan was being bludgeoned. He seemed to be an expert at editing, because, with a few strokes of the keys, he apparently erased a good portion of the video.

I couldn't see, however, who was on that video killing Jordan. The man at the keyboard was blocking my view, and this frustrated me.

I held my breath, even though I knew that the shadowy figure at the controls couldn't see me.

Then I woke up. I looked around, and the dogs were on the bed, giving me my morning kisses. This was their way of telling me that they needed to go out, and I laughed and opened the door to let them out. Then I put my running clothes on, and grabbed a protein bar while I fed the dogs and gave them fresh water. I kneeled down and pet both of their heads while they ate.

"You guys be good, mommy is going to go for a run."

They looked at me as if they understood, and I smiled. One thing was for sure – no matter what was going on in my life, these two dogs were my constants. They were always glad to see me, and they gave me unconditional affection and love. My life might've been stressful – Slade's moods were giving me fits, and my job, in general, was extremely challenging – but I could always look forward to the two dogs giving me kisses when I got home.

I headed out the door, and ran to the boardwalk of the beach. There were already people around, even though it was 5 AM. Not a lot of people, because the restaurants weren't quite open, but, as I got further down the board-walk, I started passing enormous homes with large patios. These were the beach houses lining Mission Beach, whose boardwalk connected to Pacific Beach, and most of these homes were available for short-term rentals. Once in awhile, I would catch somebody sitting outside one of those homes, sipping coffee, and I would wave and they would wave back.

As I ran, there was something, in the back of my mind, that was nagging at me. There was something in my dream that seemed to have been cut off, but I realized that it might not have been cut off at all. I did wake up seemingly before I saw who altered the video, but there was something in the back of my mind that nagged me. I *did* see who had altered the video, but the memory of that was hazy.

I tried to concentrate on my dream, as my legs and feet pounded the pavement. I had no idea if that would definitively would show who killed Jordan, but I had the feeling that this was another lead.

But what about the marijuana pill? That was the last thing that the spirit had shown me, and I figured that was a solid lead once Santino gave me the name of Michael. But it might've been deliberate misdirection on Jordan's part. He apparently wanted our firm to go in the direction of Michael, even though Michael was dead, because perhaps Jordan wanted to get the associates of Michael into trouble.

Then again, maybe this dream was just another piece of the puzzle. It would be, definitely, if I could just remember the part where I saw the face of the man in the hoody.

This was incredibly frustrating. The answer was right there, and I was getting closer and closer to it. Yet it seemed to be so far away.

I finally was done with my run, and I went home, showered, and packed the dogs up for their day at the day care. I dropped them off, and went into the office and prepared for another day.

Malcolm appeared soon after I arrived. "Good news. The lead that Santino gave about Michael has led the prosecutor to file drug charges against Michael's associate, Gianni. Gianni was apparently also involved with the marijuana pill transaction with Jordan. The prosecutor doesn't know if Gianni is good for Jordan's murder, but he's in custody right now, and Hilary is trying to find some proof to make a murder charge stick. I'll keep you posted, but Santino got his deal. We're going to plead him out today."

"That's good," I said. I felt preoccupied for some reason as Malcolm spoke to me. Slade was bothering me, of course, but there was something else. Something that I couldn't put my finger on.

"Is there anything wrong?" Malcolm asked me.

I shook my head, trying to shake off the horrible feeling I had right at that moment. "No. What time are we pleading out Santino?"

"1:30. We did a good job for him."

"Yes." I took a deep breath. That nagging feeling that I got when I was running, earlier, was getting more and more unsettling.

"Serena, you look pale. Are you sure you're feeling okay?"

"Actually, no," I said. I attempted to stand, but my legs felt wobbly beneath me.

"Let me get you a glass of water."

I just nodded my head and said nothing. I was unable to speak. I gripped the side of the desk with my hand, because I needed the desk to steady me. My hand was shaking, absolutely shaking.

Malcolm reappeared with a glass of water, and I took it with a very shaking hand. "Must be blood sugar issues," I said to him, gulping down the water. "I sometimes have a problem with that."

But I hadn't had a problem with blood sugar for quite

awhile. I'd long since learned how to eat before and after my run, so, usually, my blood sugar was steady. Nonetheless, I reached into my bag and brought out the nuts and dried fruit that I always carried with me for a snack. "This should make me feel better."

Malcolm was looking at me strangely. "I hope that it does. You're really looking pale and clammy."

I took a deep breath, and then my legs just gave way beneath me.

And that was the last thing that I remembered.

Chapter Twenty-Seven

I woke up in the hospital, and my brother Luke, of all people, was standing by my bedside.

"Kid," I said to him, stretching out my arms. "What are you doing here?"

"I got a call. I guess that you have me down as your next of kin," he said, hugging me back. It was so strange, knowing that Luke and I were okay. He hated me for so many years, and it wasn't until his beautiful fiancée, Dalilah, convinced him to give me a chance that he actually did. We'd been close ever since.

"Where is that beautiful lady of yours?"

"She's out in the hallway. You want to talk to her?"

"Of course. Bring her in."

At that, Dalilah came in and she, too, gave me a long hug. "Serena, we've been so worried about you," she said to me.

I furled my brows. "How long have I been down? I remember being in my office and not feeling well, and then, the next thing you know, I'm here and you guys are too."

"You've been out for about six hours. They haven't been able to revive you, either."

"Six hours? How did you guys manage to get out here so quickly?"

"Dalilah's father flew us in on his plane. We came out here as soon as we got the call." Then he shrugged. "Eh, it gives both of us an excuse to see you."

Dalilah smiled. She looked amazing, although she looked like she was about ready to burst.

"Dalilah, you look like you're going to have that kid at any moment. You're lucky you're already in a hospital."

She laughed. "Egads, I never thought that I could feel so shitty and so amazing, all at the same time. Luke and I can't wait to meet this little girl."

"Me too," I said. "Ah, well, it's great to see you guys, but I have no idea why I'm here. All that I know is that I started to feel really awful, and shaky, and then, the next thing you know – boom. Down for the count."

Luke and Dalilah didn't exactly look worried, so I felt that there probably wasn't some terrible disease that I was suffering from. "The doctor is around," Luke said. "Let me try to find him for you."

Dalilah took my hand. "We were so worried," she said. "We miss you so much."

"I miss you guys too, but you can't beat the weather out here. I know, it's pretty hot right now, but in December, when I'm on the beach and you guys are buried under 8 feet of snow, I'll be pretty happy that I'm here. Although I'd love for you guys to be out here with me."

She smiled. "That would be great to live out here, but Luke is doing so well in New York, you just won't believe it. He has so many wealthy benefactors lining up for him, he can't keep them all straight. He might do a half a million in commissions this year, and more lined up next year. I couldn't be prouder of him."

"Well, after what you guys went through, you deserve all the success and happiness in the world."

"And so do you. So, tell me, any man on the scene?"

I felt myself blushing. For some reason, I didn't want to tell Dalilah about Slade just yet. For one, we were perpetually on shaky ground. And, for another, it was difficult to explain that Slade was my client, or my team's client, and that we were kind of sort of together. So, I shrugged. "A man here and there. I've tried Internet dating and a matchmaker, but nothing has really stuck."

Dalilah looked at me sympathetically. "You'll get there. Look at Luke and me. He saw me naked when we first met." She was referring to the fact that she was Luke's nude model when they first met.

Then she giggled, and I felt charmed by her lilting and melodious laugh.

I wanted to tell her that the man that I was falling for was somebody that I saw naked right away as well, but I couldn't bring myself to. I just wasn't ready to talk about Slade to anyone just yet. I mean, I told Malcolm, but that was because I had to. But I didn't have to spill the beans to Dalilah, so I didn't.

At that, the doctor came in to see me. "Hello, Ms. Roberts," he said to me. "I need to talk to you about some things. Do you want to speak to me alone or do you want your brother and sister-in-law here?"

"I want them here, of course," I said, taking their hands. They were on either side of me, standing by the bed.

The doctor nodded. "Well, we're not immediately able to tell exactly why you lost consciousness. There's nothing regarding your vital signs that are immediately jumping out at me. We could certainly do more tests if you like, but it seems that you are perfectly healthy."

I nodded. "Okay, then, I guess I can just be released?"

"I don't see why not, although I would like for you to follow up with your primary care physician. It's not common for a perfectly healthy 28-year-old to lose consciousness without there being some kind of underlying health issue."

I knew, deep down, what the problem was. It had to do with the dream that I had, and the fact that I thought that I knew who it was who was erasing the video in the control room. But I couldn't be sure. It was just a feeling that I had, and the spirit was giving me the signals.

I wondered if Malcolm owned a hoody.

———

Luke drove me home. "Dalilah and I are totally excited to get to the beach," he said. "I've been working so hard that we're going to treat this as a little vacation. I mean, if there was a serious health issue with you, we wouldn't be, but, since you seem to be fine, we're going to take advantage of being out here in the sun."

I looked over at Dalilah in the backseat. "Dalilah, you look like you're going to be going home with a new person. When are you due?"

"Any day. I'm actually overdue, so I was afraid to fly, but I called my doctor before I left to come here, and he said that I'd be fine."

"Well, then, it's probably better that you actually do have the baby here. Luke needs to find you an ob-gyn stat." I shook my head. "I'm really happy that you guys came, but you both took a huge risk in coming out here. And Dalilah, you're not going to have your doctor available when you deliver."

Dalilah put her hand on my shoulder. "It's okay. Luke was very concerned, as was I. We're happy that you're fine, though."

I wasn't fine, although physically, I was. I suddenly knew that Malcolm was behind all of this. At least, he seemed to be behind the erasure of the video. Why he was, I didn't yet know. The spirit didn't implicate him in the murder, although that was increasingly a possibility.

Looking back, I was surprised that Malcolm had been so accommodating to me. Allowing me to get the clothes from Jane was something that I was surprised that he'd do. But, then again, he probably didn't necessarily think that I'd actually be able to get anything off of those clothes. Malcolm pretended that he believed in me, but something told me that he really didn't.

But his encouragement of my relationship with Slade suddenly made perfect sense. He wanted to throw me under the bus when Slade was inevitably convicted. That was when I knew that Malcolm was going to try to throw the case. That would be a perfect alibi for him – he wouldn't look incompetent when Slade went down for murder. He could merely say that it was my fault – I was sleeping with our client, and therefore, my judgment was clouded and I did an incompetent job.

He was a slick one, that was for sure.

How was I going to approach this, though? I had no clue why Malcolm would be involved in Jordan's murder, or even if he was. He most certainly, however, was involved in the cover-up. It certainly looked like he might've been involved in Jordan's murder. He might've done it.

I suddenly knew that I needed to talk to Slade. I never

found out exactly why Slade hired our firm for his case. He had his pick of lawyers around the country. Lawyers who were extremely high-profile and were used to taking on cases such as this one. Our firm was relatively unknown, although we did defend a number of locally high-profile cases. We never, however, had defended something quite like this.

Why would he hire our firm? Did he know Malcolm? Was Malcolm a friend or an acquaintance of Jordan's? What was the association there? After all, Malcolm had to have the code to get into that lab, otherwise he wouldn't have been able to get into the lab to erase that video.

There was another missing puzzle piece, and it, quite frankly, was driving me nuts.

Dalilah was looking at me, a concerned look on her face. "What is it, Serena? We lost you there."

I shook my head. "Oh, nothing, nothing. I was just thinking about a case that I have."

"Well, you need to relax right now. This job seems to be taking a lot out of you."

I smiled, and reached behind me to pat her hand. "I love you, you know that? Luke did well. Who would've thought?"

Luke smiled. "Oh, I know, I'm a lucky, lucky guy. Can't wait to walk down that aisle. Kiss the girl. Can't wait."

I knew that Luke and Dalilah had earned this happiness, but I couldn't help but feel a pang. I had such a complicated relationship with Slade, one that was constantly on the rocks. I knew that Slade's murder case was most of the reason why there was so much tension, and I was looking forward to the time when that wasn't being held over our heads.

But there was still so many secrets that were being withheld, and Slade wasn't an open book, by any means. It seemed like, every time I turned around, there was something new coming out, and all of these new revelations made me feel that I couldn't trust Slade at all.

We got to my house, and Luke and Dalilah put their bags down. "What a cute place," Dalilah said. "And so close to the beach."

"Yes. Well, let me show you to the spare bedroom."

I took them into the spare bedroom, and they both sat down on the bed. Luke's arm was around Dalilah's shoulder protectively, and Dalilah's hand was covering her bulging belly. She rubbed it thoughtfully.

"Do you know of any doctors around here? As you said, I have a feeling this baby is going to be born while we're out here visiting you."

"Let me go into the living room. I have a business card for my doctor, and I'll call him and see if I can't get you a referral." I shook my head. "I love you for coming here, but you shouldn't have taken that risk."

I went into the living room, and I gasped.

A strange man was standing there with a gun.

Chapter Twenty-Eight

I was shaking in my shoes when I saw this man standing there. He had dark hair, was over 6 feet tall, and was dressed well. Although I didn't quite know why he was there, I had a good idea. Slade was right – you shouldn't mess with these mafia types.

He narrowed his eyes, and I drew a breath. "Who are you?" And then I immediately thought of Dalilah and Luke in the bedroom. I knew that I had to save them. My life might be in danger, but I had to save them at least. They were innocent. "Excuse me, I'll be right back."

He shook his head. "No, you're coming with me."

"Okay, but let's go immediately." I had to get out of there before this man, whoever he was, knew that I had two guests in the bedroom.

I felt my phone, which was in my pocket, and I felt that I might have a chance to get out of this, if the phone wasn't taken away from me. Slade would be able to find me, wherever it was that I was taken.

"As you wish," he said, waving the gun. "My car is outside."

My heart pounding, I followed him into his car, which was a black Escalade. I knew that Dalilah and Luke were going to be alarmed, to say the least, but it couldn't be helped. I was apparently going to parts unknown, and who knew if I would make it out alive?

"Where are we going?" I asked him.

He said nothing, of course.

I wondered if this was Gianni Garancino. I never met the guy, but it very well could be. I didn't know that he was already out on bail, though. At any rate, it was clear that this guy was at least associated with the mobster. I assumed.

Finally, he spoke. "I'm taking you to the person who hired Gianni."

Gianni was a hired gun? Was this person, whoever he was, admitting that Gianni did it? Did Malcolm hire Gianni?

I had no clue, none whatsoever, but I knew that I was soon going to find out. The whole mystery was soon going to be revealed.

Whether or not I lived to tell the tale, though, remained to be seen.

"I'm not going to hurt you," he said. "But I don't know if I can say the same for the boss of this operation."

I wanted to ask him thousands of questions, but I just didn't know where to start. And I knew that he wasn't going to answer them, anyhow, so I just kept my mouth shut.

We were soon on the Five going north. When we got out of the city limits, I knew that we were heading to LA. I closed my eyes, and tried to get a read on this guy. I wanted to see if I could figure out what his intentions were with me. All that I sensed, however, was that he was calm. And why wouldn't he be? This was a job for him, apparently one that he'd done 100 times before. Him kidnapping me was the equivalent of my going into a deposition – just another work duty.

I surreptitiously patted my phone, knowing that Slade might be able to find me in time. I was terrified, however, that this man would end up taking my phone if he knew that I had it. Frankly, I was surprised that he didn't pat me down before taking me out of the house. He would've surely thrown away my phone if he knew that I had it on me.

We sat in the SUV, both of us not saying a word. I was terrified to say anything, and this man wasn't up for chatting, either.

———————

After a couple of hours, we pulled up to an enormous mansion. This place was easily as big as Slade's Malibu home, and, like Slade's home, it was situated behind a large gate. The driveway was long, and the SUV finally pulled up to a circle drive that had a fountain in the middle.

I looked at this man, and he got out of the SUV, and came around and opened my door for me. "Get out."

I took a deep breath. I wished, at that moment, that I had studied Karate and had mastered that instead of my running. As it was, I had no means of self-defense, and I felt like I was completely at the mercy of this man.

He led me, with the gun planted in the small of my back, into the home. "Wait right here," he said, after he led me into an enormous den. "Don't even think about running, either. There are cameras everywhere, and if you run, then I'll immediately chase you down, and I will kill you."

I felt chilled when he said that last line, because I had zero doubt that he would kill me for any reason at all. So, I sat down on the couch and tried to tune into the vibrations around me. I couldn't pick up anything, though, which frustrated me. I also silently tried to summon Slade in my head. I knew that he didn't believe in psychics, but perhaps, just perhaps, I could get on his wavelength to let him know that I was in serious, serious trouble.

It was then that I regretted the fact that I didn't tell Dalilah anything about Slade. If I were a normal girl, gushing about being in love, I would've told her everything about him. Then, when Luke and Dalilah discovered that I was missing, maybe Slade would've been the first person they would've called.

As it was, I had to rely on the fact that Slade was tracking me like he did before. But what if he weren't? What if he'd given up on me? The last time I saw him, he seemed upset that I continued to go against his wishes regarding Santino, and he seemed like he might've been completely through with me. What if he were completely through with me? I might be killed here and nobody would even know.

I couldn't help but think that I made this bed myself with my reluctance to get close to Slade, and my secretive nature. If only I would've said something to Dalilah. If only I would've listened to Slade about Santino. If only this, if only that. It didn't really matter. I was in the situation that I was in, and nobody was going to come and save me.

After what seemed like forever, the brute who kidnapped me summoned me to follow him. "And don't get any ideas," he said. "You need to speak with somebody."

I followed him through the maze of a house, feeling more and more apprehensive as I went. This house was as big as Slade's mansion, and it seemed like forever before I finally was led into a room.

Where I saw somebody who was the last person I ever would've imagined.

"Hello," Charlotte Boswell said to me. "So glad that you could make it."

Chapter Twenty-Nine

I shook my head rapidly, trying to get my bearings about this. "I'm so sorry, I don't quite understand what's going on here?"

She laughed. "I figured you wouldn't. I'm here to tell you to back off the Garancinos. You need to stop going down that road yesterday."

"Why do you care?"

She shrugged. "I just do." Then she narrowed her eyes, and I suddenly knew exactly what was going on.

"You hired Gianni."

"You can never prove it."

My heart started to race. Was this the real reason why Slade was so adamant about my not going after Michael and Gianni? Was he somehow in cahoots with Charlotte? He knew that if I started going down the road of getting Gianni and Michael, that it would all eventually lead to Charlotte? Was Charlotte the person he was protecting, not me?

I started to feel sick. Was I being played all along?

I felt like I had nothing to lose. "You don't think that Gianni won't give you up when push comes to shove? You're sadly mistaken. There's no way that he isn't going to roll on you."

"He won't. He's a good soldier. He'll take his prison term like a man. And I have the trump card, which you would've known if you would've done your homework."

"What do you mean?"

"My father is the godfather of the Garancino family."

"Your last name is Boswell," I said lamely, but I knew that she probably changed her name to make her sound less ethnic. That was a common thing with Hollywood starlets. Like Ann Bancroft's birth name was Anna Maria Italiano.

At that, she started to laugh. "You're not that naïve, are you, Serena?"

She was right. I didn't do my homework on her. I didn't feel the need to. She seemed so insignificant in the whole scheme of things. Still, it was unusual that the fact that she was an apparent mafia princess wasn't in the news more often. Usually, when there was a star as big as she was, that kind of thing became common knowledge. Not that I kept up with the supermarket tabloids.

I made a mental note to keep up on the gossip more in the future. If I only would've known that Charlotte was related to the Garancinos, I would've put two and two together a lot sooner, and maybe, just maybe, I wouldn't have been in my present predicament.

I shook my head. This was all so surreal.

"Yes, so, I'm pretty well-insulated from this whole Jordan mess," Charlotte said.

"Why would you do something like this?"

"You'll never know. But I'm going to let you go. Gianni is going to beat this, but I want you to do your part. You need to talk to the prosecutor about dropping the charges against him. I want you to go to your boss, Malcolm, and tell him that you're not going to defend Slade by implicating Gianni. I want you to not bring Gianni into Slade's case at all."

"I won't do that. Slade's life is on the line here. I've found a guy who's good for the crime, so that's where it's going to lead. You can do what you want to with me, but I won't back down when Slade is facing the death penalty."

She crinkled up her face and snapped her fingers. "As you wish."

At that, the goon who brought me into this house took me forcefully by my arms and dragged me off. I had no idea where he was taking me, but I knew that it wouldn't be good.

To my dismay, when we got to a door that led into a room in the house, the goon patted me down. He took my cell phone, and I despaired. He then threw me into a dark room that had no ventilation, so it was sweltering. There was nothing in this room, at all, just a concrete floor. It had no windows, so I couldn't see a thing at first. Then my eyes adjusted to the darkness, and I still couldn't see anything.

I was essentially left, and there was a good chance that I would be left there for good. No food, no water. Just wasting away in the darkness, completely alone. I couldn't imagine a worse fate for me.

I knew what Charlotte was doing. She was going to keep me in this prison until I panicked and told her that I was going to do what she asked.

My mind started to go into survival mode, but I also thought about Slade. I'd fallen in love with him, and I would do anything for him. That was the main reason why I was put into this cell. I wouldn't do what Charlotte asked for me to do because I didn't want to give up on Gianni taking the rap for the murder of Jordan. I couldn't, because, if I did, Slade was back to square one. I was going to keep him out of prison, no matter what it took.

My mind also ran to Malcolm. What was that dream about? The spirit was misdirecting me? Or was Malcolm still involved with this whole affair? If so, how did that relate to the fact that Slade hired our firm in the first place? Why would Malcolm not try to stop me from implicating Gianni if he was behind it all? I was totally confused, and, I had to admit, I started to question whether Malcolm was involved after all. I didn't exactly remember seeing his face in my dream. I only saw a figure in a hoodie, who very well could've been Gianni.

But, then again, my reaction to being around Malcolm was so strong…

I was completely confused.

I figured out who was behind the killing of Jordan – it was clearly Charlotte. She hired Gianni to do it, and he carried out the killing like a good soldier. But that didn't fill in many of the missing puzzle pieces. Why did Charlotte do it? Did Slade know that Charlotte was behind it all, which was why he was so adamant about my not implicating the Garancinos?

Augh! I had to shut off my brain.

Then I thought about something else. I had to close my eyes and try to contact Jordan. I didn't have an article of his clothing, though, so I had no idea if it was going to work out. But maybe he had some answers for me.

That wasn't going to help me get out of this situation, of course, but it might help me get some answers on all of this.

So, I concentrated. "Jordan," I summoned. "You

showed me in a dream that Malcolm is behind this. You didn't show that Charlotte was. Please communicate with me. Show me the answers to the questions I seek. Please."

I waited a few minutes, but nothing happened.

I then tried to get into Charlotte's head. I closed my eyes, trying to summon her and her thoughts. But she was probably too far away, because I heard and felt nothing.

Then again, Charlotte probably actually was a sociopath, which was why I felt nothing.

Malcolm was, too. He must've been. I never got an inkling that Malcolm was anything but above-board. The fact that I felt no guilt or remorse coming from him told me that he didn't feel those things.

I finally lay down my head and tried to sleep. It was impossible, though. How could I sleep when I was in a dark cave and I had no clue if anybody was even going to feed me or give me water? For all I knew, they just put me in here to rot.

Don't panic, Serena, don't panic. But telling myself not to panic was like telling the sun to stop shining. It wasn't working, of course.

After a few hours, I wanted to bang my head against the wall. There was no doubt about it. I was really starting to panic.

But, to my absolute relief, the goon who kidnapped me peeked his head in the door. "Are you ready to do what Charlotte asks?"

My heart raced. Getting a conviction against Gianni was Slade's only chance. "No."

He slammed the door again.

And I was, once again, alone in a dark room with no hope for survival.

It seemed like days that I lay there on the concrete floor. Time had no meaning. I was beginning to panic as I felt myself getting dehydrated. I was also starving. The room had no ventilation, and it was June, so I was also roasting.

Yet I couldn't give in. I was left there to die, but at least Slade would possibly have a chance to beat the rap. Charlotte couldn't threaten everyone on the legal team, could she?

Right then, when I was at my most desperate, I saw him. Jordan. He was standing right there in front of me, as plainly as if he were alive. I reached out to try to touch him, but, of course, there was nothing there.

"Jordan?" I said to him. "Why are you here?"

He spoke. "You're finally at the point where you're actually ready to see me. To speak with me. I need to tell you what you need to know."

Finally. "Please tell me. Although I don't know what good it'll do now. I doubt that I'll see the outside of this cell alive."

"Ask me any questions. I'll answer them all."

"Who killed you?"

"Who killed me or who was responsible for my being killed? Because those are two different things."

"Gianni killed you. I know that."

"Gianni didn't kill me. He had nothing to do with it. Michael neither."

I shook my head. "I'm so confused. Why did Charlotte all but tell me that Gianni did it?"

"Gianni is not exactly her favorite cousin. They've had many arguments over the years, and more than one falling out. So, she wants you to believe that it's Gianni, when it's not."

"But she wants me to lay off of Gianni. That's why she threw me in here."

"She threw you in here because you're getting too close to who really did this. It wasn't Gianni. But Gianni isn't going to take the rap for killing me, either, without singing like a canary about who really did this. That's why she needs for you to lay off of him."

My heart started to pound. I didn't want to ask the next question, but I felt that I had to.

"It wasn't Slade, was it?"

"You need to trust Slade more. He loves you. And, no, it wasn't him."

Relief poured through me. I finally knew, for sure, that Slade didn't kill his business partner. I vowed to finally trust him from that point on.

"So, who did it? Who killed you?"

"Malcolm did it."

My heart started to race. I knew that he was in my dream, altering the video. But I never imagined, never in a million years, that he would have actually done this.

"I don't understand. Why? And why has he been so encouraging with me, as far as not trying to block my way when I wanted your clothes? And how did he get involved with the case in the first place?"

"One question at a time."

Another deep breath. "Why did he do it?"

"Charlotte persuaded him to. Malcolm met Charlotte at a fundraiser, and he became obsessed with her. He has always wanted to be on the arm of an A-list actress, so when she said 'jump' he said 'how high?'"

"So why did Charlotte persuade him to do it? What did she have against you? And how come I never picked up on the fact that Malcolm was behind this?"

"Malcolm is apparently a sociopath. You always feared that a true sociopath could get in under your radar, and he did. As for Charlotte, as obsessed as Malcolm was with her, she was just as obsessed with Slade. They dated for awhile, but he got bored and dumped her. She vowed her revenge, and having me killed, and framing him, was the perfect way of getting this revenge."

"Okay. Now, how did Malcolm get involved with this case?"

"It was sheer genius on his part. Since he knew that Slade would be finding my body, and he knew when Slade would be finding me, he knew approximately when to show up at the police station. He ran into Slade at the station, pretending that he was there to meet with another client, and then used his charm to convince Slade to hire him. Basically, he was hired because he was the first attorney Slade met, and, since Slade was in a very poor mental state at the time, he was easily persuaded to hire Malcolm and his firm."

I shook my head. Something wasn't quite adding up. Yes, I could understand that Malcolm could be very persuasive and charming, and that he got Slade at a bad time. But, that still didn't entirely make sense to me. Slade could have his pick of law firms. He could literally afford the best attorney in the entire country, and the best attorney in the country would've been eager to represent him. I imagined that high-profile celebrity attorneys were lined up at his door. So why would he continue to retain Malcolm's firm? Our firm was well-regarded locally, and our firm did have its share of very high-profile local cases, but nothing like Slade's case. Nothing even close.

"Okay. So, Malcolm caught Slade when he was vulnerable. But why didn't Slade switch attorneys once he came to his senses?"

"He was going to. He was in the process of doing just that. He had some interviews lined up with all the heavy-hitters in the business. But then he met you, and he decided to continue on with your law firm. You changed his course single-handedly."

His words were registering with me, and I knew that Slade was right when he said that he fell for me at first sight. Just as I did for him. Now that I finally knew that Slade was innocent of Jordan's murder, I was finally able to admit to myself that I was in love with Slade. And he apparently felt just the same way about me.

Which made my present situation all the more tragic. I certainly wasn't going to give up on Slade's defense. But, then again, if I died there, all alone, then it was going to be up to Malcolm to defend Slade. Malcolm, who clearly was going to throw Slade under the bus, any way that he could. He had to. He was the "other dude," after all.

"But what about that marijuana pill that you were showing me? How does that fit into all of this?"

"I was trying to get you to think about the possibility that a mobster was involved in the case. I didn't know what else to do. You were blocking me, for the most part. You didn't really want to communicate with me, so I was only able to show you very limited pictures. The marijuana pill was the best way to get you to start thinking about drug dealers. You didn't take the bait, though, so I was disappointed in that."

"But a drug dealer didn't do it. Malcolm did it."

"He might've done it, but Charlotte was the one who was responsible for putting it all into motion. I knew that if you followed the trail of Jordan's drug problem, that you would eventually be led into the right direction on this. I apologize that I couldn't have been more clear with my hint to you."

"Okay. So, I need to tell Charlotte that we'll lay off Gianni. Now that I know that he didn't do it, there's no need for me to continue to tell her that we'll keep pursuing him."

That didn't exactly solve my problem, though. Charlotte knew that I was onto her, of course. I doubted that she knew that I was now onto Malcolm, though. Regardless, Charlotte was dangerous. She might just leave me here to die anyhow, just because I now knew what was going on.

"I have another question," I said to Jordan. "Why didn't Malcolm try to block me from implicating Gianni? Doesn't he know that Gianni is going to rat on him if he gets the chance?"

"Malcolm thinks that he's insulated from what Gianni has to say about this case, but he's sadly mistaken there. He clearly underestimates Gianni. Charlotte has no such delusions about Gianni. She knows that he's very intelligent and can be very persuasive. That's why Charlotte is angling to get you off of Gianni's trail, while Malcolm is encouraging in pursuing him as an alternative suspect."

This changed everything, of course. I couldn't think clearly, but I knew, from that point forward, that I could tell Charlotte that I would stop going down the Gianni path. If I had my way, I'd tell Malcolm that pursuing Gianni wouldn't be prudent, and I'd also talk to the prosecutor and tell her that Gianni wasn't good for the murder.

But then again...Gianni was going to "sing like a canary," according to Jordan. He'd be the one, therefore, who could implicate Malcolm. As crazy as that was going to sound. I doubted that he could get the prosecutor to even believe him. That made a whole lot of sense, which was why Malcolm was so eager to pursue him. He knew that Gianni telling the prosecutor that Malcolm was behind it all would be crazy talk.

I shook my head. The entire thing was becoming way too complicated. Malcolm did it. Okay. Now, how would I go about proving that he did it? I couldn't very well go to the authorities and tell them that Jordan told me who killed him. I knew law enforcement officials well enough to know that they generally wouldn't believe me.

I had to make a decision soon. Would I tell Charlotte that I would call off the dogs with regards to Gianni? Could I even do that? Malcolm clearly wanted to go ahead and implicate Gianni. Or, at least, he wasn't adverse to doing that. And the prosecutor was going to think that I was nuts for trying to convince her to drop her pursuit of the mobster.

Perhaps it was too late. Maybe that goon wouldn't even return to let me out of my prison. Maybe I'd never see anybody ever again.

Then the door opened. The person who was standing there wasn't the goon, though.

It was Slade.

Chapter Thirty

"Slade," I said. "What are you doing here?"

He came over to me, and kneeled down beside me, cradling my head against his chest. "I'm so sorry that I couldn't come sooner. I was with my mother in the hospital, and I wasn't paying attention to my phone. I had it on an alert system that would tell me if you were going out of town. I've been very aware that you're in danger, and I knew that if you were going out of town, there was a good chance that you were not leaving on your own free will. I came here as soon as I could."

"I don't understand. How did you get in here to see me?"

"I just did. Please don't ask that question, Serena. You're safe, that's all that matters."

I felt confused, so confused that my mind wasn't registering the absolute joy that I should've been feeling that Slade was there, and I apparently wasn't going to die in that hole. There was something that was off about Slade right then. He was hiding something, I knew that. Something that I probably shouldn't know.

I tried to stand, with Slade gently attempting to help me up, but my legs collapsed. I was weak from not eating or drinking for however many hours I was in there, and I was shaking all over. So, Slade picked me up, gently, as if I were a Fabergé egg. I wrapped my arms around his neck, and he put his hand in my hair and kissed my forehead.

"I love you, Serena," he said.

I said nothing, but just wrapped my arms around him tighter. After Jordan appeared to me, and told me, definitively, that Slade was innocent of Jordan's murder, I finally felt that I could fully trust him.

He carried me through the house, and, to my surprise, nobody was around anymore. Or, if they were, they weren't standing in our way.

"I'm taking you to the hospital," he said.

Back to the hospital. But, I had to admit, I probably needed to go.

He handed me a bottle of water. "Sip this," he said. "Don't gulp it down like I'm sure you want to. It'll make you sick." He shook his head as he put the car into gear, shaking his head while mumbling about how Charlotte was an absolute psycho. Still, he gripped my hand the entire time.

I lay down in the front seat, feeling extremely fatigued and light-headed. "How long was I in there?"

"Three days." He rubbed my hand thoughtfully. "I know this because when I finally turned on my phone, I saw that you were taken to Los Angeles over three days ago. I assume that you were put into that hole shortly after you got there."

Three days. Three days of nothing but darkness. No food, no water.

No hope.

I wanted, so badly, to tell Slade what Jordan told me in that room. But he didn't believe that I could talk to spirits. He really wouldn't believe me when I told him that I saw him only after I was completely broken down. I knew the truth, though. I knew that I only became truly open to seeing Jordan when I was at the point where I felt like I wanted to die. My defenses were completely down, which was why I was able to see Jordan so vividly. As Jordan himself told me, I wasn't ready to communicate with him before, which was why I was getting his messages in tiny fragments.

Once I was in the hospital, and given IV fluid and rest, I knew that I was going to have to tackle the issue of Malcolm. How was I going to prove that Malcolm did it? Was Gianni going to rat Malcolm out? Could I somehow, someway, find that missing part of the video? Was everyone going to think that I was crazy?

We got to the nearest hospital, and Slade gently carried me out of the car and into the ER. "I need a bed right now," he said when he got to the reception desk. "I'll pay any amount of money."

While he was negotiating with the lady at the reception desk, I sat in a chair, feeling weaker and weaker. I vaguely saw that Slade was filling out paperwork, and then he came and got me. He was pushing a wheelchair, and he lifted me onto the chair and pushed me through the double doors.

"You're going right to a private room," he said. "I arranged that personally."

"Thank you," I said weakly. "Dalilah and Luke. I need to call them. They're probably frantic by now."

"I'll call them and tell them that you're safe. Let's just get you into your room and get some fluid and nutrients in you. That's most important right now."

He wheeled me into a private room that was the nicest hospital room I'd ever seen. It had hardwood floors, pictures on the soothing green walls, and a vase of flowers on a table. There were nurses waiting for me, and I soon was in a hospital gown, and an IV was hooked up. I felt the liquid flowing into my arm, and I drifted off to sleep, feeling that I was safe at last.

Chapter Thirty-One

I woke up sometime later, and Slade was sitting by the bed. He was holding my hand and staring at me, and I felt a bit startled when I saw him.

"Slade," I said to him. "I'm feeling much better now."

"I'm sure you do. You've been resting for about 10 hours, and the hospital has been pumping fluid and nutrients into you the entire time. You should be able to eat solid food today and drink water on your own."

"Did you call Luke and Dalilah?"

"I'm not sure who they are, and you didn't have your phone with you, so I wasn't able to look up their numbers."

"If I could use your phone to call them, I would deeply appreciate it."

"Of course." At that, he handed me his phone, and I dialed it.

Luke picked up on the first ring. "Hello?" He sounded frantic.

"Luke, it's me. Serena."

"Oh, thank God. Thank God. Dalilah and I called the

police when we went to the living room and you were nowhere to be found. They've been searching for you ever since."

I smiled, in spite of myself. "She needs to not get worked up. She's..."

"She had the baby. It's a beautiful little girl, and we named her Skylar. Thank God you're going to be able to meet her. I was thinking the absolute worst."

"I'm fine," I said, although I was feeling anything but. There were too many unanswered questions in my mind. How did Slade manage my release? Was Charlotte still going to have it in for me? How was I going to get the prosecutor to drop the charges against Gianni? Slade evidently knew that Charlotte was involved with the mob, so what did that mean? How was I going to pin the murder on Malcolm? Slade still wasn't out of the woods, and he wouldn't be, unless I could somehow, someway, find the proof that was necessary to show that Malcolm did it.

"What happened to you?"

"It's a long, long, long story. But I'll be coming home soon. Maybe today or tomorrow."

"Well, get home. We need to see you and make sure that you're okay. We were so worried."

"I know that you were. I would apologize, but it wasn't my fault."

"No need to apologize. We're just happy that you're safe. Get home, we need to see you before we take off for New York again."

"I'll be home soon."

At that, I got off the phone. Slade was still staring at me, and clearing the hair off my face while he gently kissed me on the forehead. "I'm so relieved," he said. "Now, will you finally take my advice, and stay away from these mobsters?"

"Slade, Charlotte is a mobster. Or her family is. Did you know this? And was that one of the reasons why you wanted me to lay off the Garancino family?"

"I knew that her family was a prominent mafia family, yes. Of course I knew that she was a Garancino. And, yes, that was one of the reasons why I urged you not to mess with Gianni or Michael Garancino. I knew that Charlotte was capable of anything. I've dealt with her for many years, and I've seen it first-hand."

"Why didn't you tell me?"

"It's not important."

"But it *is* important. It is. You withheld that information from me."

He sighed. "Charlotte and I have gone through a delicate dance. I don't think that you would quite understand the intricacies of my relationship with her."

I wasn't liking what I was hearing from him. "What does that mean?"

"I know things about her that she doesn't want to get out. And she knows things about me as well. We've been in a Mexican standoff for quite awhile."

I wasn't liking the sound of that. "What do you mean, she knows things about you? And what do you know about her? And if you're in a Mexican standoff, like you say, how did you get the upper hand? You had to have gotten the upper hand, otherwise she wouldn't have just let you spring me from that prison."

Things were starting to not make sense again. I was just getting to the point where I trusted Slade. Jordan told me that Slade didn't kill him, and that was that. I knew that Slade wasn't capable of a brutal murder like that. But now that he was saying that he and Charlotte were involved in a "Mexican standoff," which meant that there are two parties

273

who cannot bring one another down because both parties have equal danger in doing so, it changed everything again.

Slade's eyes looked pained. "Serena, there are some things that you don't know about me. And, I'm sorry, but they're secrets that I just can't tell you right now."

I felt tears coming to my eyes. Just when I was turning a corner with him, I find out that there is something else out there.

"Serena, I love you. I wish that I could tell you everything, but I just can't right now."

I put my chin out. "Slade, I love you too." There, I said it. The one thing that I couldn't imagine that I would say to any man ever again. Except Luke, my father and my other brothers, of course. "I wish that you could know that nothing you tell me about yourself will affect how I think about you."

He kissed my forehead again, and sat on the bed with me. He stroked my arm, and I leaned my head against his chest. I listened to his heart beating, and I felt comforted.

I knew that this comfort wouldn't last long. There was too much that was out there, just waiting to leap out and get me. Malcolm was going to have to be brought down, and I had no idea how to do that. And Slade was hiding a deep, dark secret.

But, for that moment, I felt that I needed to savor the feeling of him holding me and stroking my hair. The piper was going to have to be paid, of course.

Tomorrow.

Next in the Temptations series

vinci-books.com/twisted-temptations

Serena's quest for the truth behind Jordan Harris's murder takes a heart-wrenching turn.

As Serena relentlessly pursues the truth behind Jordan Harris's murder she discovers a devastating revelation, which threatens to shatter her world.

Turn the page for a free preview…

Twisted Temptations: Chapter One

I rested comfortably in the hospital bed, with Slade lying next to me. I could hear his heart beating as I lay against his chest. His skin felt incredibly warm, and I opened up the buttons of his shirt and put my hand on his incredibly hard pec. Even though I was exhausted from my ordeal, and still felt incredibly weak, I also found myself feeling very turned-on. I was safe, Slade was there with me, and his smell of clean aftershave and man was making me tingle. It didn't help that he kept bringing my face to his and would give me light, feathery kisses that would deepen before he would abruptly stop, telling me that I needed my rest and we couldn't possibly make love in that hospital bed.

I knew that he was right about that. Making love in a hospital bed wasn't a good idea, considering how often the nurses would come in to monitor my blood pressure and check on me. Even though I had a private room, there was no way to put out a "Do Not Disturb" sign, so Slade and I weren't truly alone.

Nonetheless, I was starting to crave him again. Now that

I knew that he was not guilty of Jordan's murder, I felt that I could truly open up to him. And, the fact that he came to save me meant a lot to me as well. I was worried, of course, about what kind of deal he had to make with Charlotte to get me out of that hell-hole, but that was another matter for another day.

At some point, of course, Luke and Dalilah came to see me with their new daughter, Olivia. They came in while Slade and I were cuddling on the hospital bed, and they both looked surprised to see Slade, to say the very least.

Dalilah had a bouquet of flowers in her hand, and Luke was carrying little Olivia in a swaddling cloth. The baby was only a few days old, but I could already see both of them in her beautiful little face.

"We have to stop meeting like this," Luke said, addressing me, but looking right at Slade.

"I know."

"Do you mind telling me what happened?"

I took a deep breath. "I seem to have run afoul of some mobsters. I'm defending one of them, and, well, let's just say that my defense of one of the mobsters didn't sit to well with the person that I was trying to bring down."

Luke immediately looked worried. "Serena, you're not in trouble are you?"

Just then, Dalilah put the flowers on a table, and she approached Slade, her hand out-stretched. "I'm Dalilah, Serena's future sister-in-law, and this is my fiance, Luke, who is Serena's brother."

Slade gave Luke and Dalilah both his free hand, while his other arm was tightly wrapped around me. "Slade Bridgewell."

Dalilah raised an eyebrow at me, and it didn't take an empath to figure out what she was thinking. *You lied to me when you said that you didn't have a man in your life.* She didn't looked pissed, though, merely amused.

Slade stroked my hair while I talked with Luke and Dalilah. "Let me see that little baby," I said. "Bring her here."

At that, Luke handed me the swaddled infant, who was fast asleep, but making faces as newborns do. "Who do you think that she looks like?" Luke asked me.

"Hmmm," I said, looking at the child's perfect rosebud lips and tiny little nose. She had a tuft of hair on her head already, dark hair, which meant that she took after Luke in that regard, as Dalilah was a deep ginger. "I see both of you, to be perfectly honest. It's hard to tell at this point, although she is a beautiful child."

Slade was mesmerized with the little girl, and he reached over to touch her nose. She didn't stir, but continued to sleep soundly. Just like my two dogs, I thought – this little baby was like all tiny infants, and would probably sleep through an earthquake. Not that there were any earthquakes in San Diego, of course.

Which reminded me, of course, about Bella and Gigi. "My dogs. Oh, crap. They're still at the day care. Not that they mind it, but I can't believe that I forgot all about them."

Slade kind of nudged me. "That's to be expected, Serena. You survived being kidnapped and thrown into a hole and left for dead. Your survival instinct kicked in, so little things like your dogs still being at the day care are probably the last thing on your mind." Then he kissed my forehead lightly. "But, don't worry, when you were sleeping, I called the day care place and made sure that they're okay there. They moved them into the doggie hotel, and the attendant said that they're having a ball playing with the other puppies. So, don't worry. They're safe and sound and will be waiting for you when you get out of here."

I let out a sigh of relief, and I gripped his hand tighter. "Thanks for doing that, Slade. That's wonderful that you know my needs without my even saying a word."

"Well, I know how much those dogs meant to you."

"Wait, so you have dogs?" Dalilah asked. "What kind?"

"French bulldogs. They've always been my favorite. I got two litter mates from the rescue agency. They're names are Bella and Gigi. I didn't pick out the names, but they fit."

Dalilah giggled. "I can't wait to meet them."

"How long will you guys be in town?"

Dalilah shrugged. "Luke has to be back in a couple of weeks, because he's starting a new painting that's been commissioned by one of the big hotels. Of course, he can get started here. We've talked about it, and we'd really like to stay awhile, to make sure that you're doing okay. It seems that you have a lot on your plate."

"Well, that's an understatement, of course. I've got a ton of stuff to do, and I take the bar this weekend in Sacramento." I didn't mention, of course, that Slade's case was my top priority. I didn't quite know how to tell them about Slade and who he was, although I had the feeling that Luke and Dalilah already knew. They paid attention to the news the same as anyone else, and I could see in their eyes that they were regarding him just a bit warily.

Slade seemed to sense that I was wanting to talk to my brother and future sister-in-law alone, because he offered to go to the vending machine and get me something to drink. "What would you like?" he asked me.

"Well, you know that I don't drink a lot of pop, so if they have some kind of tea just bring me that. Otherwise, a bottled water would be great."

He pointed at Luke and Dalilah, both of whom said the same thing as me. Tea if they have it, water if they didn't. "Thanks," they said in unison.

At that, Slade got off the bed and disappeared from the room.

I took a deep breath as Dalilah took my hand. "Oh, my god, that's Slade from the news casts. Everyone thinks that he brutally beat his business partner to death. I hate to ask this, but what are you doing with him?"

She seemed very worried, and I loved her for that. I saw in Luke's face that he, too, was worried. "Slade is actually a client of the firm's. I'm on his legal team for his case. I can't really tell you much more than that, though. I will tell you definitively that he didn't do it."

"How do you know that he didn't do it?" Dalilah asked. "I've seen the news, and it looks very bad for him. All the pundits think that he did it."

"Of course they do. They do because they're lazy and so are the police. I remember, years ago, that there was a murder case that involved a woman that was sleeping with a congressman. Chandra Levy was the girl's name. She was found dead in the woods. The congressman's name was Gary Condit. The pundits made this Gary Condit look guilty as hell, for a variety of reasons. Ruined his career and his life. Turns out his only crime was sleeping around on his wife. Some random person actually killed that poor girl, but you would never know it by watching the news that summer. That whole thing happened because of a lazy press and lazy police-work and tunnel vision."

Now that I knew that Slade was innocent, and I knew who did it, I was prepared to make a full-throated defense for him, no matter who asked me about it. "Okay," she said. "I just don't want you to get involved with…"

"A murderer?" I finished her thought for her. "Don't worry, I'm not." Of course, I *was* involved with him before, even though I didn't know for sure if he was a murderer or not, so I don't know what that said about me.

"Yes." Dalilah was still looking worried. "How do you know that he didn't do it?"

I sighed, looking at Luke, who now had little Olivia and was also looking at me with the same worried look on his face as Dalilah's. Would Dalilah understand the spiritual message from Jordan? I knew that Luke was going to call bullshit on the whole thing, so I was prepared for that. But Dalilah had the same abilities as me, even if she had a hard time acknowledging them.

I took a deep breath. "Jordan told me that Slade is totally innocent."

"Jordan. The victim?" Luke was incredulous. "What's that supposed to mean?"

"Now, Luke, you've always known that I can sense things. Talk to spirits."

"I've known nothing of the kind. You've always said things like that, but…"

"But what? I don't know how it is that you still don't believe me. I expect this from dad, Amy, Chris and Mark but not you. You're engaged to somebody who has the same abilities as me, after all, so you better brace yourself."

Dalilah was quiet, and pale, getting paler by the second. "She's right," she said to Luke. "I do know things. I've covered it up all my life, but somehow, when everything started to calm down between you and me and the whole Nottingham situation, I've started to…see things. I can't explain it, though."

"Oh my god," Luke said. "Okay, Serena, so you're involved with a guy. The whole world thinks that he brutally beat his business partner to death. And you're okay with being involved with him because of some hocus-pocus message that you hallucinated?"

I crossed my arms. *Thank god I didn't tell him that I saw Jordan when I was in that hole, after not having eaten or drank anything for days. He would really think that it was all a hallucination.* "You can believe what you want, Luke. Listen, I don't need the lecture from my baby brother. You haven't exactly been the paragon of great decision-making."

"I just don't want to see you end up hurt or dead, that's all. Just be careful."

I took his hand and squeezed it. "I am careful. He didn't do it." My heart quickened as I braced for the next question. Because I had no idea how I was going to bring Malcolm down. No clue whatsoever. I was going to have to find that video that was missing, somehow, someway. That was the only thing that I could think of that would show definitively who killed Jordan.

At that, Slade came back into the room. I hated to think that he might have heard what I was saying to Luke and Dalilah. I didn't want him to know that they were so suspicious of him, although I was quite sure that he was used to the suspicions. "Here," he said, handing me a bottle of water. He then handed Luke and Dalilah their bottles of water as well. "I looked for some iced tea, but they weren't selling that at that particular machine. I can keep looking for you if you like."

"No, this is fine," I said, opening up the bottle of water and taking a sip. "Thanks for this."

"You're welcome," he said with a smile.

Olivia woke up, and Luke handed the little girl to Dalilah. "Well, I think that I have to feed and change this little one," she said. "We better go. We'll be back to see you tomorrow, though, unless you're home."

"I should be home tomorrow. The doctor needs to come and check on me, though, but I would imagine that I can go on home. There's nothing really wrong with me, after all. I feel great, too."

At that, they both kissed me on the cheek and left. Slade climbed back onto the bed with me. "They seem nice," he said. "I'm sure that they warned you away from me, though."

"They did. But I think that I put them in their place."

Slade was quiet for a moment, just stroking my hair. "Do you now believe for sure that I didn't do it?"

"I do."

"What changed your mind?"

It was my turn to be quiet. I didn't know what to tell him. Like Luke, Slade didn't believe in my powers. He was going to scoff, I knew. But maybe he wouldn't. Maybe, since I now believed him for sure, he would be grateful for Jordan's message.

But probably not.

"I don't know, I just had an epiphany."

"An epiphany. Well, Serena, I don't know what brought the epiphany on, but I'm glad that you finally believe me. Now we can move forward with our relationship and not have that hanging over our heads."

He interlaced his fingers with mine and kissed me on my cheek, then on my lips. "I can't wait to get you alone. I've thought of little else since I found you, I'm ashamed to say."

I felt the tingles when he said that, as I thought of his lips exploring every inch of my body. I examined his beautiful hand, that was gripping mine. And, just like that, I thought of something.

"You're left-handed," I said. "At least you eat with your left hand."

"Yes, I'm left-handed. Why do you ask?"

I shook my head. The investigators didn't indicate if the killer was left or right-handed, and I had no idea if they could tell something like that from the crime scene. What I did know was that Malcolm was not a lefty. He was right-handed, like most of the world.

I knew that I was going to have to speak with the investigators on this case. It was something that so fundamental, I was surprised that I didn't think about it. Surprised and a little ashamed that something so simple escaped me. I realized that I was relying on Malcolm's analysis of the case, and not being proactive enough. I trusted that Malcolm was on the up-and-up, and, now that I knew that he wasn't, I was going to have to do the investigation that he no doubt was neglecting to do.

"I need to speak with the investigator for the police on your case." My heart started to pound. "I need to see if they were able to tell if the killer was left or right-handed."

Slade was quiet. A little too quiet. "That's a good idea." That was all that he said, though.

I looked at him. "Slade, what is going on? You've done very little to help with your own defense. In fact, you've thwarted me when I tried to go down a path towards finding out who really did this. Now, I'm telling you that I need to speak with the investigator about whether or not the killer is left-handed, and you don't exactly seem enthused."

He sighed. "Sometimes I wish that you weren't involved in this mess. I'm glad that you are in that, if you weren't, I never would have met you. But, Serena, you're mixed up with some dangerous people because of me. You were kidnapped because of me. I wish that you could just live your life without all this danger hanging over your head all the time. If something happened to you because of something I did, I honestly don't think that I could forgive myself."

"I am involved in this mess, and you should be too." I shook my head, trying to shake off the feeling that Malcolm wasn't the only person who was trying to throw his case.

It seemed like Slade himself was throwing it as well.

Twisted Temptations: Chapter Two

"Slade," Charlotte was saying to me. She was sitting by the side of the pool, and I was in the water, lounging on an air mattress. "Where are we going tonight?"

I put my head on the pillow of the mattress, and my hands went into the water. I floated lazily to the side of the pool and shoved off the wall again. "I don't know. I have to study, so maybe we need to take a rain check."

I might have only been 18, but I was already in college, having been admitted to UCLA when I was just 16. Charlotte had a hard time trying to understand that, of course. She was my age, but had just graduated high school, as most people my age had done. She didn't have the kinds of pressures that I did. I put these pressures on myself, because I wanted, more than anything, to make something of myself. If anybody had asked me why, I probably couldn't answer them. It was embarrassing for me to admit the truth – I needed to take care of my mother. Not Helen, of course. She didn't need anyone's help. Well, maybe the help of a good shrink, not to mention rehab. But monetarily? She didn't need a thing.

My mother, on the other hand, was a completely different story. She was a convicted felon. Nobody would hire her. Not that she was well-off even before she killed my father. She wasn't, because she was a woman of few skills aside from raising a family. Her felony black mark therefore was just one thing that kept her from making a living. As it was, she was working for a fleabag motel as a maid, making precious little.

I knew that I was going to have to get out of school soon and get a job that paid well enough that I could buy her a house and make sure that she had food on the table every evening. So, when I was accepted to UCLA at the age of 16, I jumped at the chance to go. Helen and Scott were paying for everything, of course, so I knew that I didn't have to worry about financial aid and scholarships and all of that.

"Another rain check?" Charlotte said. "You're getting very boring, I hope that you know that."

"Well, you might think that I'm boring, but I see myself as driven. I'm driven to get out of school as soon as I can. You know that I'm going to soon be studying for my PhD as soon as I get out of UCLA, too, so you might as well get used to my not paying as much attention to you as you might like."

She rolled her eyes. "Listen, I'm busy too. When I'm not in school, I'm at a photo shoot, yet I still try to put you first."

I didn't roll my eyes back at her, yet I wanted to. I simply didn't have time for her bullshit. I had a path in life, and I was determined to follow it as quickly as I possibly could. The sooner I could get out of school and start making some serious money, the sooner I, and my mother, could start to live the way that we wanted to.

She took a sip of her drink and looked at me. "I know that you want to take care of your mother, but why can't you just get the money from Helen and Scott to help her live?"

"You know why." The short answer to that was that Helen and Scott didn't even know that I was still in contact with my mother. They would have blown a gasket if they knew. Helen made it clear, all those years that my mother was in prison, that I was to cut her out of my life. She refused to take me to see my mother in prison, and, when my mother was released, she lectured me about how I was never to see her again.

That's how much bullshit Helen brought to me. She couldn't control me now, of course, as I was of age. But, even when I wasn't of age, I still managed to sneak out at least once a week and see my mom. I would tell her that I was going out with the guys, and she didn't bat an eye. More often than not, I used my allowance to buy her food and I would take it over to her where she lived, which was in Watts. When I turned 16 and started working nights at a convenience store, I used that money to help support her. It was always difficult, though, because she was working, but making minimum wage, so I worried about her constantly.

I knew how much she was suffering. I was suffering right along with her. My father was a bastard, an absolute drunk bastard. He beat her constantly, and she took it. She tried to leave several times, with me in tow, but found that the battered women shelters refused to take animals. That was a deal-breaker for her, because we had a Sheltie, and my mom knew that the dog would be in grave danger if we just left her there at the home. She didn't have the heart to take the dog, Tara, to the animal shelter. All the no-kills were full, so my mother knew that poor Tara probably wouldn't find a home. She had a soft-spot for animals, which was where I got it, I guess.

So, she returned, and took the abuse. She always kept me out of it, though. She protected me, and told me to lock myself in my room whenever they would have a fight. It wasn't until he turned on me and beat me so badly that I went to the hospital, that my mother decided to finally take action. The night that I got back from the hospital, she shot him in his sleep. "You can do what you want to me, but I've always warned you never to touch Slade," she said with gritted teeth to the corpse. "You didn't listen to me."

The bottom line was that she killed my father to protect me. I would never forget that. I couldn't. When she got out of prison, I knew that I had to keep seeing her and doing what I could to protect her and make sure she had what she needed. I even tried to hire a lawyer to sever my adoptive parents' rights to me, so that I could return to my mother, but no lawyer would take that case. They all said that I was going to need permission from Helen and Scott, because there wasn't a reason to sever their parental rights. That was an impossibility, considering how controlling Helen was, so I never did return to my mother's home.

"Okay, then," Charlotte said. "I guess I'm just going to have to find another boy. Somebody who has some time for me."

I shrugged my shoulders. "If that's what you feel you need to do."

She made a face, but I knew that she was only bluffing.

They always said that the person who has the most power in any relationship is the one who cares the least. That certainly was true in my relationship with Charlotte. I couldn't care less about her, and I pretty much had her wrapped around my finger. Not that I intended it to be that way, but that's how it was. She had been hanging out with me for two years, begging for the scraps that I would give her. I didn't want to be cruel to her, because I did like her well enough, but my life was such that I simply didn't have the time to give to her. If she wanted to hang around and take my scraps, that was her problem, I reasoned.

"I don't know why you don't see what you have with me. I don't want to sound like a conceited bitch, but I know that I'm going to when I tell you that everybody considers me to be a hot girl. Everyone. Everywhere I go, I turn heads and men are constantly asking me out. I turn them down for you, and you don't even care."

I knew that Charlotte was a "hot girl." She didn't have to bring that to my attention, that was for sure. It was plain that she was truly stunning. Long legs, taut stomach, large natural breasts, big blue eyes and beautiful dark hair. She was an in-demand model, and had been since she was 15 years old. She was already offered a slew of cosmetic contracts, and, now that she was graduated from high school, she was able to take her pick. There was even talk of her being the "face" of Lancome. Victoria's Secret was going to feature her in their next big fashion show in New York. Charlotte was going places, that was for sure, and any other guy my age would be jumping at the chance to be with her.

Suffice to say that I wasn't any other guy my age.

Oh, well.

"Charlotte, I've told you before. You're free to do what you want. You're young, you're gorgeous, and you're soon going to be a superstar. Don't let me stand in your way. If you want to hang around, great. If you don't, well, I don't blame you. But I'm not going to change my study schedule to accommodate you. You know this, so you can act accordingly."

She narrowed her eyes, but said nothing. "Okay, then, I guess I'll go and see that new movie with Astor." Astor was her closest girlfriend. She was, like Charlotte, wealthy and completely smoking.

"Go for it."

———

I got home that night, which was the palace where Helen and Scott lived, and I went to my room to study. I got a phone call about midnight. As I recognized my mother's number, I immediately picked up. It wasn't like her to call me in the middle of the night like that, so I figured that there must have been something wrong.

"Mom, what's going on?"

All I heard was heavy breathing. And then I heard screaming.

That was all that I needed to hear. I raced out of the bedroom, and ran down the steps to my car. I was more than stunned to see Charlotte, who was drunkenly standing outside the house. She had a handful of rocks in her hand, like she was going to use them to tap on my window, which is what she did a lot. Whenever I didn't pick up the phone, she would appear outside my window and throw rocks at it until I would open the window to tell her to quit. Then she would inevitably shout something at me, usually about how much she was in love with me, and I would, just as inevitably, shut the window and ignore her for the rest of the night.

"What are you doing here?" I asked her, although I already knew.

"Was in the neighborhood," she slurred.

I then thought of bringing her to my mother's house. Something told me that, whatever was happening over there, it would be a good thing to have backup. Even if that backup was 115 lbs on a good day, and three sheets to the wind. "Get in the car."

"Oh, joy, we're going for a ride."

"Yes, we're going for a ride."

At that, she got in the car, and we took off. "Where are we going?"

"To my mother's house."

"In Watts?" At that, she buckled her seat belt and locked the door. "You're going to get us jacked, you know that, don't you?"

I knew that she was probably right. I was driving the Audi, which was given to me by Helen and Scott on my 16th birthday. I usually drove my beater 17-year-old Corolla, which I bought with my own money before the Audi gift, when I went to see my mother, but I couldn't take the chance that it would break down before I got to her. She was clearly in trouble, and this was confirmed when I tried to call her back in the car, and the phone went straight to voice mail.

"What is going on?"

"I don't know. I just know that she called me just now and didn't say anything, but started to scream. That's all that I know."

I felt like puking. I saw a red light ahead, and I gunned the car through it. I prayed that there wasn't a cop that was at the intersection with his lights off. I had been caught, more than once, blowing through a red light while there was a cop waiting. I somehow knew that every minute counted, and the ride from Helen and Scott's house in Brentwood down to Watts was going to take too long as it was.

I might have felt like puking, but so did Charlotte. I looked over at her, and her face was green. "You have to slow down. I've had a lot to drink tonight, and I'm about to hurl."

"I'm sorry, Charlotte," I said, and I was truly sorry for driving so fast that she felt like throwing up. I was dragging her along on this, after all, and she had no idea what she was getting into. Not that I exactly knew what I was getting into, but I knew that, whatever it was, it wasn't good. And Charlotte was going to have to witness it.

I started to regret having her come along, but that was neither here nor there. She was along, and that was that. It was a spur of the moment decision, and hopefully one that I wouldn't rue later.

The neighborhoods started to get sketchier and sketchier, until I finally came to a stop outside my mom's apartment. Charlotte got out of the car, stumbled really, and made a face. "If I wanted to throw up in the car, I really want to throw up now." She gingerly stepped over the broken bottles, trash and condoms that were littering the sidewalk. "Really, Slade, these people just don't seem to care about how their streets look, do they?"

I sighed. She was absolutely right, but she had to understand that, when you didn't have the basics, such as safety, enough food and a sound shelter, it was very difficult to care about anything else. Maslow's hierarchy of needs demonstrated this – you have to have your basic needs met before you can desire higher needs, such as having a clean living environment. If the people living around here didn't care about the trash outside their homes, there was a good reason for it.

She gripped my hand, and leaned into me. "I never thought I would be around here after dark. Oh, what am I saying? I never thought that I would be around here, period."

"Charlotte, again, I'm sorry for bringing you here. But my mom is in trouble. I'm almost positive of it."

She gripped my arm, having let go of my hand. She looked around her, as if she was afraid that somebody would just jump out of the shadows to attack her.

We walked into the front door of mom's building, and up the creaky stairs that always smelled like urine and curry. At the moment, only the urine smell remained. I doubted that anyone was cooking at this time of the night. I tried not to breathe in too heavily, and Charlotte was evidently doing the same. But she wasn't able to stand the smell, and the puke that was threatening in the car finally was released. She heaved in the corner, and I rubbed her back and held her hair while she did it. After she was done, I made a mental note that I would have to clean it up after we saw my mother. There was no need to add to the disgusting stench of the stairway.

"This is just so gross," she said to me, as we made our way all the way up the steps to the top floor, which was where my mother lived. "Why do we have to do this again?"

"Because," I said to her. "She's in trouble. I'm now sorry for dragging you along."

"Let's just get this over with." She gingerly stepped along the creaky wooden floor, as if she was afraid that she would be stepping on bodily functions. Not that I blamed her. I was afraid of the same thing, usually. Not at that moment, though. I was simply afraid that I was going to walk into my mother's home and see that she was dead.

I got to her door and opened it. "Mom?" I called out.

That's when I saw her. And him. She was standing over a lifeless body of a man who I didn't recognize. She was shaking, from head to toe, and didn't even appear to recognize me when she was looking right at me. She had a gun in her hand, and she kneeled down to the man, her hand on his wrist. She shook her head rapidly, and then lay down on top of the dead guy.

"Mom," I said to her, approaching her gently and slowly. "Who is that?"

I apparently startled her, because she popped up onto her feet and she pointed the gun right at me. I put my hands up, realizing that she was in some kind of altered state and there was a danger that she would shoot me. Charlotte, for her part, was standing right next to me, but she hid behind me when my mom pointed the gun at us.

"Margot, what did you do?" Charlotte asked her. "What happened?"

Mom started crying as she put down the gun, and she came over to me and threw her arms around me. She sobbed and I wrapped my arms around her. "Shhhhh," I said to her gently. "Mom, you have to calm down so we can help you. Let us help you."

She just shook her head and continued to sob loudly. Charlotte was sobered up by the whole thing and she went over to the dead body and picked up his wrist. I guessed that she wanted to be really, really sure that the guy was dead. I could tell that he was though, just by looking at him. He was perfectly still, his mouth wide open, as were his eyes. His face was a terrified mask.

After about an hour, my mom was finally cried out, and she seemed to be ready to talk. I made her some hot tea and sat down next to her at the tiny kitchen table. "Okay, mom, you need to talk," I said to her. "Who is that guy in the living room, and why is he dead?"

"He, he, he," she began, and then shook her head. "Oh, my god, I'm so ashamed."

"Mom, it's okay," I said. "But you need to talk to me. I need to know what happened, and I need to know how I can help you."

She took a deep breath. "His name is Hugh. I think that his last name is Robbins. Hugh Robbins."

"Okay. Go on." I felt surprisingly calm, considering the circumstances at hand.

"He's a prison guard. He was one of my prison guards." She had a handkerchief in her hand and she was twisting it around and around and around. "He wanted to go out, so we went out." She shrugged her shoulders. "I get lonely too, you know."

I nodded my head. "I know. Okay, so the two of you went out."

"Yeah. We went dancing and we had a very nice time. He showed me to the door and I thought that was the end of it, although I did want to see him again sometime."

"Okay. Sounds fine so far." It sounded fine, but it very clearly wasn't fine. Something happened, and I was getting impatient to find out what that something was. "So, what happened?"

"Well, I went inside my apartment and I was planning to turn in, so I took a shower and everything. Brushed my teeth, washed my face, you know the routine. When I came out of the bathroom, he was standing there in my living room. Hugh. Was right there," she said, pointing to the couch. "He was there, just kinda waiting for me. He had this look on his face." She shuddered as if she was remembering the look on this Hugh's face. "I asked him why he was there and he said that he forgot something."

I nodded my head. I knew where this was going, and it wasn't pretty. "Okay. So, he told you that he forgot something. What was this something that he forgot?"

She shook her head. "He came over to me and put his hands on me. I was scared. I really don't know him that well, Slade. He was a strange man in my house and I got scared. I was so scared that I ran into the bedroom and I got my piece."

She started to cry again and I held her head against my chest. "Mom, tell me what happened. Why did you shoot this man?"

"I shot him because I was scared. I don't know why, but when I saw him standing there in my living room like that, I started to think about all the prison guards who tried stuff with me and some of the other girls in prison." She looked ashamed as she cast her eyes down to the ground. "I was raped in prison by a guard. It wasn't Hugh, it was a different guard, but, I don't know, Slade, I started to think of that other guard when I looked at Hugh. And, well, he started toward me, and I panicked."

Grab your copy...
vinci-books.com/twisted-temptations

About the Author

Annie currently lives in San Diego with her two fur-babies, Bella and Toby, and her significant other, Joey. When she's not writing, she's busy reading, cycling all over town, watching cooking shows or classic old movies on TCM (Cary Grant is her favorite) and occasionally watching trashy television shows.